Finding Fae

El Holly

El Holly

Edited by Laura Cossette

Book cover art designed by RLSather, SelfPubBookCovers.com/ RLSather

ISBN 9798749991666

Imprint: Independently published

Contents

This is the fairy-land; O spite of spites!
We talk with goblins, owls and sprites.
~William Shakespeare, *A Comedy of Errors*

Chapter 1

Move-ins and Breakups

Breakups are like broken noses; they both suck. A lot. And they both give you that eyes-stinging, face-numbed-with-pain feeling.

Okay, I've never had a broken nose. But I imagine it has to feel similar to this.

"In 1.2 miles, turn right."

The robotic female voice of the car's navigation system cuts through the silence, and I glance out the window at the familiar landscape rushing by—monotonous lines of tall evergreens, with the occasional driveway. I avoid looking up front, even when I hear the woman in the passenger seat shifting to look at me.

"Almost there," she says. I feel my jaw tighten at the pity coating her voice. I know if I looked, I'd see the same feeling in her eyes. Two pools of warm, blue sympathy.

I wish she'd stop trying to be nice to me right now.

"Okay," I finally say, keeping my voice as distant as possible. I hug my backpack to my chest.

"Do your parents know you're coming back today now, instead of Sunday?" the man in the driver's seat asks.

No, I think.

"Yes," I say in a way that invites no other questions. I squeeze my backpack even harder, like I'm a drowning person and it's the only thing keeping me afloat.

Silence settles on the car again. Truthfully, I prefer the awkward silence to the forced conversation.

My mind runs through the events of the past few months, as if this time, maybe, I can make sense of it.

Damian and I had hit a rough patch. At least, that's what I was calling it when I talked to Maggie and Cam about it. He just didn't seem to want to do anything with me. We even went a whole week without talking.

And then today. We started the day early, in Damian's car, the trunk stuffed full and bags stacked high in the backseat. There was even a backpack shoved between us in the front seat.

I should've known then that something was off, that our rough patch was worse than I had thought. If there's anything I've learned about Damian after ten months of dating, it's that he loves reaching for my hand during car rides. One of my favorite things about Damian was how his hand would always find mine when we were driving anywhere.

Instead, we spent the four hour car ride from Duluth to Winona separated by a backpack filled with an inexplicable number of shoes. Seriously, Damian has an unhealthy obsession.

I remember studying what I could see of him over his bag of shoes between us, taking in his thick eyebrows, his square jaw, and his blonde hair gelled back out of his face. Not for the first time, I wondered to myself how we had ended up together. Him, the consummate jock, and me, the ADHD girl with a penchant for Shakespeare.

The answer to that is a forced collaboration during science class. He'd shown up late, and I needed a partner for the lab that day. Fast forward ten months, and we're still together, he's off to college, and I'm along for the ride to help him move into his dorm and to visit for the weekend before I head home.

"What?" he'd asked me when he noticed me staring at him. We were driving through Lake City, and I could see sailboats sprinkled across the lake, little triangles of color amidst the blue waves.

"Nothing," I'd said quickly. "You're cute, that's all."

The fact that he didn't quite meet my eyes should've been another red flag in a long line of red flags I kept ignoring because I didn't want to see them.

Even when we'd gotten out to stretch, he'd been distant, rushing into the Kwik Trip for snacks and leaving it just as quickly after I had used the restroom. I ended up talking to his parents as we stood in line to buy pop and gas. Their car was also filled to the brim with their son's worldly possessions. By the time we got back to the cars, he was already waiting in the driver's seat.

I thought it had been nerves, you know? He wouldn't be the first college freshman nervous to move away from family and friends.

But then, when we were helping him move into his dorm, his roommate, Chet, destroyed that illusion for me.

Damian's parents had gone back down the three flights of stairs to grab another load, leaving me in the tiny, humid room filled with boxes. The air already smelled like a sweaty locker room. Or maybe that smell always pervaded the halls.

I was bent over one of Damian's boxes labeled "Shoes," opening it with a box cutter, when I heard Chet whisper to Damian, "Thought you said you'd be flying solo when you got here?"

Damian, who is all too familiar with my uncanny hearing, lowered his voice, making it impossible for me to hear the reply.

My cheeks flamed and I whirled around. "Flying solo?"

I meant to say it calmly. Really. But the thing is, my temper's always close to the exploding point. The insecurity I'd felt this summer during our rough patch and the "something's off" sensation I'd had this morning bubbled up from my stomach and burned in my throat. "Is that what you and Chet have been chatting about all summer since you met online?" I choke out. "There are lots of single, college girls to meet together, huh?"

Damian shot Chet an angry look, then turned to me. "It's not what it sounds like, Eevee, it–"

"It sounds like you're breaking up with me so you and Chet can be each other's wingmen."

The way his face looked–shocked, surprised, with just a hint of guilt–said it all.

I barely heard his explanation through the blood rushing in my ears.

"I just know I can't do distance," was part of it.

Chet interrupted with a helpful, "Damian needs to be free to do what he wants, not tied down in some high school romance."

"Shut up, Chet," Damian and I had snarled in unison.

Damian's parents entered the scene just in time to see me running out into the hall, screaming "Have a nice life, you jerk!" to Damian over my shoulder.

And when it came time for his parents to leave, I left with them. They've been overly nice to me ever since, which I hate. They even helped me cancel my train and bus tickets for Sunday.

"We're here," Damian's dad says, pulling me out of my swirling thoughts. I see him peer out the front window to my house. "Looks dark, are you sure your parents are home?"

"I know where they hide the key," I reply, ignoring his question.

To his credit, he doesn't press it.

As I unbuckle, Damian's mom says, "I'm so sorry, dear."

"Me too," I manage to choke out. "Thanks for the ride home."

Before she can say anything else, I slam the car door closed and run up the driveway and into my house.

*****

My bed is so wonderfully soft and welcoming. I dive into it, burrowing under the covers, then pull my phone out of my pocket. What I didn't tell Damian's parents is that the entire rest of my family is camping at Lake Carlos State Park this weekend and won't be back until Sunday, which is when I was supposed to get back as well.

Still under my covers, I unlock my phone. No new messages. My finger hovers over Damian's name, but I can't bring myself to block him. Not yet.

13

I send a quick text to my best friends Maggie and Cam instead.

E: *im home. Damian broke up w/ me.*

Setting the phone down, I finally lower the stone walls I'd thrown up around my heart when Damian said he was through with me, and my tears do their best to drown my face.

That's how Cam and Maggie find me an hour later, hiding under my covers and sobbing uncontrollably.

*****

"You're worth ten of him, Eevee."

I give Cam a watery smile and they pass me a can from their backpack.

"What's this one?" I ask, cracking it open before they can answer.

"Winter's Dream. A cranberry sour. From last winter's batch," they reply.

"Tasty." I give them a more genuine smile, then set the can down to pull my long hair up into a messy bun on the top of my head. After hours of crying, my face feels stiff. The relief in Cam's eyes is palpable as they lean back and crack open their own can.

"You changed your hair color," I notice for the first time.

Cam keeps most of their hair buzzed short, leaving the right side longer, between chin and shoulder length. Every few months they change the color of their longer hair, just to switch things up.

"Change is good," Cam says.

"I like it," I tell them, as they rake their fingers through it. "Teal is a great color."

"Maggie helped me with it earlier today," they say, giving Maggie a nudge with their shoulder.

Maggie, who had been looking at her phone, glances up at Cam's hair, then over at me. "We would've had you join us, E, but you-"

"I was on my way to Winona with a lily-liver'd boy who was too cowardly to tell me he wanted to break up with me before I went on a four-hour road trip with him."

"Ooh, you know Eevee's mad when she starts dishing out the Shakespeare," Cam exclaims, a gleam in their eyes. "Which one's that from?"

"*Macbeth*," I answer promptly, then quote, "'Go, prick thy face, and over-red thy fear, then, lily-liver'd boy.'"

"Now you've done it, Cam," Maggie says with a groan. "She's gonna be quotin' Shakespeare all night now."

"I can stop when I want," I protest.

We dissolve into giggles. For just a few moments I forget about my lily-liver'd ex.

Maggie pulls us out of my bedroom and into the living room, setting up Netflix. Once we're settled, she runs to the kitchen to rummage through the freezer.

She's almost as familiar with my house as I am. My parents love her. They'd probably adopt her if she didn't have parents of her own. Instead, they just invite her on all our family trips with us. They invited her to Lake Carlos with them this weekend, even though I wasn't going to be there. She declined, but only because she works on Sunday morning.

I hear the beep of the oven, and Maggie reappears, plopping down next to me on the couch.

"Pizza will be ready in ten minutes," she declares as she steals the remote from Cam and starts scrolling through the rom-coms.

"You're a goddess and a lifesaver," I proclaim solemnly, throwing my arm around her.

She laughs. "How much of that Winter's Dream have you had?"

I swirl the can around, weighing its contents. "Only half so far, why?"

Shaking her head at me, her fluffy black Afro bouncing with the movement, she grins. "You're a lightweight, E."

"Am not."

"Whatever you say." She shoots me one of her killer smiles, the one that lights up her whole face.

*****

One pizza and three cheesy rom-coms later, and I'm the only one awake. Cam, who had commandeered my dad's easy chair, is lightly snoring, the ends of their teal hair fluttering with every breath. Maggie is sprawled out next to me on the couch, her chest rising and falling steadily.

"Don't go on social media tonight, E," she had warned when she caught me reaching for my phone between movies. "It's not going to help anything."

And I know this. But I can't help myself.

I swipe and unlock my phone, hesitating only briefly when I notice a new pic from my little sister, Amelia, on Snapchat. I open it, and see a picture of a glowing campfire with a perfectly poised roasting stick hovering above it, a golden brown marshmallow at its tip.

Finding Fae

It's so melty it's practically falling off the stick. The words "Nailed it" dance across the bottom. It fades to reveal her next pic, which shows the marshmallow in the fire and crying emojis next to it.

I send her a quick reply, *Tragedy in two acts, marshmallow edition*, then open up Instagram.

I immediately wish I hadn't. I can practically hear Maggie's voice in my ear: "Told you."

The very first story in my feed is a post from Damian. The picture shows him and Chet, their eyes glazed with who knows how much cheap beer, and their arms around two girls who, I grudgingly admit to myself, are gorgeous, though their too-wide smiles and red Solo cups tell me they're probably drunk as well.

#collegelife is the only caption.

I can't help it. I click on his profile, and my stomach drops.

Where it used to say, "HS grad, proud bf, fitness fiend, sports fan" in his bio, it now reads, "WSU undergrad, single & ready to mingle, sports are life, life is sports."

My nose wrinkles in disgust and I hate how my heart breaks even more. Not even twelve hours after breaking up with me and he's moving on like the last ten months meant nothing to him. I scroll down and look at the picture he'd posted.

There are three comments on the picture already.

From some girl's profile I don't know: *ur so hotttt* 😍😗🖤

From another unknown girl's profile: *can't believe that crazy ex dumped u!! who could leave something that cute?!*

Below that, his response: *ikr*

Well, Damian's never been prolific with words.

Still, I see red. I type out an angry response. *He broke up with me, not the other way around...*No. I delete it before I can send it. I don't need to prove his lie is true by acting like the "crazy ex" he claims me to be.

Get a grip on yourself, Evelyn Gray Acker, I admonish myself. Before I can think about it, I block him on Instagram, then go through all my social media accounts, blocking him over and over.

Finally, I'm left with our texts. Ten months of messages. Before I block him there, too, I type, *You are not worth another word, else I'd call you knave*, and hit send. Using the Bard's words from *All's Well That Ends Well* for a final line feels right, though the irony of the play title is not lost on me (it'll probably be lost on Damian, however).

It's two in the morning, but I know he's a night owl. I wait until the message says "Read," then block him before he can reply.

A pop-up window displays after I hit block. "Delete messages?"

This time, I don't hesitate. Letting out a satisfied growl, I press yes.

Chapter 2

Rash Decisions

I stand in front of my bathroom mirror, locked in a staring contest with my own reflection. My whole body, my brain, my heart, everything feels numb, and my reflection has a hazy, unrealistic quality to it that's probably due to the lack of sleep.

Turns out it's hard to sleep right after you've been dumped, even after you've done a therapeutic social media purge of the poisonous, bunch-backed toad who used to be your boyfriend. (Shoutout to *Richard III* and April 23's quote from my Shakespearean Insults calendar for that phrase.)

My phone lights up with a Snapchat pic from Amelia. "I know why I'm up, but why are you?" I mutter, picking up my phone and clicking on the message.

A picture of her face lit by her phone's light pops up. *ur snapchat location says ur in Duluth??* Her eyebrow is raised at the camera, demanding an answer.

tell u Sunday. go to bed. I type quickly, then set my phone back down on the bathroom counter.

Where was I? Ah, yes. Locked in a staring contest with myself.

I had found my way into the bathroom adjacent to the living room when, after tossing and turning for a bit, I knew sleep wouldn't find me. My family calls this bathroom the girls' bathroom, as it's shared by me,

Amelia, and our youngest sister, Jess. It's decently sized, as far as bathrooms go, but it's always littered with makeup, damp towels, hair spray, curling irons, and the like, so it feels small. We've tried to reason with mom and dad that one of us should also use the boys' bathroom on the second floor, since there's two of them and three of us and they're hardly in the bathroom for long, but apparently our bathroom assignments are non-negotiable.

I study my reflection. My eyes have bags under them, and my hair in its messy bun is disheveled at best. My eyes are red-rimmed from crying and lack of sleep, and I don't see any of my usual vibrance. I look defeated.

I let my hair out of its messy bun and take another sip of the last can of Winter's Dream, tasting the tart bubbles on my tongue. It really is good. I'll have to tell Cam their parents should offer it again this year at their family brewery.

Gazing at my reflection, my eyes follow the waves of my long brown hair, funky curls in it now from being up in the messy bun for hours. A memory of me and Damian rises unbidden in my mind. His lips pressed against mine, heat flooding my body, his hands tangled in my hair.

My stupid, traitorous brain.

I watch as my reflection's eyes well up with tears. As stupid as it sounds, all I want right now is for him to call me and tell me it was all a mistake, that he wants me back, that I'm worth the effort, that he wants to make it work long distance.

Stupid, traitorous heart.

I swipe at my eyes, then check my phone. 4:23 in the morning. I should really be in bed, but I can't sleep. I should try though. One look at the way my face sags and my eyes droop tells me I need it. Besides, sleep would help that growing ache I feel in my chest. As Shakespeare says in *Cymbeline*, "He that sleeps feels not the toothache." Or, in my case, heartache.

I pull out the bottom drawer of the vanity, where all my toiletries are crammed together in no logical arrangement whatsoever, and grab my brush, yanking it angrily through my hair.

"Never cut your hair, Eevee." I can hear Damian's voice in my head as I extricate the brush from a particularly large snarl. "You're so beautiful with long hair." How many times had he whispered that to me? In class, in the movie theater, his fingers twisting strands of my hair as he spoke?

I lower the brush and set it on the bathroom counter. Before I can think about it, I sneak to the kitchen to grab the pair of scissors my mom always keeps in the silverware drawer, then dash back to the bathroom, closing the door behind me.

Leaning over the sink, I study my reflection, frowning at the sheets of hair framing my face. I lift the scissors. With a snip, a chunk of my hair swirls through the air and lands in the sink.

"You have princess hair," Damian's voice whispers.

"Then you must be my prince," I remember saying back to him.

Letting out a sob, I attack my hair, tufts of it flying around me, until my head and my heart both feel lighter and my ears no longer echo with the memory of Damian's words.

I pause, my hands shaking, and stare in horror at the uneven mess atop my head.

I must have screamed, because the door behind me bangs open, and Maggie runs in.

"What's wrong?" Her hands fly to her mouth, and her brown eyes blink at me. "Oh, E…"

"What is it?" Cam asks as they peek around Maggie. Their eyes widen. "Whoa."

"I look awful!" I sob.

Maggie gently takes the scissors from my hand. "You definitely wanna cross hair stylist off your list of potential jobs," she says. Behind her, Cam's face breaks into a crooked grin.

I cover my eyes. "Can you fix it?" I ask.

I peek between my fingers to see Maggie biting her lower lip and narrowing her eyes. "Maybe." She turns me around to face the mirror and lifts the scissors. "Do you trust me?"

My laugh sounds jagged and raw. "Yeah, I trust you."

"Want me to help, too?" Cam asks from the doorway.

"Sure," I say. "There's another pair of scissors-"

"In the office. Yeah, I remember. I'll be right back." Cam leaves and Maggie sets to work on my head, turning my chin this way and that, and making careful cuts.

By the time Cam joins us, Maggie's already evened out almost the entire right side of my head. Cam starts in on the other side, and all I can hear is the sound of scissors and the murmur of my friends as they collaborate.

"There," Maggie says, her tongue sticking out and her right eye closed as she makes one final snip. "Done."

I've spent the last twenty minutes with my eyes closed, or looking at Cam and Maggie's reflections, not daring to look at my own. Slowly, I open them and look at myself in the mirror.

The princess with long, wavy hair is gone. In her place is a pixie. My hair is close-cropped, shorter on the sides and longer on the top. Maggie must have done some styling near the end, because my hair is spiked up.

"How'd we do?" Cam asks, smiling at my reflection like I might break into a thousand pieces if they're not careful.

"I think it really brings out your eyes, E," Maggie says reassuringly.

"Yeah," I say, a smile growing on my face. "Yeah, it does."

*****

When mom and dad return on Sunday with the rest of my siblings in tow, they don't see my do-it-yourself haircut as a positive transformation.

Mom sits me down in the living room. Around the corner, I can see my brothers, Greg and Charlie, gawking at me.

"Boys, we're having a private conversation," mom scolds them. "You both have bags to unpack. Go!"

They may only be eight and six, but everyone in the Acker family pulls their weight. Greg's usual job after camping trips is to unpack his bag and gather up everyone's laundry. Charlie, the youngest, only has to unpack his bag and put away the toys he'd brought with him.

As mom turns back to look at me, her eyes glance up at my hair, then away, as if she can't bear to look at what I've done to myself. Dad walks into the room like he's stepping on hot coals and sits on the edge of the couch next to me, regarding me carefully.

"Is everyone occupied?" mom asks him, and he nods. She lets out a shuddering sigh, then shakes her head, her white blond hair catching the light of the August sunset and burning red. "Why?" Her voice is quiet, and she's still not looking directly at me.

"You mean this?" I ask, running my hands through my short pixie cut. Shrugging nonchalantly, I say, "Felt like a change, that's all."

"Eevee," dad says, a warning in his voice. "Talk to us."

Sighing, I tell them an abridged version of events from early Friday morning until now.

"Oh, Eevee," my mom says. She reaches out tentatively, but I lean back, away from her hands.

"I don't want your pity," I say more harshly than I intend.

"Damian is not worth destroying your hair over, honey," dad remarks, disappointment in his voice.

"I didn't do it just because of Damian," I protest. His disappointment in me stings. Where is their rage at the callous way I've been dumped? Why are they focused on my hair and not how Damian's a grade A spineless jerk? "You know, I could've done so many worse things. At least hair grows!"

"Yes, I suppose…" Dad exchanges a look with mom. "But still-"

"But nothing!" I shout, standing up. "It's done, okay? Damian broke up with me, and I cut my hair. End of story." I stomp out of the living room and up to my bedroom, slamming the door behind me.

Chapter 3

Insults of the Shakespearean Variety

I think Mr. Jenkins, my math teacher, is intentionally trying to bore us to death. The minutes in his classroom drag by like sprinters with concrete blocks for shoes. It's only the third day of the school year (almost two weeks since my humiliating trip to Winona and back), but he's already having us copying down equations and whipping out our calculators.

Glancing down at the notebook on my desk, I grimace. Well, we're supposed to be copying down equations, anyway. The notebook page I've been writing on has some doodles on it. Nothing fancy, I'm not artsy like Cam. But mindless squiggles adorn the page with–I lean closer and squint–a few numbers and letters, which might be equations, but may as well be messages in Klingon for how well I understand them.

"Mister Bradleigh?"

I stop trying to decipher my doodles and look up, shocked. I'd consider Mr. Jenkins boring, sure, but I haven't gotten the sense in the last three days that he's insensitive. From my spot in the back of the room (my preferred location in any class), I can see Cam's shoulders hunch forward as they slide down in their chair. Mr. Jenkins is looking at them expectantly.

"Are you serious?" I exclaim before I can stop myself.

"A problem, Miss Acker?" he asks dryly, shifting his attention from Cam to me. The skin around his eyes is saggy, giving him the appearance of a mournful basset hound. When I don't answer, he raises his eyebrows. I make an effort never to speak in class if I can help it, and I can see some of my classmates whispering and pointing at me in surprise. I also used to hide behind my hair, too, but my post-Damian pixie cut I gave myself a few weeks ago has not grown out long enough for that yet.

"Don't," Cam mumbles out of the corner of their mouth, but it's as if they're speaking from far away.

"Cam told you, literally only days ago, that they use they/them pronouns. Don't you think calling them 'mister' is a bit callous?" My heart has, illogically, moved from my chest to my throat and is beating so hard I worry it'll burst.

Mr. Jenkins blinks slowly at me and I notice a few of the classmates near the front of the room shifting nervously in their seats. A few others have their phones out, probably live-streaming this.

I don't care.

I raise my chin, daring him to respond.

"Miss Acker," he drawls, "I have called my students 'miss' and 'mister' for decades. And if Mister Bradleigh has a problem with it, he can bring it up with me himself."

My whole body goes rigid, and I feel as hard and cold as stone. When I speak, my voice is just as cold. "Thou art the son and heir of a mongrel bitch, Mr. Jenkins."

Mr. Jenkins' paunchy face drains of color faster than my sister Jess can solve a Sudoku puzzle, which is saying something, because Jess is prodigy material when it comes to Sudoku.

"Office. Now."

Cam watches me with wide eyes filled with betrayal, only making me feel worse. I gather up my scribbles–let's face it, they don't qualify as notes in the strictest sense of the word–and stuff them into my backpack before stalking out into the hall.

When I'm no longer in view of the classroom, I lean on the cool, metal lockers lining the hallway, feeling my legs shaking beneath me like a newborn foal's. I left my bravado behind in Mr. Jenkins' room, and I try calming myself down with a few deep breaths, though they don't seem to do much except make me feel light-headed.

Heart still hammering away at my ribcage, where it has settled after jumping to my throat during my exchange with Mr. Jenkins, I inch my way through the halls to somewhere I've worked hard to avoid in my three-plus years at Duluth High–the principal's office.

As I enter, the secretary places the black office phone on its hook and gestures to the chairs alongside the wall opposite the door.

"Principal Lowell will see you shortly-" he glances down at the sticky note in his hand "-Evelyn."

I make my way to the line of chairs he indicated and deposit my shaking body into the one in the corner farthest from the principal's office door and closest to the exit. Out of the four chairs, only one other is occupied, by a fellow senior I know only by sight and name–Quince Florentz. All I really know about him is he runs with the theater crowd; if there's a school play, he's in it. I'm not a huge theater person, but I did go see Duluth High's production of *Much Ado About Nothing*, because Shakespeare. He did a passable Benedick, I suppose.

He's staring at me like I'm the most interesting thing in the room, which, considering the only other person besides the two of us is the wizened secretary with a double chin and age spots on his bald head, I guess that's fair. Still, for the second time today, I miss my long hair. It was a convenient shield to hide behind.

"What?" I ask him, still on edge from telling off Mr. Jenkins.

He studies me for a moment. His eyes are brown, like mine, but where mine are tawny with green flecks, his are so dark they're almost black. There's a twinkle in them now, though.

"Are you new here?" He tilts his head, the sharp lines of his jaw on full display. Inexplicably, I feel an urge to run my fingers along that jawline. As if he can hear my thoughts, he flashes me a mischievous smile.

I scowl, cursing my cheeks for betraying me so heartily. I can feel the heat rising in them.

"I've gone to this school district my whole life," I say, coating my words with cold disdain.

"Oh." He leans forward, unbothered by my tone, placing his elbows on his knees and his chin in his hands. "I don't think I've seen you in here before."

"Stop acting like you're the bad boy in the office all the time, Quince," the secretary says in a weary voice, his eyes on the crossword puzzle in front of him. "You and I both know you're only waiting to be picked up for a doctor's appointment."

Quince shoots me an annoyingly unapologetic grin, and sits back in his chair, shrugging. "Jeeves has me there."

An exasperated sigh issues from deep in the secretary's chest. "My name is Mr. Jives, Quince, as you well know."

The office phone buzzes, and Mr. Jives answers it. When he restores it to its hook, he gestures for me to come forward.

"Principal Lowell will see you now," he says, jabbing his thumb unnecessarily at the door behind him labeled, in large, bold print, OFFICE OF THE PRINCIPAL.

As I make my way to the door, I can feel Quince's gaze on my back like two small flames.

I close the door behind me and stand awkwardly in the space between the door and Principal Lowell's desk, unsure if I should sit or not. Principal Lowell is typing furiously on her keyboard. With her severe bun and navy pantsuit, she looks more suited to corporate America than to running a public high school.

She pauses, her hands hovering over the keyboard, and skewers me with her stare, her gray eyes as severe as the bun on her head.

"Sit," she says, before returning to what I assume is an email.

I comply, sitting on the edge of one of the leather-lined chairs in front of her desk and setting my bag by my feet.

She finishes whatever it is she was working on, then swirls her office chair to face me directly, steepling her fingers in front of her face.

The silence is painful.

"Look, Principal Lowell-"

She raises a finger. "Your mother is on her way to pick you up. Until she arrives, care to-"

"Am I suspended?" I interrupt, feeling all my sweat glands activating at once. Why else would she have my mom picking me up from school?

"No," she responds, but it's too late for my sweat glands, which are in full swing. I feel a bead of sweat trickling down the small of my back.

"Oh, good," I whisper. "So, why…?"

"I just think you and Mr. Jenkins need some time to cool off. Seeing as it's the last hour of the day, your mother has decided to come and drive you and Amelia home. I'm having Mr. Jives contact Amelia's seventh hour teacher right now so Amelia knows not to take the bus today. As for your punishment." She eyes me over the rim of her thick-framed glasses. "I've chatted with Mr. Jenkins and we think a week's worth of detention should do."

My lungs seem suddenly devoid of air. I've never had so much as had a warning from a teacher before, let alone a week's worth of detention. My specialty is doing well enough in my classes to get by and staying invisible as much as possible. The worst thing any of my teachers ever has to say about me (until today) is that I'm quiet and space out a lot in class.

"Now. Care to explain your actions?"

I look at my shoes, studying the dirt smudged into the creases and folds. They're my oldest, and most comfortable, pair of sneakers. It's been years since I've had any kind of growth spurt, so my shoe size has remained a solid seven since I first started at the high school.

Still focused on my shoes, which are easier to look at than the critical woman sitting across from me, I tell Principal Lowell everything that happened in Mr. Jenkins' class.

When I finish, I peek up at her. Her face looks grave. "Those are some serious allegations you've made against Mr. Jenkins."

"There were kids recording the whole thing," I say. "If you don't believe me-"

She holds up a hand to stop me. "I believe you." She sighs. "Still, your response crossed a line, Evelyn."

My mom enters Principal Lowell's office just at this moment, and I'm forced to recount the whole exchange a second time. I avoid looking at my mom as I talk, but I imagine her normally round, kindly face growing hard with anger and disappointment. A quick glance at her shows me that I'm right, though there's a stony edge to her features, and her arms are crossed. She's not looking at me, but at Principal Lowell.

When I finish by saying what my punishment is to be, Principal Lowell jumps in. "As you can see, Mrs. Acker, Evelyn's behavior today was inexcusable-"

"So was Mr. Jenkins'," I protest, just a hair shy from yelling. "He's a–a boil, a plague sore, an embossed carbuncle-"

"Evelyn," mom interrupts in her stop-talking-or-else voice. She turns back to Principal Lowell. "Obviously Evelyn spoke out of line, Ms. Lowell, but I hope you plan to do something about Mr. Jenkins' utter lack of respect for the pronouns Cam uses. They deserve to have people, especially people in authority like their teachers, use their proper pronouns, just like everyone else. If I don't hear that Mr. Jenkins has had some consequence for his actions, you can expect to see me at the next board meeting!"

Standing, my mom pulls on my arm.

"Come along, Evelyn," she says, her voice as hard and cold as iron in Antarctica. "Let's wait in the car for Amelia."

I grab my bag and stand.

"And, Ms. Lowell-" my mom's voice has a high-pitched, hard candy sweetness to it- "given this is Evelyn's first offense ever, I think it's only fair to shorten her punishment, don't you?"

The lines in Principal Lowell's face deepen when she looks at my mom, and her mouth purses, like she's just smelled something rotten in the state of Denmark. Even though she's sitting and my mom is standing, they almost see eye-to-eye.

"One detention, then," Principal Lowell finally says, her tone even. "To serve as a warning."

As we exit her office, Mr. Jives waves goodbye to me with one hand while filling in a box on his crossword puzzle with the other. The four chairs are empty.

Back in the car, I buckle into the passenger seat and look at my hands as I hear mom turn the key in the ignition and shift in her seat.

"Mom, I-"

"I don't want to hear it, Evelyn Gray."

"But-"

"Your father and I didn't get you that Shakespearean Insults calendar for you to memorize it and use the phrases on your teachers!" she bursts out.

"I know," I say quietly.

She sighs. "I just don't know what's gotten into you lately. First the hair, and now your first ever detention?"

Out of the corner of my eye I can see her shake her head.

We spend the next fifteen minutes in tense silence until Amelia scrambles into the backseat, babbling excitedly about her day. I can tell she's intentionally avoiding any gossip she may have heard in the halls on the way to the car, for which I'm grateful.

*****

I'm not at all surprised when my parents say they want to talk to me after dinner.

I am surprised when I walk into the living room to see my dad playing with a thick, sealed envelope in his hands.

"Am I grounded?" I ask when mom joins us, before she can even sit down. More than anything, I want to get this conversation out of the way. I have world religions homework due tomorrow, and I need to text Cam and Maggie. They both messaged me after school, but I haven't responded yet. Cam's only message to me is ingrained in my brain though: *u shouldn't have done that without checking with me first.* I still don't know the best way to apologize to them, but I've been turning around various apologies in my head all evening.

"No, not this time," mom says, sitting down next to dad. "But, Evelyn-"

"Yes, I know, next time, don't angrily quote *King Lear* at my teachers," I finish.

"Well, that's a given," she replies. I think I see the slightest smile curling on one side of her mouth, but then it's gone. "No, what your dad and I wanted to talk to you about tonight is something else."

It's now that I notice the name on the envelope in my dad's hands: EVELYN GRAY ACKER.

"What's going on?" I ask, still eyeing the envelope suspiciously. I haven't applied to any colleges yet, and besides, the yellow manila envelope is devoid of any college insignia.

"We've been worried about you, honey," my dad says carefully, as if saying the wrong word will set me off like a bomb. Well, given how I've acted lately, I guess I don't entirely blame him. He grips the envelope and looks to mom for help.

"We just think you're heading down a self-destructive path," she explains, "and, well…"

My dad thrusts the envelope at me. "We decided to give this to you ahead of time."

"What is it?" I ask, turning it over in my hands. It's hefty, filled with what feels like a manuscript's worth of paper.

"You know how you always used to ask us to tell you about your birth parents?" my mom asks, her voice quavering.

"Yes…" I say slowly. I had asked more as a kid. My parents had made it pretty clear that, given my adoption was a closed adoption, they couldn't tell me much. I've always wondered about them, though. My birth parents. The envelope suddenly feels like it's filled with rocks.

"We were planning to give it to you as part of your graduation present next summer," mom says. Her hands flit nervously at her sides and my dad takes them in his own.

"What is it?" I ask again.

"It's information from the adoption agency," dad replies.

I feel my hands start to shake as I look down at the envelope.

"About your birth parents."

Chapter 4

Apologies and Envelopes

Questions swirl around me like debris caught in a tornado. Will I find out why my birth parents didn't keep me? Do I want to know? Have they ever tried to find me? Do they even care about me anymore? Have they forgotten me? Where are they today? Will I find out where they live, so I can go visit them if I want? Do I even want to? After all, they decided to have me adopted. Why didn't they want me?

On my bed in front of me: my world religions textbook, open to a page on Islam, a notebook with exactly zero notes taken in it, and the envelope my parents gave me an hour ago, still unopened.

I pick up my phone for the hundredth time, re-reading my messages from Cam and Maggie. I have a new notification on one of my social media sites, but I ignore it. The after-effects of my run-in with Mr. Jenkins have settled in my gut like acid. I never meant to hurt Cam in the process. I open the text from them and read it again. *u shouldn't have done that without checking with me first.*

I start a response, then delete it. After doing this about ten times, I finally send: *im so sorry.* ☹️ *i kno u dont like the attention-it's why we've been friends since 2nd grade. remember? 2 invisible kids saw each other in Ms. Keller's class. BFFs in invisibility ever since. idk why i blew up at Jenkins. next time i promise 2 check w/ u b4 i say anything.*

      I hit send, then consider obsessively watching my phone to see when Cam has read the message, but instead switch to the texts from Maggie. I have twelve texts from her I haven't responded to yet. She's one of those people who texts a little, then sends, then texts some more, so her recipients, like myself, end up with a whole chain of texts to read.

M: *omg*

M: *omg E!*

M: *seriously. is what im hearing true?*

M: *DID U SHOUT AT JENKINS??!?*

M: *just confirmed w/ Cam. YOU DID.*

M: *omg.*

M: *Cam says u quoted SHAKESPEARE AT JENKINS. U R MY NEW HERO.*

M: *real question. can the NSN cover this story?*

M: *everyone's talking about it anyway*

M: *Cam says no, but if you say yes, maybe they will change their mind??*

M: *let me know asap!!*

M: *???*

      I feel slightly panicked as I type.

E: *yes i yelled Shakespeare at Jenkins. NO the school podcast can't cover this story, Mags!!* 🫠

      As soon as it's sent, I see the "Read" notification appear below it, followed by the "..." that lets me know Maggie is typing.

M: *MY HERO. FR.*

M: *ok ok. I will tell the others at NSN we can't do the story.*

M: *IT'S SUCH A GOOD STORY THO!!!*

M: *and u kno im always looking for a good scoop*

Before I can further reiterate that she is NOT to use what happened in Jenkins' class as a featured story for the school's podcast, she sends another text.

M: *guess ill have 2 look 4 something else*

M: *so r u & Cam ok??*

I flip back to my messages with Cam. My last message has been read, but they haven't responded yet.

idk, I text to Maggie.

M: *they just hate being the center of attention*

M: *u 2 have been friends 4eva-ur gonna be fine*

In my head, I think, *I hope so.* To Maggie I text, *yeah probs.*

M: *r ur parents mad?*

M: *did they ground u??*

I glance at the manila envelope labeled EVELYN GRAY ACKER.

E: *no. but they did give me a packet of info on my birth parents.*

Her responses show up rapid-fire.

M: *wait. WHAT.*

M: *WHAT DOES IT SAY, E??*

My stomach tenses. *idk. i haven't opened it yet.*

I can practically hear her rolling her eyes at me.

M: *E.*

M: *Eevee...*

M: *OPEN THE DAMN PACKET ALREADY!!*

Laughing despite myself, I type: *k fine.*

M: *AND TEXT ME AFTER!*

I type, *i will. promise,* then check my messages to Cam one last time. Still no response, so I turn my attention back to the yellow envelope on my bed.

Simultaneous waves of heat and icy cold wash over me as I pick up the envelope and turn it over, running my fingernail under the seal and opening it. The envelope shakes in my hands as I draw out the official-looking papers and set them on my bed.

At the top are what look like medical records. A quick scan of these tells me my parents are of average height and weight. Their names are blacked out, and I try not to be too disappointed. According to my birth mother's medical record, she has brown hair and eyes, like me. My birth father is listed as having blond hair and green eyes. Both were deemed healthy, according to the report.

I take in any information I can. A lot of information is blacked out, like their names on the first page. Addresses, birthdays, and names of family members are all blacked out as well. On my birth father's medical record, there's a note that heart disease runs in the family, and that he enjoys running and playing guitar. My birth mother's record shows she has no living family, and I feel a sharp pang in my chest, a mixture of pity for this woman I've never met, and betrayal. As much as I love my life with my parents and siblings, it's hard not to feel betrayed by this person, my birth mother, who had no other family and still decided to have her one blood relation–me–put up for adoption. In the notes section, it's written that she likes to paint and lift weights.

The two medical records are thick and had taken up most of the room in the envelope. Beneath them is a large, periwinkle-blue envelope. In loopy writing on the front is written "To Our Daughter." I open it and pull out a card with a teddy bear holding a heart-shaped red balloon. On the balloon is the text "THINKING OF YOU."

I hear my phone ding, but can't let go of the card in my hand. When I open it, a picture and a folded piece of computer paper fall out. The message in the card is simple, written in the same looping handwriting as on the front of the periwinkle envelope.

We love you so much, little one. You are special—more special than you know. We hope your adoptive parents can give you the life we can't.

Love,

Your birth parents

I set down the card, blinking tears away, and pick up the picture. The small bubble of excitement I'd felt at finally being able to see my birth parents is popped and disappointment clogs my throat. The picture is of a baby, presumably me, in a hospital bed. I have a medical band around my left ankle, and my lips are pursed in a pout, eyes squeezed shut. The label on the back says: "September 15–the day you were born." I flip back to the front, looking more closely at the baby. At me. My very first picture, maybe even taken by one of my birth parents. Next to me is a little baby doll with an orange dress, almost as big as I am.

My phone dings again, and this time I check it. Two new messages, both from Cam. My stomach writhes nervously.

C: *i forgive u.*

C: *but next time, let me stand up for myself? i was gonna talk to Jenkins after class about using they/them and mx instead of mr. until u said something.*

A crushing weight, which has been with me since this afternoon, lifts from my chest.

yes of course!! im so sorry again. forgot our #1 rule: be visible enough to be invisible, I quickly text back.

C: *and don't u forget it* 😜

C: *now what is it im hearing from Maggie about ur parents giving u info on your birth parents??*

I peer down at the envelope's contents now strewn across my bed like flowers.

E: *not as exciting as it sounds. medical records, lots blacked out. a card w/ a pic of me when i was born. & a letter i haven't read yet.*

They respond almost immediately. *thats more than u knew before tho! read the letter, maybe it has more info in it??*

k, I type, then set my phone aside. Unlike Cam, I don't hold out hope that this single piece of computer paper will reveal much.

I unfold it to see a typewritten letter.

Dear little one,

We write this letter with tears in our eyes. How we wish it could be different, that we could raise you ourselves and be a happy family. But our lives are in danger, and we can't risk yours. You are too precious to us.

As we write this, you are asleep in your bassinet. It's a miracle–you usually wake up every hour on the hour. By the time you get this letter, you'll have graduated from high school, according to the adoption specialist we've been talking to at the adoption agency. Congratulations, and how exciting! Your whole life is ahead of you. We hope you follow your dreams, wherever they take you. We can't ensure you the same opportunity, as much as we want to.

It hurts to say this, little one, more than you can imagine. But there's an important reason we're writing this letter. We want to be perfectly clear–the information you've been given on us is as much as is safe for you to know. Do NOT look for us. Enjoy your life with your family. From what we've heard of your adoptive parents, they sound like kind, loving people.

Forget about us. Do not come looking for us. It would only put us all in danger.

Live your life to the fullest, and make us proud.
We love you so much.
Love,
Your birth parents

Confusion clouds my vision. What kind of danger could my birth parents have been in, that they felt it necessary to tell me, not once, but twice, not to look for them? I start imagining all kinds of scenarios, each crazier than the last, involving the Mafia or some other criminal organization hunting down my parents.

I blink a few times and scrub at my eyes, then look at the letter again. For the first time, I notice a little arrow on the bottom right hand corner, pointing as if to tell me to flip the page. Curious, I turn the letter over.

On the back side is a post-script, written in the same looping handwriting as on the enclosed card, but the loops are bunched and cramped, as if hastily written. The words are scrawled in a dark red ink.

P.S. I don't have much time to write this. Your father and I are fae. I know we said not to find us, but I can't stand the thought of not seeing you ever again. I want to see you someday. If you decide you want to find us, just know there will most likely be danger. When you are ready, go into nature. You've lived so long in the human realm, coming to the fae realm won't come naturally to you right away. Find a mushroom circle, or a still pond, or a tree with a hole in it. You'll know what to do from there. When you are ready, follow the clues.

Below this are two lines, which seem to have nothing to do with anything else my birth mother has written.

The Mage Stone, they call it, rests on the plains.
Take note of its western face when it rains.

I read the postscript hastily at first, then, my confusion thickening like fog around me, read it again.

Your father and I are fae.
I want to see you someday.
When you are ready, follow the clues.

Chapter 5

Late Night Conversations

My hands shake so badly it takes me three attempts before I am finally able to snap a picture that isn't blurry. I quickly send the picture to Maggie and Cam in our group chat with the text: *message from my birth mom*

As I wait for their replies, I read my birth mother's note again; the dark red ink stands out in stark contrast to the plain computer paper. I run my finger along the cramped loops of her handwriting, wondering why she wrote it, and what was going through her mind when she did. I frown at the last two lines, trying to puzzle out their meaning.

The Mage Stone, they call it, rests on the plains.
Take note of its western face when it rains.

They seem so random and disconnected from the rest of her message, almost like a puzzle I'm supposed to decode.

I set the letter down on my lap. Why would she go through the effort of writing an entire letter with my birth father saying not to find them, multiple times, and then hand-write a note telling me to look for her on the back of that same letter? It makes no sense.

Your father and I are fae.

Fae. What does that even mean?

My phone dings with a message from Maggie.

M: *E?*

M: ...

M: *is this a joke?*

Not a joke, I begin to type. Her next message arrives before I finish.

M: *there's nothing on there??*

I blink. What? The picture sent, didn't it?

A text from Cam appears.

C: *yah, i see a blank piece of paper?* 😊

Did I take a snapshot of only part of the page and not realize it? I scroll back up to the picture. It definitely sent, and it's definitely the whole letter, but none of my birth mother's writing is there. Suddenly my hands feel clammy. I look down at the letter on my bed, where I can clearly see my birth mother's strange, rushed note. Why do her words disappear when I take a picture of them? I stare at the picture on my phone. It's the back of the letter, alright, but it's blank.

When I scroll back down, my whole body as cold as Lake Superior in winter, I see Maggie's already sent a couple of new messages.

M: *it sux u didnt get the info u wanted*

M: *we r here 4 u, E*

My brain, frozen as it is, has a hard time comprehending her texts. Finally, it dawns on me. She thinks the picture I sent, of the empty letter, has a...what, a symbolic meaning to it? Of not finding out what I wanted to from the packet of info on my birth parents?

C: *u have an awesome fam. sry ur birth parents info was disappointing. but Maggie & i are here to talk if u need*

I feel my brain thawing out enough to cobble together a response to them. Deleting my previous text, I send instead: *thx guys. ur the best. talk tomorrow?*

My phone dings merrily with their responses, but my attention is on the note from my birth mother. I pick it up again, my eyes narrowing as I hold it up a few inches from my face to examine it.

Why can't Maggie and Cam see the writing on it?

That line jumps out at me again. *Your father and I are fae.*

Fae.

When I come out of the cold in the winter time and start to warm up too quickly, my whole body tingles. That's how it feels now, except my heart is also beating about a million miles a minute.

Maggie and Cam can't see my birth mother's message, almost like magic. As in, fairy magic. Fae magic. My hands still tremble as I move my world religions book to the nightstand. I can finish up my homework later.

Settling back on my bed, I pull up a search engine on my phone and type in "fae." So many results come up, it's overwhelming. I quickly dismiss many of the blog posts, trying to find articles about the fae in folklore. Soon, so many tabs are opened on my screen, it's hard to keep track of it all. Fae are mentioned in the folklore of many different European cultures, it turns out. Celtic. German. English. French. Slavic. And fae is an umbrella term. I scroll through pictures of goblins, nature spirits, sprites, and more. Self-consciously, I reach for my ears. They don't feel pointed, like many of the fae in the pictures.

Before I know it, I'm down one of the many rabbit holes the internet has to offer, bookmarking countless websites to read later. It's one of my rare moments of hyper-focus, and of course, it couldn't have happened with my homework.

I'm drawn out of it only by a new notification alert. I have a few unread notifications on my different social media sites, including a follow request on Instagram from, of all people, Quince Florentz. I hesitate, then accept his request and follow him back before opening up my internet tab and resuming my cyber quest.

From what I can tell, most lore has the fae clearly split between good fae and evil fae, however, the good fae are also described as mischievous. Even though I'm not entirely certain I am fae (I'm still entertaining the possibility of some kind of picture glitch and a lack of sanity on the part of my birth mother), I find myself slightly offended by the bad reputation the fae seem to have in literature.

"Eevee?" a soft voice asks at the door.

I set my phone down and stuff all the papers–the medical records, the card and picture, and the letter–back in the envelope.

"What?" I call back quietly. I have no idea how long I've been researching the fae, but my phone's low battery light is blinking at me from where I threw it on the bed, so I know it's been a while.

Amelia cracks open my door and a black streak of fur pushes past her and hops onto the end of my bed, curling up into a buzzing fluffball.

"Hey, Slinky," I whisper, scratching under his chin.

Amelia sits next to me on the bed.

"You wanna talk about it?" she asks.

I cross my legs under my body and pick up the envelope, turning it over in my hands.

"I dunno. It's weird, you know? I've never known my birth parents, so I dunno what I was expecting. The medical records are good to know, I guess, but…"

"It still feels like something's missing." She nods knowingly at me, and I feel the urge to hug her and to cry. When did my little sister become so grown up?

"Do you ever wonder about yours?" I ask her, watching her heart-shaped face closely. She may be a freshman in high school this year, spending more time on her phone or with her friends than with me, but I still remember how excited I was when my mom and dad came home from the airport with her. She was this tiny two-year-old with the biggest brown eyes I'd ever seen on a little kid. I had made her a card, with my grandmother's help, taking time to cut out the shapes and write the words "Welcome Sister" on the front in my scraggly, six-year-old handwriting. When I had held it out for her, she grabbed it and crumpled it, and we both had cried. I think my mom and dad wanted to cry, too.

I'm pulled out of my reverie when she shrugs one of her shoulders and says matter-of-factly, "I was left at the orphanage. Yeah, someday I'd like to visit Ecuador, and maybe even see the orphanage where I lived for the first few years of my life, but this-" she gestures all around her- "this is my home."

"Mine, too," I assure her, when I see the uncertainty in her doe eyes.

"So you're okay?"

"Yeah, I'm okay. I'm not planning to do anything crazy just because I have this info now," I say, laughing.

"Good." She stretches out next to me on the bed. "Now tell me *everything* about what happened with Mr. Jenkins."

*****

Amelia finally leaves to go to bed an hour later, and my desire to do my world religions homework is at its lowest point of the evening.

"In the morning," I mutter. I plug in my phone, which is still blinking a low battery warning at me, and get up to brush my teeth. Slinky stays on the bed, fast asleep in his favorite spot (which also happens to be where my feet usually go).

When I crawl under my covers and close my eyes, I can see the letter from my birth mom as if it's seared to my eyelids. Questions pile up on one another and thoughts race around my brain like kids on a sugar rush. I groan and sit up. It's going to be one of those nights.

I skim Cam and Maggie's messages, then scroll through my Instagram newsfeed. I have a new direct message, which I click on absent-mindedly.

Q: *embossed carbuncle. now THAT'S a phrase you don't hear every day.* 😊

Q: *(confession: i had to look up how to spell embossed carbuncle)*

Heat rushes to my face. Luckily, Quince can't see me, so I can be as cool and witty as I want with my reply.

E: *i save the best insults for the worst kinds of ppl*

I hit send, then click on yet another article on the fae. Before I can read too much, another message pops up from Quince.

Q: *how does one earn an insult like that?*

Q: *asking for a friend.*

Despite myself, I smile.

E: *if u want 2 kno what Jenkins did, y not just ask?*

Instead of going back to the article on the fae, I scroll through his Instagram pictures as I wait for him to respond this time. Obviously, he's having a bit of insomnia tonight, too. Or maybe he's always up at 1:30 in the morning on a school night.

Most of his pictures are of him in large group photos of cast members from different shows. One picture stands out to me, as it's one of the few he's posted that isn't related to theater. It's of him and another kid I recognize from school, Jim Mortensen. Quince is holding the phone for the selfie, and they're both grinning widely. They're sitting in a small wooden boat I'm surprised can hold their combined weight without capsizing, and their faces are tanned. What really draws me to the picture, aside from how happily Quince is smiling, is the look in his eyes, both delighted and mischievous. I wonder what trouble he and Jim had gotten into that day?

I scroll back up through his pictures and see I have a missed message from him.

Q: *nah i get the gist of what happened with Jenkins. i mostly wanted to say hey. and use the phrase embossed carbuncle. it's a good one, i'm saving it.*

it's Shakespeare, I type, then add, *so i can't claim credit.*

Q: *do you usually quote the Bard when you're mad?*

I grin, then send a quick reply. *maybe*

My eyelids feel heavy as I wait for his reply and yet I think there's no way I'll fall asleep.

Q: *ok this is gonna seem random, but it's your birthday soon, isn't it?*

Well, now even my eyelids aren't tired.

E: *how did you know?*

I don't usually do much to celebrate my birthday. To me, my adoption day, or my "gotcha" day, as my parents call it, is more cause to celebrate. It's the day I joined my family.

Q: *oh god you think i'm a creep. i just have a weird sixth sense when it comes to people's birthdays, that's all, i swear.*

Still a little suspicious, I type back, *i don't think ur a creep. just maybe next time u predict someone else's bday, start w/ proclaiming ur birthday-sensing ability first* 😜

Q: *so you're saying I announce it like a parlor trick?*

E: *yeah, the Great Birthday-Guessing Quince*

Q: *how'd you guess my magician name?*

I smile, snuggling down under my covers.

E: *thats my weird sixth sense*

Q: *noted. so how are you celebrating your birthday? you're turning 18 right? excited for your extra abilities to kick in?*

Raising an eyebrow, I type, *u mean like my ability to vote and buy cigarettes and lotto tix? yeah, totally stoked*

He reads my message almost immediately, but his response takes a while. I'm almost asleep when he types back.

Q: *yeah. that's what i meant. what else would i mean?*

Not sure how to answer that question, I simply say instead: *no idea*

I lock my phone and set it on the nightstand before he can respond and, though questions still lurk at the back of my brain like monsters under the bed, I find myself drifting into an uneasy sleep.

Chapter 6

Coincidences

Cam is quieter than usual as they drive us to school. For the last two years, their parents have allowed us to take the Bradleigh family van to school on Fridays. It's a beat-up, rusted thing with an inoperable CD player and windows which stick sometimes when you roll them down, but it's a step up from the painfully boring bus rides every other day of the week, so we don't complain (too much).

I ignore the nugget-sized pit of worry in my stomach that formed after the first few minutes of stilted conversation with Cam, and focus my nervous energy on scribbling down some passable answers for my world religions homework I'd abandoned last night. I'm so focused I don't even notice we're at school until I hear Maggie's voice.

"E? Eevee? Earth to E!"

Blinking, I look up and to the right, where Maggie is standing and tapping on the van's passenger side window. She holds up her phone and points at it with the emphatic energy of a hockey coach.

"Shit." I stuff my mostly finished homework in my bag and scramble out of the van.

"How long were you calling for me this time?" I ask as Maggie, Cam, and I rush to the front doors of Duluth High amidst the horde of tired teens.

"Long enough," she replies, grinning. "I've got Journalism first period and I need to finish editing my article that's due today. See y'all at lunch!" With that, she's maneuvering the crowded halls, nose already buried in her article.

Even on the best of mornings, I'm not a morning person, and today I'm feeling the effects of my late night researching fae and talking with Quince. I shake my head in Maggie's direction, jealous of her seemingly effortless ability to be awake before nine in the morning.

"See you," Cam says as well. I catch their arm as they're turning away, and they raise an eyebrow at me.

"We're good, right?" I hate the idea that Cam might still be mad at me. They don't get angry easily, like I do, but where my anger burns bright and is gone in a flash, theirs is like a slow-burning ember and they can hold onto a grudge for a long time.

Now they're giving me an exasperated look, which is better than anger, I suppose. "Yeah, of course we're good, Eevee. Why do you ask?"

I let go of their arm and shrug. My hand raises to tuck my hair behind my ear, then I remember I don't have long enough hair to do that anymore. Habits, even small ones, are hard to break. "I dunno, you seemed quiet in the van this morning."

They open their mouth, an uncomfortable look on their face. Just then, the warning bell rings, letting the students of Duluth High know we have two minutes to get to class before we're marked tardy. At the sound, Cam jumps and their mouth snaps closed.

53

"It's nothing, don't worry about it," they say over their shoulder after I call out to them. They continue walking away, slouching through the hall in their eternal attempt to make as little of an impact as possible on the people around them.

The nugget-sized pit in my stomach doubles in size, though now I'm worried that something's going on with Cam they're not telling me about.

I ponder the hypocritical nature of wanting Cam to tell me what's bothering them when I'm not planning to tell them about possibly being fae (still figuring out what that might mean) as I speed-walk to my first period class, backpack slung over my shoulder. No time to drop off my bag at my locker this morning, unfortunately.

*****

I really don't want to lug around my backpack all day, so I dash to my locker to deposit my bag as the bell signals the end of first period.

Across the hall, the last person I want to see today is leaning on a locker, looking casually confident as he runs his fingers through his black hair and says something to the girl next to him, who blushes and laughs.

Ugh. Quince "guessing-birthdays-is-my-sixth-sense" Florentz, who could possibly be a new friend if I wasn't so confused by his sudden interest in me.

For a moment, I think I see the air shimmer around him, like how the air looks above a paved road on a hot day, but I blink and it's gone.

"I need to get to bed early tonight," I mutter to myself. I shove my bag in my locker and extract the materials for my next class, hoping I've remembered everything for once. When I turn around, the girl–I think her name is Laura?–is talking animatedly to Quince, but his dark eyes are on me.

It's at this moment I wish I'd put more deodorant on this morning. There's an intensity to his gaze I can't quite explain, other than it's like he's trying to see through me and it's working.

In a panic, I realize he's no longer leaning on the lockers but coming toward me, Laura trailing behind him, still talking excitedly, oblivious his attention is elsewhere. I tear myself away from his gaze and turn my speed walk into a near jog. Though I'm tempted to look behind me, I don't, and I rush into my world religions class a minute before the bell, sweaty and red-cheeked. Mrs. Merriweather looks at me curiously, but says nothing as I slide into my seat in the back and plunk my textbook on the desk.

I busy myself with finishing my homework until class starts, keeping my gaze on the desk and nowhere near the window or the door.

*****

My study period is a welcome relief, and I sincerely mean my "*TGIF*" text I send to Cam and Maggie between classes. My exhaustion has only gotten worse as the day has worn on, my conversation with Cam at lunchtime was less-than-fruitful despite Maggie's and my best efforts to get them to open up about what's bothering them, and I've officially spotted Quince no less than three times today, after hardly seeing him at school before (other than our conversation in the office yesterday). Twice in the hall and once at lunch (which is suspicious, as I don't recall seeing him at our lunch before). Am I just noticing him more, now that we've met and had a late night conversation about Shakespeare and eighteenth birthdays?

Determined to forget about Quince Florentz for a bit, I sit myself down at a computer in the library. I have some research to do for my small animal care project on local veterinarians, a project I'm actually looking forward to since I want to go to school to be a vet tech, but my brain, as usual, has about ten thousand thoughts rushing through it haphazardly, including one I've been unable to fully ignore since I read the words in my birth mom's note last night: *Your father and I are fae.*

I open a new tab in the browser and, after a quick look around to make sure no one is nearby, type the term "faeries" in the library's online catalog search box and hit enter. Immediately I realize my mistake, as most of the results are for fiction books. I change my filters to include only nonfiction books and refresh the search.

One page comes up with six book results. I quickly jot down a couple promising titles, including W. B. Evans-Wentz's *The Fairy-Faith in Celtic Countries,* then clear my search and exit out. As I move to stand, I see, with a touch of irritation, Quince "coincidentally-keeps-showing-up-wherever-Eevee-is-today" Florentz strolling into the library as if he owns the place. He saunters over to the librarian's desk and leans over it. I watch as he passes her a note with a smile and a low murmur.

Internally, I'm rooting for Ms. Bates to kick him out, as she is a notorious stickler for the rules and doesn't let anyone into the library who isn't supposed to be there, but instead of sending him back the way he came, she's smiling back at him and nodding.

Now I know I didn't get enough sleep last night, and my caffeine at lunch was clearly ineffective, because I swear I see the air around Quince shimmer again, just as it had done this morning. As soon as I try to focus on the shimmering, though, it's gone.

My heart rate skyrockets as I see him looking around the library.

"Don't notice me, don't notice me, don't notice me," I whisper, sliding down in the blue plastic seat.

To my horror, he plops down in the seat next to me. I rush to cover my notes on fairy books.

"Impressive," he says, too loudly for my taste.

Ms. Bates fails to uphold her stickler-for-the-rules reputation yet again. She looks over to us, whispers "Quince!" with a smile, and shakes her head good-naturedly at him.

I roll my eyes. She's obviously not going to kick him out of the library anytime soon.

"I mean, it doesn't work on me, of course, but I bet you use that trick on fireflies all the time, huh?"

"I don't know what you're talking about," I respond in confusion. No louder than he'd been talking, but Ms. Bates shoots me an irritated look and puts a finger over her lips in warning.

Anger floods my mouth, leaving in its wake a metallic taste. Quince is watching me with, infuriatingly, amusement.

"What do you want?" I ask in a whisper once I see Ms. Bates resume her task of checking in a stack of library books.

His smile is easy-going, but his eyes are a mix of questions and–unless I'm totally misinterpreting from my quick glance up at him–excitement? Anticipation?

"Why didn't I know about you before yesterday?" He pretends to type something on the computer in front of him.

"Uh..." I say, ever the smooth talker without Shakespeare to rely on. Shakespeare. Of course. I smirk at him. "Because 'Your abilities are too infant-like for doing much alone?'" Thank you Shakespeare, and *Coriolanus*, and my mom and dad for that Shakespearean Insults calendar.

Quince is not one for hiding his emotions, apparently. At the taken aback, hurt look on his face, I quickly add, "I don't know, big school?"

He shakes his head. "I know all the others at the school, but not you. Why?"

Now I'm confused. "The others?"

"Yeah, I mean, there's not that many of us. We're a tight-knit community."

It dawns on me. He heard me quoting Shakespeare yesterday, and started his text convo with me by mentioning the quote. "You think I'm a theater person!" He opens his mouth, then closes it. "Yeah," I go on, shrugging awkwardly, "I'm really not. Can't sit through a musical for the life of me. I just really like Shakespeare. He's got a way with words, you know?"

I leave a befuddled-looking Quince at the computers and escape for the bookshelves, hiding in them until I think he's gone, or at least forgotten about me.

I feel foolish. Here I thought he was interested in me, but now I know he's probably just recruiting for the fall musical.

I glance at the ancient clock on the wall. Five more minutes until next period. I pull out my hastily scribbled list of books on fairies and squint at it, trying to decipher my own handwriting.

Staying as hidden as possible, I make my way to the nonfiction section and grab a few titles from the shelves, then tuck them under my other books.

Turning toward the checkout desk, I jump a foot in the air.

"Now what?" I ask, my nerves fraying and my anger spiking again.

Quince holds his hands up in surrender. "Don't hit me," he jokes. "I just wanted you to know the bell's about to ring."

"I'm aware," I snap. His eyes flick to the section I had just left. "Just, uh, getting books for a world religions thing on, uh, folktales around the world." I try not to wince at my awful excuse. I've never been great at thinking on my feet. "See ya!"

Before he can answer, I rush away, though no matter how quickly I check out my books and walk through the halls to my next class, I can't shake the feeling that I'm missing something and that I'm not the only one with a secret to hide.

Chapter 7

Off the Beaten Path

I'm elbow-deep in soapy dishwater and the dish machine is roaring and whooshing and clanking. It's almost as if the machine is competing with Mike's 80's playlist he's always blasting through the speakers above the oven. Despite the cacophony around me, all I can think about is a continuous loop of my birth parents, Quince, fairies, Cam's evasiveness, and my unfair detention coming up next week.

When my shift ends, right after the brunch rush, I clock out of Gramp's Diner and wave goodbye to my replacement, Robby, the afternoons and evenings dishwasher. As I exit through the back door, I'm distracted from my thought loop by a demanding meow at my feet.

I look down to see the familiar scraggly body and one-eared head of the stray cat who lives behind the diner.

"Hey, Scamp." I kneel down and scratch him behind his one ear and he purrs, blinking up at me expectantly. He always seems to know when my shifts are over. "I'm sorry, buddy," I say to him when I realize what he's expecting. "I forgot to grab some scraps for you today." He gives me a wounded look, almost as if he knows what I'm saying, and arches his dusty-colored back, stalking away with his tail swishing.

I watch him go, feeling more guilt than probably strictly necessary. I don't usually forget to save him scraps. He was there after my first shift at Gramp's six months ago, and ever since then, I've saved him scraps of food in a napkin to give him after my shift. My coworkers call me a big softie, and Mike, the cook, always glares and says, "I don't cook fer that fleabag, y'know!" when he sees me saving the food, but no one has stopped me from doing it, either.

"I'll save extra for you tomorrow!" I call after Scamp's retreating back. In answer, his tail whips haughtily around the corner of the building and he's gone.

I make my way to my mom's car and roll the windows down as I drive. It's a hot September afternoon, but when the wind blows I can smell just a hint of autumn in the air, like it's sticking its foot in the door to peek in and whisper that it's coming to visit soon. Mom's letting me borrow the car all day so I can do my homework and visit Maggie at her work (win-win). Greg and Charlie have somehow convinced mom and dad to let them have a bunch of friends over today, so the house is overrun with elementary kids and their energy and, more likely than not, their shrieking. Less than ideal conditions for doing homework, which is why I'm happy to escape to a coffee shop for the afternoon.

Maggie is at the counter when I walk into the shop, sporting a bright red scarf on her head. The smell of roasted coffee and the sounds of espresso machines at work greet me like an old friend.

"Thanks for stopping at Java Jive, come again soon!" The girl working the drive thru window has one of those incessantly perky voices, and I see Maggie cringe when the girl says into her headset, "Hi there! Welcome to Java Jive! What can I get for you today?"

"Hey Mags." I step up to the counter after the person ahead of me walks to a table with a mug of coffee in each hand.

"Hey there, E. How was work?"

"Busy. Have you heard anything from Cam?"

"Nada." She shakes her head. "You think they're okay?"

I shrug as she pours me my usual, a large mug of medium roast, black. The Java Jive boasts environmental awareness, only buying sustainably sourced coffee and offering reusable mugs for those staying in the shop to drink. No mug is the same as any other. Maggie says the owner went around to different thrift stores and stocked up when the Java Jive first opened. The mug Maggie hands me today is white ceramic with the phrase "Nifty and Fifty" on it in bold, black print.

"Thanks," I say, taking the mug from her and handing her some cash. "Keep the change."

She drops the coins in the tip jar. "They'll talk when they're ready, I'm sure."

"I guess," I say, blowing on the steaming coffee in my hands. "When's your break?"

She checks the clock. "In about an hour?"

"Cool. See you then?"

"You know it."

I make my way to my favorite table in a dimly lit corner of the cafe, and set my overfilled mug down, careful not to spill any of the precious elixir, before digging my homework out of my backpack.

With caffeine and an impending timeline I'm able to focus in on my work due Monday in math–though the entire time I work, I curse Mr. Jenkins and Principal Lowell, because Monday is also when I have detention.

When my coffee mug is empty and my math homework is done, I check the time on my phone. Still about twenty minutes until Maggie's break, if she's able to take it on time. The line for the register snakes through the shop, and the voice of the girl working the drive thru window is more shrill than cheery when she says, "Thanks for stopping at Java Jive, come again soon!"

I unlock my phone and see I have a message from Amelia in Snapchat. It's a video of Greg, Charlie, and six of their friends all running around the living room with balloons in hand. I don't have to turn on the sound to know there's a decent amount of shrieking happening as well, like I predicted. Her next message is a picture of her with wide eyes and an exaggerated expression of horror on her face. The text on the picture reads "*save me!*"

I take all my textbooks, notebooks, and folders out of my backpack and arrange them in an impressive-looking pile on the table, then take a picture, adding the text: *ok but it'll cost u.*

She opens my message immediately and sends a rapid-fire response: *im honestly considering that tradeoff!*

I shake my head, smiling, then check my other notifications. Nothing on Instagram from Quince since our weird encounters yesterday. I'm mostly relieved. Deep down, maybe a little disappointed, too. I guess now I've made it clear I'm not interested in doing theater, he's given up on his recruitment efforts.

Pocketing my phone, I put all my books and materials back in my bag except for the books I checked out yesterday from the library and start to flip through them. They were written long ago, in the early twentieth century, and the words swim before my eyes, skating off my consciousness like stones skipping over water. This happens sometimes when I read. It has nothing to do with interest or desire or whatever–I want to read the books in front of me. But it's like my brain decides on its own that the words are boring and no matter how much I try to focus my attention back on the pages in front of me, my brain keeps saying, "What about this? Or that?"

I've read the same sentence at least twenty times in a row now and am no closer to remembering or comprehending it. I drop my head in my hands, angry I can never get my brain to focus when I need it to. The chair next to me scrapes as it's moved back, and Maggie sits down across from me. I rush to shove the books into my bag, mumbling the same lame excuse about world religions homework I'd given Quince yesterday. She raises an eyebrow at me but only says, "You know, for someone whose hearing is as good as yours, you sure are startled a lot, E."

"My super hearing is only as good as my focus," I joke, "so, not so great most days."

We contemplate Cam's behavior and Mr. Jenkins' bigotry for the next fifteen minutes, until she's called back by her harried-looking coworker, Jeff. I grab my bag and bring my mug to the dishes tray, having given up on being able to concentrate on any more reading this afternoon, and head out.

The late afternoon sun feels good on my face. I look up at the clouds in the sky, and a thought pops into my head as if it's been waiting for a moment just like this. *Go into nature.*

This thought sticks with me on the drive home, replaying in my mind. I hesitate at a stop sign, then, instead of turning left to head home, I go right and make my way toward North Shore Drive, the scenic road north of Duluth.

Living in Duluth, I'm never too far from nature. As I drive north, I have the sparkling blue waters of Lake Superior on my right, and a forest to my left. Though I love Lake Superior, I keep an eye on the trees as I drive today. I slow down and pull off to the side of the road when I spot what I'm looking for: a dirt path winding off into the woods.

I unplug my phone from the car charger and set it on battery saving mode. Remembering Amelia's Snapchat sleuthing after my breakup with Damian last month, I disable my location as well.

This moment is for me, no one else.

As I hike along the path, swatting at the occasional mosquito, I repeat the words of my birth mom's note to myself in my head. "Go into nature...Find a mushroom circle, or a still pond, or a tree with a hole in it. You'll know what to do from there."

After fifteen minutes of hiking, I've spotted ten squirrels, four chipmunks, a bold rabbit who stared at me for a minute before hopping off into the woods, and many birds, especially crows.

No mushroom circle or hole in a tree yet, though. Not that I'd know what to do if I found one, despite my birth mom's confidence that I somehow would. I've given up on finding a still pond, as this path doesn't appear to lead to any creeks or rivers or other bodies of water, at least, not yet.

Up ahead, a huge crow caws. I look up to see it perching on a low-hanging branch of a large, twisted oak. Most of the tree is dead or dying, its branches skeletal. Two or three branches boast a few leaves, already yellowing. Near the base of the tree, about knee-high, is a knotty hole.

My breath catches in my throat. Above me, the bird watches as I step closer to the tree. Remembering where I am, I stop at the edge of the dirt path and do a quick check of the foliage around the base of the tree. I can practically hear my dad's voice in my head. "Leaves of three, let it be." Though I don't recognize any of the plants in front of me, none of them have the leaves of three I've been taught to look for to spot poison ivy. I step up to the ancient oak.

Now what?

Cautiously, I lean over and peer into the hole in the tree. It's mostly empty, with some rotted wood in the bottom. A squirrel racing through the underbrush makes me jump–I'll never understand how something so little can make so much noise. It's an ordinary squirrel in an ordinary forest, though. Nothing more.

I go back to contemplating the hole in the tree. Am I supposed to stick my hand or my head in it? Stare at it for a certain amount of time? Say "Open Sesame" three times in a row? I feel dizzy and disoriented, thinking of it all.

"Whatever's in that hole must be fascinating," says a voice right behind me.

Chapter 8

Fae Encounters

He's just a hiker. An ordinary hiker, in an ordinary forest, on a normal path, in Minnesota.

I don't have to turn around to picture him. Probably bearded, with gray or balding hair or both. His voice sounds old. I bet he's wearing shorts, as any respectable Minnesotan does for most months of the year. Perhaps over his t-shirt he's got a flannel overshirt, or maybe he's been hiking for a while and he's got it tied around his waist, going for practicality over style. His feet are shoved into department store tennis shoes.

I think all this in the space of a few seconds. Forcing out a laugh, I shake the dizziness from my brain and turn toward him. "Oh, yeah, holes in trees are always fascin-"

I face him and my voice catches in my throat, as if the words had been snatched away before I can stop it.

The image in my head of a normal Minnesotan hiker shatters.

In front of me stands a man, his mouth and eyes open wide. My face must mirror his naked surprise because he's not like anyone I've ever seen before.

He's short, maybe about three feet tall if he's straightened out, but he stands hunched over, one of his hands clutching a gnarled staff, his other clutched at his heart over his brown robes. His skin is a mottled green, and his eyes a shocking yellow; in fact, his face looks more frog-like than human, with a flattened nose and an oversized mouth, made broader by the way it's gaping at me.

My curiosity overcomes my temporary loss of speech. "Who–what–er, I mean, hi." Remembering my manners, I offer him my hand. He doesn't move to shake it, though. His jaw is still dropped open, and his eyes remain glued to my face.

I pull my hand back, blushing and confused, and that's when I see the trees behind the small frog-man. Beneath me, my legs suddenly feel shaky, like I'd been walking for fifteen hours, not fifteen minutes.

One thing's for sure: I'm not in Minnesota anymore.

We are surrounded by trees in the ripe stages of mid-to-late autumn, with leaves of red and gold and sunset orange. When a wind whispers through the trees, it whisks away some of the leaves from the branches, tossing them through the air until they float to the forest floor. Some leaves rest on a circle of stones. Light undulates across the surface of the stones in movements and patterns unrelated to the sunlight streaming from above.

My gaze shifts from the odd stones and leaf-carpeted ground to the frog-man again. He's still staring at my face, though his jaw is no longer gaping open like a fly trap, and his eyes shine with an excitement I can't explain.

"Can I help you?" I ask somewhat irritably, because honestly, what gives him the right to just stare at people like this?

Seeming to recover his senses, the frog-man clears his throat. "Yes, you can," he muses, though I'm not sure if he's actually talking to me or to himself. His voice isn't just old, I realize, but also a bit croaky. I hadn't noticed that before.

"Are you lost?" I realize how ridiculous it is for me to ask him if he's lost when I'm the one internally freaking out about not being in Minnesota anymore and not sure if I know how to get back and also definitely lost myself.

"Lost?" His laugh is croakier than his voice, and almost too cheery. "No, not lost. But you can help me. It's been a long time since I've had company."

Ah, that's why. He's lonely.

Planting his staff in the ground, he straightens his back a bit. "You may call me Folsom."

You may call me. His words remind me of something I'd read on a number of the websites about the fae a couple nights ago. Unlike the library books, which my brain had decided were unworthy of my time this afternoon, I had spent hours on different fae-related websites, and many of them mentioned the power of names. The common thread? Names have power, and it's generally not a great idea to tell a fae your given name, unless you want them to have power over you.

Lonely or not, I don't want to give Folsom an opportunity to have power over me. "My friends call me E." I attempt a warm smile, looking down at him.

"Well, E, your company is welcome. What brings you to this part of Elfaeme? Not many travel to my little corner of the fae realm."

"Adventure." I may only have a rudimentary knowledge of fae, established from a few hours of website research, but it's just common sense not to spill your guts to a stranger.

He blinks at me with his yellow, protuberant eyes. "Would you like me to show you around?"

I hesitate, regarding him warily, and look back to the hole in the tree which, I can only assume, brought me to the fae realm. Do I dare leave it? What if I can't make it back?

His foot taps the forest floor impatiently with a dull thud-thud-thud.

I look around me, memorizing the trees, the path, the tree with the hole in it, as best as I can. "Sure," I reply. "I'd love a guide who knows this area of Elfaeme well."

"It's settled then," he wheezes. "There are many wonderful places to visit in this remote corner of the realm. Satyr Grove. Dragonfly Falls. Dryad Woods. But," he taps his chin thoughtfully, "my personal favorite is the Reflecting Pool."

"They all sound wonderful!" I exclaim, truly excited, because it's dawning on me. I'm in the fae realm. Where my parents are from. Where I'm from. The two lines from my birth mom's note, pop into my head:

The Mage Stone, they call it, rests on the plains.
Take note of its western face when it rains.

Too bad we're in the middle of the woods on a sunny day. I have no idea how to even navigate the fae realm. Apart from getting here, I realize I'm woefully unprepared to start searching for anything in that rhyme.

Folsom prattles on about the Reflecting Pool and other things as we walk, but he's worse than my grandpa Ben when it comes to circuitous stories, and I soon tune him out. He takes slow, careful steps, pausing often to look around, though I have no idea for what. I can feel impatience curdling in my chest at the pace. To distract myself, I look around.

I still can't believe I'm here. That this place, Elfaeme, the fae realm, is real, that my parents are fae. That I'm fae. I don't feel any different from the Eevee I was before reading the note or coming here.

The trees here keep catching my eyes. They have this timeless quality to them, like they've been around forever and a day and will continue to be here for at least double that time. Their branches intertwine with each other, creating what would probably be a thick canopy if it weren't for the fact that most of the leaves were on the ground. Late afternoon sunlight beams down between the branches, illuminating the multicolored forest floor. There's hints of life in the trees, scuffling sounds and twittering of birds all around us, but no other fae that I can see aside from Folsom (and myself, I guess).

When Folsom stops and looks around yet again, I ask him. "Aren't there any other fae who live here? What are you looking for?"

He turns to me, regarding me warily, like I caught him in the act of doing something he shouldn't. "Is that a trick question?"

My eyebrows knit together. "Why would it be?"

"Why indeed?" he asks himself. He blinks up at me, first with one eye, then the other. "The Reflecting Pool is not far now. Come."

I grumble to myself about frog-men who don't answer questions, but follow regardless. My mind is racing. Have my birth parents been here before? Where is here, in relation to the rest of the fae realm? Is there a map? Taking my phone out of my pocket, I snap some pictures of what I'm seeing, then switch the camera mode to take a picture of myself. My heart stops. The image on my phone's screen. It can't be me. It has to be me.

It is me. The figure on the screen is wearing the same red and white checkered shirt with the "Gramp's Diner" logo emblazoned across the upper left. As I bring the phone closer to my face, the image zooms in on a face that is mine, just...different. My light brown eyes with their green flecks are almost glowing. The skin on my temples is covered in what looks like inked orange flowers, but when I rub my face, the images stay. And, what is that...that thing over my shoulder?

I try and peer over my own shoulder, then gasp. Wings. Iridescent orange wings are attached to my back. What? How? Why couldn't I feel them before? I reach over my shoulder and feel where they attach to my back, then try flexing some muscles to get them to move. My fingers trace over two neat holes in my Gramp's Diner shirt where the wings poke out. As I angle my phone to snap some pictures of my wings as best I can, I can't help but think to myself that I'm going to have to buy a new work shirt now, which sucks. Then I feel my wings again and grin. Cam and Maggie are not going to believe this. I can't send the pictures, though, because my phone has no service. Apparently the fae realm doesn't have cell phone towers.

"We're here," Folsom says. I pocket my phone. Folsom has a nervous energy about him as he shifts from one foot to the other.

I have no idea why he's nervous. This place is amazing. The Reflecting Pool lives up to its name and reflects the scene above it: bright blue sky, trees ablaze with leaves, and not a cloud to be seen. The surface of the pool is only marred by leaves landing on it. Other than the occasional ripple, it is completely still.

I step up to the edge of the pool and look downward. "It's beautiful."

"I know."

Folsom is at the edge of the trees, still shifting from foot to foot. He moves his staff from one hand to the other and clears his throat. "Right. Stay here. I'll be back."

"Wait, what?" I gaze for a moment at my reflection–my glowing eyes, floral patterned face, and my wings peeking out above each shoulder–then look back up at him. "Where are you going?"

"Just stay here until I return," he presses. "Promise me."

Warning bells erupt in my head, sounding very much like the tornado sirens that go off in Duluth on the first Wednesday of every month. Another piece of advice I had read on the websites the other night: be careful about entering into binding agreements with the fae, or you'll be held to them, and they'll often find loopholes that will keep them from holding up their end of the deal. Well, I'm a fae as well, aren't I?

"I promise I'll stay a while." Hoping my face looks innocent, I add, "The pool is so pretty, isn't it?"

"Very," he says. I give him a dazzling smile. "Right, then." He clears his throat and pauses, seeming to weigh his options. Finally, he says, "I'll be back."

With that, he shuffles off into the trees, leaving me truly alone in the middle of the fae realm for the first time since I arrived.

I breathe a sigh of relief. He could have tried to press me to make my promise more specific. I think he would have, if I weren't over two feet taller than him and a lot younger. As it is, promising to stay by the Reflecting Pool "a while" is vague enough, so I don't feel bad when, after ten minutes, I stand up to leave. I breathe deep, then listen, trusting my super hearing to pick up any suspicious sounds. After making sure I can't hear his distinctive shuffling steps in the trees, I head back the way we came.

My heart pounds in my chest as I walk, trying to avoid making too much noise. It's hard, with so many leaves on the ground, and I wince each time I step and they crunch and crackle beneath my shoes.

How do I get back to Minnesota? The sun is now burning orange, and I panic, walking faster. Who knows how much time has passed since I left? I've seen enough movies about parallel worlds with Cam to know the time doesn't always match up. For all I know, I'll get back to find a hundred years has passed and I'll call myself Eevee Van Winkle.

I'm running now. I don't care if Folsom hears me; even if he does, I doubt he can catch up to me. My wings flutter uselessly behind me–if I can fly, I don't know how yet. I stop running, feeling dread coursing through me. Looking from left to right, I force myself to take deep breaths. I don't recognize this part of the path. Just as I'm about to turn around, I see a side path that I had missed, and I head down it, breathing a sigh of relief when I see the circle of stones with their odd, light-shifting surfaces. The stones I had seen when I first arrived in the fae realm.

Breaking into a run again, I make it to the knotted oak with the hole in it that had started this whole adventure. I don't know why Folsom wanted me to wait, but I trust my instincts and know I should get out of here. I stare at the hole in the tree. "Come on, come on," I whisper. "I need to get back." I glance around at the darkening woods around me, at the leaves fluttering through the air, then force my gaze back to the hole. "How did I do it before?" I mutter, leaning closer and peering inside it. It's still as empty as it was earlier. Sighing in frustration, I straighten up and sway on the spot, lightheaded. In the distance, I hear the sound of a truck rumbling down the road.

A truck!

Impulsively, I hug the old oak tree, then run down the path. I don't care that my face is red or that sweat is pouring down my back as I get to my car parked on the side of the road. I fumble for my keys and accidentally press the alarm button, which makes me jump about a foot in the air. Turning off the car alarm, I unlock the front door and slide into the driver's seat, my whole body shaking. Impulsively, I reach over my shoulder to feel for my wings. They're gone, of course, or I'd have felt it when I sat down. The holes where they had poked through my shirt are gone, too, which is a relief. I hadn't exactly been thrilled with the idea of needing to replace my work shirt.

My phone dings and beeps with missed messages and calls. I glance at the clock on the dashboard. Craptastic. I told my parents I'd be home by five at the latest, and it's six thirty. I send my mom a quick text, *be home soon. sorry im late, im ok*, and pull the car out onto North Shore Drive, heading home as quickly as the speed limits allow.

Chapter 9

Telling the Truth

We're back in the living room again. My parents are sitting on the couch next to each other, looking at me with disappointment in their eyes. It's 8:30 at night, so Greg and Charlie are already tucked into their beds, though I doubt they're asleep yet. Amelia and Jess are supposed to be in their rooms working on homework, but I'm willing to bet one or both of them are eavesdropping at the bottom of the stairs, where they're out of sight but not out of earshot. I'm itching to go to my room, like the rest of my siblings, and text Cam and Maggie everything that happened this afternoon. I have photographic evidence now, not just a picture of a blank sheet of paper. Excitement hums in me, even as I wilt under the combined stares of my parents.

I wonder what Cam and Maggie will say? I can imagine it now. Cam, sweet as ever, will say they always knew I was special. Maggie will probably jokingly ask if she can do an exposé on me for North Shore Notorious, the school podcast. She wouldn't mean it, though, not for something like this.

I'm so lost in my thoughts it takes me a minute to realize my dad is talking now, and another minute to focus on what he's saying.

"-maybe a mistake to give you that info on your birth parents when we did, Evelyn. You've been distant ever since, and-"

My mom sobs. "I feel like we're losing you!"

I look at them both, then. Really look at them. Mom's white blonde hair is up in a bun for the night, but wisps of her hair have already escaped the bun and are framing her face, which is round and red-cheeked. Dad looks tired; big, puffy bags sag under his eyes and his shoulders are slumped. He takes off his glasses and fiddles with them.

"You are not losing me." I get up and smush myself between them on the couch, taking one of their hands in each of my own. "You're my mom and dad," I tell them firmly. "Nothing will change that. Not information on my birth parents, not even if I meet them someday."

Mom lets out a shuddering breath, and I feel tension leave her. The smile she gives me is a little more relaxed. Hesitantly, she says, "And we'll be here for you if and when you do meet them, Eevee. You know that."

"I know." I lean my head on her shoulder, breathing in her sweet honeysuckle perfume, which always seems to linger on her, no matter how long it's been since she actually applied it.

"Was there some hard-to-swallow information in that envelope, Evelyn?"

I look at my dad, whose face is pinched with worry.

"We hadn't opened it ahead of time, out of respect for you, so we don't know what is in it," he admits.

I tell them both about the medical records and the card and picture, and they listen attentively. I don't mention the letter, with its many warnings not to go looking for my birth parents. I don't want mom and dad to worry that I may be in some kind of danger. Mom especially. I can picture my senior year now if I let her read the letter; I'd never be allowed to go anywhere. I'd spend my days going directly from home to school back to home. She'd constantly be checking in. No, better not to mention the letter and worry them.

When I finish talking about my frustration with all the blacked out information, mom rubs my back soothingly.

"You guys really didn't know anything about what was in it? About my birth parents?" I ask.

"No," dad answers at the same time mom shakes her head. "We were just so grateful to have you. We didn't ask too many questions." He launches into a recollection of my adoption story. He and mom have told it so many times between the two of them, I practically feel as if I had been there. Which I was, for part of it, but as a month-old baby, so I don't remember it myself.

I recall the story well, though.

A young Todd and Penny Acker had agreed, early on in their marriage, that when they had jobs and a house, they'd adopt a child and start a family.

The jobs (Penny, a products data analyst and Todd, an electrician) and house (just outside Duluth) came, but their adoption journey was at a standstill for years. For their first adoption, they wanted to adopt a baby from a local Minnesotan agency, and infant adoptions were rare. There had been a few opportunities along the way, but they always fell through.

Then the adoption specialist from the agency, Martha, had called them, almost eighteen years ago now.

A couple had just given birth to a baby girl and wanted her adopted into a caring family as soon as possible. Were Todd and Penny Acker interested?

"Silly question," mom interrupts, her eyes teary as she grips my hand. "Of course we were interested."

Dad continues the story.

My parents already had a file with the agency, so it was just a matter of waiting for my birth parents' files to go through.

"Then, October 15th, eighteen years ago, we got to bring you home," my dad concludes.

It's usually the end of the story.

"Did you meet them when you went to pick me up?" I ask.

I know the answer. I've asked before.

"Not exactly."

I look sharply at my mom. Their answer is usually a straight no.

"What do you mean, not exactly?"

Dad is looking at mom as well, one of his eyebrows raised. "Yes, what do you mean?"

Mom bites her lip and looks at my dad. "I've never been sure, Todd. It's why I haven't mentioned it. But, when we were leaving the adoption agency and walking with Evelyn to the car, I saw a woman in the parking lot."

My heart races, and I remember my birth mom's hastily written note. "I can't stand the thought of not seeing you ever again. I want to see you someday."

"It could've been anyone," my dad tells her.

"Yes," she nods. "But...the calculating, intense way she looked at me..." She shakes her head. "Well, I don't know."

"It was probably just an employee," dad says reasonably.

Mom is quiet for a moment. "You're probably right." But she looks at me and I see uncertainty in her eyes.

"Now, Evelyn." Dad has a no-nonsense tone in his voice. Storytime is over, apparently. Back to the business of figuring out what to do with Eevee. "Your mother and I had thought you were mature enough to handle the information in that envelope, and that is why we ultimately decided to give it to you now instead of after graduation."

"We also thought with your current emotional state, you could use a distraction," mom adds. "Something to take your mind off of Damian."

"Well, you can't take it back," I say quickly.

"No, of course not," dad replies, looking surprised I'd even suggest it. His face settles into a stern expression. "But, Evelyn, it's not like you to cut your hair out of the blue, or to shout at teachers, or to disappear without letting us know where you're going."

"You know I don't believe that grounding works," mom says. She pats my hand, searching my face. "We just ask that you're more open with us from now on, like you were tonight when you talked to us about what was in that envelope." She smiles at me. "Thank you for sharing that with us."

I feel a little worm of guilt burrowing into my heart. But what am I supposed to say? "Yeah, you're welcome. Oh, and I forgot to mention that there was a letter from my birth parents in there, too, which implies they may have been in danger. And my birth mother wrote a note on the back of that letter, and it turns out I'm fae, my birth parents are fae, the fae realm is a real place called

Elfaeme and that's where I was this afternoon. And guess what? When I'm there I have orange fairy wings."

That'd go over well. I can already see my mom's panicked expression and nervous, fluttering hands, and hear my dad pull out his phone and mutter to himself, "Numbers for mental health institutions in Duluth, Minnesota," as he types the query into the search bar.

They're still looking at me expectantly, waiting for me to respond.

I swallow, and tell them the truth, or part of it. "Of course I'd share it with you. You're my mom and dad. And, I dunno." I shrug. "It's been a weird senior year so far." They have no idea how weird. "Between Damian dumping me, and Mr. Jenkins being a jerk, you know." They nod. "And, I totally appreciate you giving me that info on my birth parents. Some of it was a little overwhelming, but I'm figuring it out."

"You're sure?" mom asks. With her free hand she reaches up and holds my cheek, something she's done as long as I can remember.

"I'm sure."

I hate keeping anything from my parents, and that worm of guilt burrows deeper, grows bigger. I think they feel better after our conversation. I hear them talking quietly as I walk up the stairs, and dad laughs at something mom says. But I feel worse, a lot worse. My secret rests uncomfortably in the back of my throat, making it hard to swallow as I head to my room and close the door.

*****

Thoughts of mental institutions dance through my head as I pick up my phone to text Maggie and Cam. All my excitement from earlier has left me like air leaving a balloon, and just like a balloon, I feel deflated.

I pull up my picture album on my phone instead, eager to relive some of my adventure to the fae realm this afternoon. Not the parts with Folsom. Something about his interactions with me makes my stomach feel queasy with unease. But I want to see the ageless trees again. The Reflecting Pool. My wings. I can almost feel them behind me as I lean back against my pillow, phantom wings where none remain.

But as I scroll through my pictures, I grind my teeth in frustration. They're all blurred, every single picture so distorted it's impossible to make out anything in them. I almost throw my phone across the room, but stop myself just in time. I don't make all that much money washing dishes at Gramp's.

Instead of throwing it, I turn it off, and lay down on my bed. When I close my eyes, I can see the trees again, and feel my wings fluttering behind me.

I want to go back. But Folsom's strange behavior has me wondering if that's a good idea. I don't know what he wanted with me, but given that fae are known for being mischievous at best, I don't think he had plans to invite me to tea.

And even if I do go back, I have no idea where anything is in the fae realm. My birth mother's clue, the two rhyming lines of her note, runs through my head on repeat.

Maybe there's something in the books? I pull out the library books again and flop down on my stomach on the bed, flipping through them. With a purpose, my brain is laser-focused, and I scan each page for any mention of a Mage Stone, but there's none. Each page I turn, I feel a bubble of hope, and when I scan it, that bubble pops. It's exhausting, and finally I put the books back in my backpack.

The fae realm isn't going anywhere, I tell myself. I can cling to that knowledge, at least.

Chapter 10

Fae Revelations

Detention is even more boring than I thought it'd be.

Mr. Jenkins is at his desk, working. He and I have hardly spoken since the incident last week. He's called Cam by the proper pronouns in class, though, so at least there's that.

I finish my homework with time to spare. Sure, I might have rushed through a lot of it, but it's done.

I wish I could use my phone. I still haven't talked to Maggie and Cam about being fae. It's not exactly lunchtime conversation material.

Cam had seemed better today compared to how they were acting on Friday. When I pulled Maggie aside in the hall earlier today, she confirmed my suspicions.

"It's nothing major, Cam's fine. They talked with me about it over the weekend," she'd said before striding off to biology.

I'm a bit upset Cam opened up to Maggie about it, not me. Cam and I have been friends for almost a decade, and I'm the one who introduced them to Maggie, back in eighth grade, when Maggie was a new student in one of my classes and needed someone to sit with at lunch.

Maggie's like that, though; she can ease the truth out of anyone when she puts her mind to it. I know she's going to be a fantastic investigative journalist someday because of that. She's already made a name for herself around town through her work on the school podcast. There was this huge story she posted to it last year on the improper use of funds for the school's hockey team. It ended up exposing a scheme by a trio of hockey moms to funnel the fundraiser money into their own pockets. There were court trials and everything.

I glance at the clock. How has it only been a minute since I last checked the time?

Sitting here is a special kind of agony. I suck at waiting for anything, and I really want to get home so I can talk to Maggie and Cam.

I spend the rest of detention daydreaming about Elfaeme and trying to figure out the best way to tell my best friends that I'm fae.

After what seems like 342 years (at least), Mr. Jenkins finally stands. "You may go, Miss Acker," he says in his dry voice, his mopey basset hound face looking tired. "Your detention is over."

"Great. Bye!" I zoom out of there before he can attempt any conversation, not that he seemed inclined to do so.

Mom let me borrow her car today. I think it's her way of saying she still thinks my detention was unwarranted, but she doesn't say that out loud. Instead, she told me she's been meaning to catch up with her work friend, Dani, so they have plans to grab coffee together this afternoon, and Dani can drive her to and from work.

Whatever the reason, I'm grateful I don't have to wait to be picked up this afternoon. It was also nice not taking the bus to school on a Monday. I had driven Cam and Amelia to school, but since I had to stay after for detention, they've both taken the bus home by now.

I stop at my locker to drop off a few of my books. No need to bring them home with me if I've already done the work.

I turn down the hall and walk toward the doors which lead to the parking lot and drop-off/pick-up zone, near the office. There's a kid standing by the doors waiting to get picked up.

My heart simultaneously sinks and beats faster, which honestly feels strange.

Maybe he won't see me, I think, but not too hopefully. Quince, unfortunately, has been noticing me a lot this year.

I'm only feet away when he looks over his shoulder at me. His eyes widen with surprise.

"Hey, Eevee," he says with a grin.

Reluctantly, I slow my pace.

"Hey, Quince."

"Waiting for a ride, too?"

I hold up the car keys. "Driving home. I was just released from prison–er–detention."

He checks his phone. Without looking at me, he asks, "Doing anything later?"

His shyness, if that's what this is, surprises me, especially after how confidently I'd seen him talking to Laura only last week.

"Mondays are board game nights at the Acker house." I'm glad for the excuse. An evening with Quince trying to convince me to do the fall musical and become a theater person like him doesn't exactly rank highly on the list of things I'd enjoy doing tonight.

"Oh. Well, maybe another time." He looks up from his phone, a twinkle in his dark eyes. "We have lots of time, after all."

"Uh, yeah." I shift from one foot to the other. "Well, talk to you later."

As I move past him, he places a hand on my arm. I could keep walking, if I wanted, but I'm curious. The place where his hand touches my bare arm is hot.

"We really should talk soon," he says. His voice is light, but his face with its sharp jawline is dark with intensity.

I feel his breath near my ear as he leans forward and can smell his peppermint gum. "I'm faemiliar with what you're going through," he whispers.

I know my ears have not deceived me; I've learned to trust in them and their ability to pick out the sound of a pin dropping on carpet.

He didn't say fa-miliar. He said fae-miliar.

I stare at him. Our eyes lock, and I see understanding, and questions, and excitement in his.

Mine probably just show utter confusion with a healthy dose of shock.

A car honks outside, and he drops his hand from my arm.

"Message me," he says, shouldering his bag and walking out toward the car before I can answer.

I shake myself out of my shock and run after him. "Quince!"

His car door slams shut and the car starts driving away. I chase after it. "Quince Florentz! You can't just say that and walk away!"

Infuriatingly, I see him grin at me as the car turns right onto the road.

I slow down to a walk and pull out my phone.

E: *this is not the end of the conversation, Quince Florentz*

I move woodenly to my mom's car, sending her a quick text that I am on my way home. She must've been waiting for me to message her, because right away, she sends a reply.

P: *I placed an order for takeout at the Lotus Garden. Can you pick it up on your way home?*

I text her back, confirming I will, and pull out of the school parking lot. Somehow I stop at the Chinese restaurant and make it back home without remembering most of the drive.

A thrill of excited energy courses through me all night.

Quince is fae.

I'm not the only non-human at Duluth High.

Our previous conversations make so much more sense now. He'd never been trying to get me to go out for the fall musical; he'd been trying to understand why he and I have never crossed paths before if I'm fae, too.

I don't even care when Greg wins all three board games in a row and dances around the room hollering that he's the best board game player in the world. Usually his awful attitude with winning and losing bothers me, but tonight I just laugh with Amelia and Jess as Charlie scowls in the corner. Losing is hard when you're only six.

My phone buzzed a few times this evening, but Jess is notorious for sneaking peeks at other peoples' phones when she knows she shouldn't. The girl has no concept of personal privacy. I know that from the many times she's barged into the bathroom when I'm in the shower. She can't help herself. She always has to know what everyone is up to all the time. Mom and dad have told us to be patient with her, though. She spent the first few years of her life with biological parents who ignored her to the point of malnutrition and neglect, so her incessant desire to always know what everyone is doing is her way to make sure she's not forgotten.

I hug her before heading upstairs. There's not much I hide from her, but I don't want to risk her seeing any messages from Quince, just in case.

Only when Amelia has finished talking to me about some boy in her math class with, apparently, the most perfect set of shoulders, do I take out my phone.

No messages from Quince, but I see I've missed a conversation with Cam and Maggie.

M: *omg*

M: *omg*

M: *OMG*

M: *I DID IT*

M: *I APPLIED TO NY COLLEGE*

Cam's reply is so typically Cam it makes me smile.

C: *awesome. let us know when u get in!*

Not if, when. I agree with Cam, though. Any college would be lucky to have Maggie.

E: *yessss Mags!! wtg! i still need to apply to the Duluth business school's vet tech program. i keep forgetting*

As usual, Maggie's response is lightning fast.

M: *u got time!*

C: *yeah, don't sweat yet, Eevee*

My fingers hover over the phone. Earlier, during detention, I'd come up with what I wanted to say to tell them about me being fae. It's nothing earth-shattering; I've decided to be as plain and simple about it as I can. I type out the message and am about to send it when an image of me in a straitjacket pops into my mind.

I delete my text, then open up Instagram. Taking a few steadying breaths, I type out another message to Quince and hit send.

Chapter 11

It's Not a Date

I sit down at a booth in the back of what must be the busiest bar and grill in Duluth. It's Wednesday, and there's no major sports events on TV that I know of, yet the place, Chummy's, is packed.

Quince should be here soon. I tap my foot as I wait, unable to contain the nervous energy that's been thrumming through my bones ever since I ran into Quince after detention.

The server brings over a water for the table, setting it down atop a white napkin.

"I'll need another water for my friend, too," I say as she places it in front of me.

She glances at the empty side of the booth and back to me, raising a penciled eyebrow.

"He'll be here soon," I add defensively at the look in her eyes.

"All right, sweetie, another water comin' up," she says in the northern Minnesotan drawl, with emphasis on the vowels and no 'g' to be found at the end of any word ending with "-ing."

She saunters away and my foot tapping resumes. I pull out my phone and scroll through it, sending a few quick messages to Cam and Maggie.

"Is this seat taken?"

I set my phone down and grin. "To take the seat, or not to take the seat, that is the question…"

"No question," he answers as he slides into the booth across from me. The plastic covered seat cushion squeaks beneath him. Shaking his head at me, he laughs. "You've got an obsession, Eevee, and his name is William Shakespeare." He grabs a menu from the center of the table and peruses it as I mockingly glare at him.

When he looks up, I crinkle my nose and say, "There are worse things to be obsessed with."

Our server returns with a second water and takes our orders. When she leaves, I open my mouth, but immediately close it. There are so many questions clambering to be first, which one to ask?

"So, this is crazy," I begin. Quince holds up a finger and pulls out his phone. Slurping his water through the striped straw, he types away.

If this were a date I'd be storming out right now. I didn't come here to sit across a booth from someone who is mentally somewhere on the internet.

You know what? I rescind my previous statement. Even though this isn't a date, I'd still be out of here under normal circumstances. But Quince had insisted we not talk overtly about the fae at school or through any kind of messaging.

So I imagine all kinds of dramatic exits and seethe internally as he continues to focus on his phone.

"Just confirming with mom that I made it inside. She's asking me when she should pick me up," he says. He looks up at me through strands of dark hair which had fallen over his eyes. "How long do you think we'll need?"

"I drove here, I can give you a ride home," I say. Mom and dad had been so excited I was going out with someone, even though I had insisted many times that it wasn't a date, that they urged me to take the car for the night. I think they see it as a sign I'm moving on from Damian. I don't think they'll mind if I drive Quince home. In fact, in their weird way, they might be excited about that, too.

"You kidding?" Quince's smile is so genuinely joyful I find myself grinning back. "Thank you! I'll tell mom not to worry about it. She and dad can have an evening to themselves."

He types the new message into his phone as our server returns with a tray of food for the booth behind me. It's loaded with heaping plates of fries and greasy burgers. Fried food smell wafts over to us and my stomach growls. I cover it with my hands, trying to stifle the sound before Quince can hear it. I think of my super hearing, though, and for the first time, I wonder if maybe good hearing is a fae ability. If it is, maybe all fae, including Quince, have it? And if so, there's no way he didn't hear my stomach complaining.

Whether he heard my stomach's pleas for food or not is hard to tell. He slips his phone into his pocket and beams at me with the usual mischievous twinkle in his eyes.

"Tell me everything," I burst out.

"Everything?" He taps his chin. "I know a lot about a lot. We could be here all night."

"Place closes at eleven," our server interjects as she refills our waters. Mine doesn't need much, but Quince's is empty. When she leaves, Quince and I look at each other and dissolve into giggles.

Our giggles subside right away, but then Quince does a deadpan imitation of our server with the dry voice and eyebrow raise and everything, and soon my stomach aches from laughing. I can see why he is cast in all the school plays. He takes on another persona like a superhero sliding on their superhero suit.

We're still laughing when our food arrives. I think our server knows the source of our amusement, because her lips are puckered like she's bitten a lemon.

"I'll check back in a bit, see how you're likin' everything," she says once both steaming plates are on the table.

"Actually," Quince smiles up at her, and this time I know I'm not sleep deprived or imagining things when I see the air around him shimmer. "We're good. Here." He hands her a twenty dollar bill and two fives. "That should cover our meals and tip. You don't need to check on us anymore tonight."

She pockets the money. "Sure thing, darlin'," she says with a smile, all signs of the sour pucker-face gone. "Enjoy your date."

"It's not a date!" we both shout.

She nods knowingly and meanders away, stopping at a few tables to grab empty plates on her way to the kitchen.

I watch her retreat in disbelief, then turn an accusing stare on Quince. "Start with that," I demand. "What did you just do? I saw that same shimmer around you last week when you were talking to Laura and Ms. Bates."

His grin is embarrassed, like a kid who's been caught in the act, and he takes a bite of his veggie burger before responding. "That's one of my fae abilities. I get it from my mom. She was a member of the Seelie Court, and a lot of the Seelie fae have some variation of the ability to charm others. Other humans, that is. Our fae abilities don't work on other fae, at least, not as well. But my dad, he was a member of the Unseelie Court, which is why we live here instead of in Elfaeme."

I nod as if I understand what he's talking about, but really my mind is whirling. Seelie Court? Unseelie Court? Different fae abilities?

He continues, his voice and face animated; his hand with the veggie burger in it gestures emphatically as he speaks. "See, the fae of the Seelie and Unseelie Courts don't mix, at least, not often. I mean, there's plenty of fae who aren't members of either Court, and they all just do whatever they want, but there's different expectations if you're associated with one of the Courts, you know?"

I know nothing, I think. "Following you so far," I say. I take a bite of my burger.

"If you're a member of one of the Courts and you join with someone from the other Court, you're kind of seen as freaks in the fae realm. That's what happened with my parents. They met at one of the Equinox gatherings, and decided to give up their seats in the Unseelie and Seelie Courts to be together. And then they had me and thought it'd be best to raise me in the human realm, away from some of the prejudice. But enough about me. Why are you here?" He pops a few fries in his mouth and munches on them, looking at me with eagerness in his eyes.

"I don't know," I admit.

He swallows and squints at me. "You're telling the truth. What do you mean, you don't know?"

I've been waiting for a chance to tell someone everything about what's been going on in my life lately. I start with what happened with Damian. A spark of happiness blooms in my throat when I tell Quince about my final text to Damian, and he applauds my use of Shakespeare's words to end the relationship for good. He already knows about why I shouted lines from *King Lear* at Mr. Jenkins, so I skim over that and skip to my parents giving me my adoption information in an effort to cheer me up.

By the end, Quince's eyes are as wide as the empty plate in front of him.

"You didn't know you were fae until last week," he says, his voice quiet. He shakes his head as if clearing it. "Wow. And you were adopted by humans?"

"Yeah, my mom and dad don't know about me being fae yet," I say. "I'm not exactly sure how to tell them the first daughter they adopted isn't human. And I'm a little worried I'd end up in a mental institution if I do tell them."

"I get it," he says. "I haven't really talked about being fae with anyone either."

I frown. "But last week didn't you say you're a tight-knit community?"

He rubs the back of his head with his hand. "I've been practicing. Once we turn eighteen and all our fae abilities are opened to us, we're also bound to the rules of the fae. And the number one rule is we cannot lie."

"But you did," I point out.

"I didn't say how many there were in the community, did I? There are lots of ways of saying something true in a way that clouds the truth."

"So it's like a loophole."

"Yeah, kind of," he answers. "We may be bound by our rules, but the fae know the loopholes just as well, if not better, than the rules themselves."

"Why bother having rules then?" I grumble to myself.

Quince laughs. "It keeps many of the fae, especially the ones not affiliated with either Court, from wreaking too much havoc." His face sobers. "But back to you."

I make a face. "Do we have to?"

"I'm curious," he insists. "It's just so weird that you were adopted by humans. Being a changeling–a fae raised by human parents," he clarifies, "is super rare. Most fae wouldn't dream of letting humans raise their children." He pushes his empty plate aside and plunks his elbows on the table, gazing at me in much the same way he had last week in the school office, like I'm the most interesting person in the room. "Fae don't have kids often, so they tend to be very possessive of the ones they do have."

"Maybe my birth parents didn't want me."

Mom and dad have always told me that my birth parents had chosen to have me adopted because they loved me, not because of a lack of love. "It's the ultimate sacrifice," mom would say, placing her hand on my cheek. "Giving up something so precious."

But the thought that maybe my birth parents simply didn't want me, or didn't want a child cluttering up their lives, has snaked into my brain on and off throughout my life, especially after reading their letter. All the references to danger in it make me think maybe it would've been too much of an inconvenience for them to have a baby around all the time.

As usual when I have that thought, my heart constricts and I'm about three feet tall.

Quince is shaking his head at me. "You don't understand, Eevee. Fae parents are super possessive of their kids. Whatever reason your parents had, whatever made them decide to have you adopted by humans, it must've been big, to push them to that decision."

He's looking at me now like I'm a mystery to be solved and I wish I could be even smaller, or invisible, to escape from that searching gaze. My heart hammers on my ribcage like a mallet on a xylophone.

"Was there anything else in the letter?"

I wish I had brought the letter with me so I could show him, but I had forgotten it at home.

"Just two rhyming lines. I can't make sense of them, though. They don't fit with anything else in my birth mom's note." I recite the lines to him and am surprised by the excitement lighting up his face.

"I know where the Mage Stone is," he says. "It's a popular landmark on the Seelie side of Elfaeme. Come on." He slides out of the booth, the plastic squeaking beneath him as he moves, and heads toward the door.

I scarf down the last few bites of my burger and grab a handful of fries off my plate, tossing a few in my mouth as I hurry after him.

The loud atmosphere and throbbing country music inside Chummy's fade as the door closes behind me. Outside, the air is cool on my skin and I feel goosebumps prickling up my bare arms. I walk over to Quince, who's standing by a bedraggled-looking tree.

"Don't tell me this tree can take us to the fae realm," I say, eyeing the pathetic tree skeptically. "Don't we need to find a mushroom circle or a still pond or a hole in a tree or something?"

"Only if you're human or have no practice traveling between Elfaeme and the human realm." He holds out a hand to me. "Coming?"

I hesitate, then wipe my hands on the side of my jeans to try and get rid of some of the fry grease.

He's waiting, his hand still held out to me, and as I place my hand in his, he grins.

Chapter 12

On the Plains

One instant I'm holding Quince's hand next to a bedraggled tree, looking out over a crowded parking lot in Duluth as the sunset sparkles over Lake Superior. The next, I'm holding Quince's hand in the middle of a field, a breeze playing through my short hair and the sun warm on my face, feeling woozy. About thirty feet away sits a large, gray stone.

Some other fae mill about the field with us, no two the same. There are a couple who look less humanoid than the rest, as if they had started out their lives as trees who had thought long ago that they'd like to try moving about on legs for a bit. One fae with a beaked nose sits atop the large stone, basking in the sun, his wings spread wide beneath him. A few, I realize, are staring at me and Quince, and unless I'm totally mistaken, they're mostly interested in me.

I turn to ask Quince if he's noticed their stares, too, and realize I'm still holding his hand, which I drop at once.

Blinking up at him, I see his Adam's apple bob up and down. He clears his throat.

"So this is what you really look like."

I'd answer, but I think I've forgotten how to breathe.

At Duluth High, Quince is considered good-looking, but that's more to do with his charisma than anything else. He's what most would term an artsy type, what with his involvement in theater.

Here, he's gorgeous. He doesn't have the same fae appearance I do at all, though I notice his eyes have an otherworldly glow to them like mine. Unlike mine, which have a soft glow, his eyes glitter like dark obsidian. Two small, black horns peek through his hair, adding to his definitely-not-a-human appearance.

I think my favorite part of Quince's fae appearance, if I had to choose, would be his wings. Where mine are more like ephemeral butterfly wings, his are feathered and as black as a raven's.

He flexes his wings, then they fold across his back. "I always miss these when I'm gone," he says, gesturing to them. "Now, let's go see if we can find anything around the Mage Stone."

He nods to the two treelike fae as we pass them on our way to the Mage Stone, and I get that prickling sensation again that their attention is on me.

The Mage Stone looms above us, its dull gray surface at odds with the bright grasses and flowers surrounding it.

"What's the big deal with this stone?" I ask. "Other than the fact it's a big rock?"

Circling the stone, Quince taps on its surface. "The Mage Stone used to be a moonstone–a magical stone fae can use to travel to different parts of Elfaeme," he explains. "It was the biggest one in the whole fae realm, and many battles were fought for control of it. Eventually, though, its magic went dormant, like a volcano, so fae can't use it to travel anymore. There's a nearby marketplace that's been set up in the last ten years or so, though, so fae still come by and see it." He circles the stone in the other direction and mutters to himself. "The western face, right?" he asks me.

When I tell him yes, he checks the sun's position and tugs me to the sunny side. I touch its warm surface, then look over my shoulder and squint at the sun. "It's not raining," I say, disappointed.

"Of course," Quince snaps his fingers. "Forgot that part of the rhyme. Well, that doesn't matter. What if we bring the rain?"

"You can control the weather?"

"No." He laughs at the incredulous look on my face. "But I know where there's a stream nearby."

"I don't have anything to carry the water with," I point out.

"Me neither," he admits, "but I thought we could use this." He unties a green hoodie from his waist. "We can soak it with water from the stream and bring it back here."

He balls up his sweatshirt in his hands and crouches, bending his knees and spreading out his wings. Without pausing, he springs into the air, and a rush of wind brushes across my face from his flapping wings.

"Coming?"

I look back at my own wings and try and flex them experimentally.

Sensing my hesitation, he lowers himself to the ground. "You don't know how to use your wings yet, do you?" He ties his sweatshirt around his waist again and fiddles with one of the two small horns that poke out through his hair near his forehead. "Shoot, I didn't even think of that, I'm sorry."

"It's fine," I say. "Really." I pull out my phone to check the time. "But maybe since our parents think we're just having dinner, we save the flying lessons for later?"

"Deal." He rubs his hand along his jaw as he surveys some trees at the far edge of the field. "It'll take us longer to walk to the stream instead of flying, but we could get there and back within a half hour if we hurry."

"That should get us back within a reasonable time," I muse.

"My thoughts exactly." He takes my hand and pulls me away from the Mage Stone to the grove of trees. Like the forest I'd been in before, these trees are in the late stages of autumn. Leaves of yellow and red and orange adorn their branches and paint the forest floor in vivid color.

Passing from the field to beneath the forest canopy is like going from outside on a warm summer's day into a room with air conditioning, and I regret my choice of a short-sleeved cotton shirt.

Quince is talking about this part of the fae realm, and I think with amusement that he must be excited to have someone else to share it with.

"We'll have to come back to the In Between in the morning sometime. The land that lies between the two Courts always begins in spring in the morning and ends in autumn by the end of the day."

I squash the happy bubbles forming in my chest at the warmth of his hand over mine with a reminder that the only reason Quince is interested in me at all right now is because I'm new and exciting. He's found out I'm fae like him, and there's a mystery about my adoption. None of that interest has anything to do with who I am.

Some animals scurry away from us as we walk, and I smile at their cheery chatter. If I concentrate, I can almost make out their thoughts about finding nuts and berries and hiding them from their enemies. Other than the forest animals, though, Quince and I are alone.

This realization hits me and I drop his hand, shoving my own hands in my jean pockets.

He continues to talk as if nothing's happened.

"Maybe once we find your birth parents they'll be able to explain all the riddles and secrecy and not-so-veiled references to danger."

I make a non-committal noise in my throat, and he switches back to talking more about the areas of the fae realm.

As much as I want to learn more from him, my mind wanders and when I blink, I see the stares of the fae in the field. It's not just the chilly autumn air around me that sends a shiver down my spine.

"Can the fae tell when someone is new here?"

He stops mid-sentence and screws up his eyes at me, so I tell him about the stares and how they gave me an uncomfortable feeling.

"And they're not the only ones I've gotten that weird feeling from," I add, filling him in about my encounter with Folsom as we walk.

We reach the stream and he kneels next to it, untying his sweatshirt from his waist and soaking it in the clear, blue water.

"You saw Folsom?" It's hard to tell what his tone of voice is, and his back is to me, so I can't see his face. All I can see is his black, feathered wings shifting as he moves.

"I did. He acted like he'd seen a ghost when I turned to face him."

He hands me his sopping wet sweatshirt. The stream water soaking through it is cold, and rivulets of water run over my hands as I hold it out in front of me.

"Do you know him?" I ask as we stride back the way we came.

"I know *of* him," he says, his voice low, as if even the trees and squirrels might listen in. I step closer to him, so close our arms almost touch. "He's part of the Unseelie Court, but barely. His family was demoted ages ago. Dad's never told me why, though he'd know. Dad was a part of the Unseelie Court for a long time and knew Folsom well."

"Any idea what he could have done?" I ask.

Quince wrinkles his nose. "Wish I knew. Whatever it was, it really angered the Unseelie King, Nightglade. And Nightglade is known for holding grudges. He's not granted any of Folsom's petitions to have his old status at the Unseelie Court restored."

"Poor Folsom," I say, feeling pity for the strange frog-creature. He'd given me a scare, sure, but anyone would have, I had been so nervous. And to be constantly shut out of the life you used to have? That'd be hard to deal with.

"He probably deserved it," Quince says. "Or not. Nightglade is also known for being a bit…" He considers his next word carefully, chewing on his cheek. "Unpredictable. Anyway, eventually Folsom gave up trying to get his old position back and lived as a hermit in an uninhabited part of the In Between. He hasn't been seen much since."

"Until I crashed in on him."

"Right. Honestly, you probably just surprised him. I don't know if he's interacted with anyone much in years."

We cross from the In Between back to the warm, summery meadow and reach the Mage Stone again. I hand over the sweatshirt to Quince, drying my hands on my jeans and sticking them under my armpits to warm them up, enjoying the warm sunlight on my back.

My hands feel less like ice blocks and more like appendages by the time Quince is done rubbing the soaking wet sweatshirt across the Mage Stone's western face.

The few fae still in the field are more interested in whispering to each other than staring at me or wondering why Quince is getting the Mage Stone wet, thankfully. The fae man who had been sunning himself on top of the Mage Stone is gone as well.

Quince steps back from the Mage Stone, a line between his brows.

"I don't see anything."

Moving next to him and looking at the glistening stone, I ask, "Maybe we need to get more of it wet?"

Some of the water had trickled down to the ground, creating a puddle at its base. I narrow my eyes. "Can I borrow that?" Without waiting for an answer, I grab Quince's sweatshirt from him and press it to the base of the stone, which was still mostly dry. I count to thirty in my head, then peel it back, like when applying a temporary tattoo.

"There!"

Quince crouches next to me as I frantically read and reread the two lines written in the same dark red ink and looping handwriting as my birth mom's note.

I run my fingers along the lines, determined to commit them to memory before the stone dries and they disappear.

"There's nothing there."

This draws my attention away from the words. "Of course there is, right here." I trace my fingers over my birth mom's handwriting.

Quince's face is pale as he pulls me up and away from the stone. "What color are the words?"

"Dark red," I answer, craning my neck to look down at them and make sure I have the wording right.

Soft fingers touch my chin and tilt my face from the stone to Quince. He brushes his shaking fingers upward from my chin and traces them over the orange flowers at my temple.

"That's not ink," he says, holding my gaze with his own. "That's blood."

I gulp. His eyes are darkly serious.

"And, Eevee, only the most powerful fae at the Unseelie Court have the ability to use blood magic."

Chapter 13

I'm a Fairy Princess, Maybe (Probably Not)

I want to joke, "So I'm like a fairy princess or something?" but I can't bring myself to say it. Jess would be thrilled if she were the one in this situation. Her room is literally covered in pictures of princesses.

Besides, Quince didn't say royalty. He'd said "only the most powerful at the Unseelie Court," which could mean any number of Unseelie fae.

Instead of joking, I do the I'm-swaying-and-may-soon-faint thing, which was not planned on my part, and find myself sitting with my left side pressed against a dry side of the Mage Stone while Quince sits facing me and jabbering away about anything he can recall about Court intrigue from eighteen years ago.

"There was the whole scandal of the Unseelie Queen Maeve up and leaving King Nightglade, but that was before you were born, and-" He stops when he sees my dazed expression. "Sorry, not helpful."

"No, it's okay." I force my face into a grin, though at the worried look on Quince's face I don't think I've succeeded. "It's interesting to hear about."

He pauses for a moment, then says, "Well, if you're sure…" At a sign from me, he goes on. "There's also the whole equinox business. Around the same time my parents got together, there were a few other members of the Courts who had married in secret, too. It was kind of a trend for a minority of the Court members–go against the grain, marry outside your Court."

"It worked out for your parents, didn't it?"

"Yeah, and some others."

"Did the trend fall out of style, then?"

Quince's wings shift behind him. "A lot of the prejudices still remain, so the Courts had noble members, who had been around for hundreds of years, suddenly dropping like flies. Either because they left the Courts or…" He draws a finger across his throat, his face grim. "It might've faded out on its own because of that. But after Maeve left him, Nightglade didn't want anyone to be happy or to intermingle so he banned all members of the Unseelie Court from attending equinox celebrations."

"Did that work?"

"Fae are masters of loopholes," Quince reminds me. "Some still go in disguise. I've seen them there."

"Oh, you go to these celebrations?"

"Every March and September. I've had to skip play practices because of it even. The equinox celebrations are the two times a year when all fae truly come together."

I pull my knees up and hug them to my chest. "Why?"

"Well, so I've told you I'm both Unseelie and Seelie, right?"

My chin bumps against my knees as I nod.

"Well, that means my fae abilities are strongest during both summer and winter. Most fae aren't associated with either Court, so they tend to be strongest during the spring and fall, especially at the-"

"Equinox," I finish. "And are the Seelie strongest at the summer solstice?"

"Yes, which leaves the Unseelie, who are strongest at the winter solstice. It's why the Courts used to gather at the equinoxes. They were-"

"On even footing."

"You catch on quick."

"Thanks." I blink up at the sky and watch a bird fly overhead. It's a lot to take in. My eyes sting, and I wonder if they'll still glow if they have tears in them.

Quince stands and checks the western side of the Mage Stone. "It's dry. Did you get the words memorized?"

I want to say yes because I had tried so hard to memorize them earlier, but I can't. My brain is doing that thing where it goes completely blank because I've overloaded it with too much information too quickly.

How many tests have I spent hours studying for and then, with the paper in front of me, blanked on everything I'd learned? Honestly, I've lost count. Cam's voice breaks through the wordless buzzing in my head.

"You know this, Eevee," the Cam in my head says. "You got this. Just breathe."

I take a deep breath as Quince picks up his sweatshirt. "It's still pretty wet. The words were about here, right?"

I rage at my short-circuited brain. It's embarrassing. Quince memorizes stuff all the time for the school plays. How does he do it and not end up standing on stage with his mouth opening and closing like a fish?

"Yeah, better check again to make sure I've got the wording right."

"If you say it to me, I'll remember it," he says.

I think he's trying to be reassuring and helpful, but I kind of want to punch him.

He finishes wetting down the spot at the base of the Mage Stone and stands, looking around.

"Most of the visitors are gone," he says, "but better whisper it to me just in case. Fae have-"

"Good hearing?"

"Like a pigeon."

I snort. "I'm sorry, what?"

"Pigeons have amazing hearing," he explains. "You should look it up sometime. They can even detect distant storms."

"Fascinating." I squat down and read through the words once in my head, then whisper, "At the center of the lake with no waves, look for the jewel in the sunken caves." I look up to Quince. "Need me to repeat it?"

"No, I've got it," says Quince "I'm-a-jerk-who-can-memorize-things-the-first-time-I-hear-them-like-it's-no-big-deal" Florentz.

Standing, I cross my arms. The sun has almost set, and though the air is summery, it doesn't have the same warmth it had even an hour ago. "Well? Do you know what it means?"

Quince lets out a long-suffering sigh. "Yes, and no." He checks his phone. "I think we'd better talk about this on the ride home. Mom's probably sent me about fifty texts, and when I don't respond right away she worries I've gone to Elfaeme unsupervised."

"Her fears aren't exactly unfounded." I nudge his shoulder with mine.

"No." He doesn't grin back at me, and guilt pricks across my skin like goosebumps. I'd been so caught up in finding my birth mom's clue and hearing everything about the fae I hadn't given any thought to Quince.

"Let's go, then. We can definitely talk in the car."

He picks up his sweatshirt and wrings it out, then fades before my eyes.

All my nerves are on fire as if someone had just poured hot coals over my body. He left me here! My mind races and I spin around, eyeing the grove we'd visited earlier. There's got to be a tree with a hole in it in there, or a mushroom circle, right?

I take a step toward it and collide into Quince, who tumbles to the ground. I'm not even sorry.

"What the hell?" My voice is shrill.

He picks himself up and scratches at one of his horns. "Sorry. I forgot you're not used to traveling from Elfaeme to the human realm and back. When you didn't follow, I figured I'd better come help."

"You think?"

"It just takes a little concentration," he explains. "Think about where in the human realm you want to go–in our case, the parking lot of Chummy's–and believe yourself there. Like this."

He disappears again, and I swear to God if this doesn't work I'm going to kill him.

I concentrate better when I close my eyes, so that's what I do, imagining the cars and the view of Lake Superior, and the pathetic looking tree we'd been standing by.

"You can open your eyes, you know."

I do, and as soon as I see him, I give his arm a light jab for how amused he sounds.

"Ow," he says jokingly, rubbing the spot I'd punched.

"Do you want a ride home or not?"

"Fine, fine. I'll stop laughing at you," he says, his hands up in surrender.

He's still smiling at me, but I let him slide into my mom's car anyway.

"Not bad for your first time, Eevee," he says. I hand him my phone and he punches his address into Google Maps. "I didn't mean to make fun of you for closing your eyes. A lot of fae do that at first to help them concentrate." He fiddles with the radio until we're listening to classical instead of my mom's favorite oldies rock station. Sitting back in his seat, he asks, "Want to hear about the first time I came back from Elfaeme on my own?"

"Duh."

"It's a pretty great story. It was winter time, and my parents and I had been visiting some of my dad's Unseelie family. When it came time to return, I wanted to do it on my own. I thought hard about the snow coating the trees like frosting and the ice sheets on Lake Superior, but I'd also been thinking about this project I'd been doing for history. Anyway, instead of ending up back here I found myself in Sweden on top of a reindeer. I didn't close my eyes, though. Maybe that would've helped."

"How old were you?" I ask, amused at the idea of Quince appearing on top of an unsuspecting reindeer.

"Fifteen," he admits as I merge onto I-35N. "Fae kids all learn how to move between realms at different ages, usually after they turn twelve. I think it's related to puberty."

I look at the directions on my phone and see there's only seven minutes left until we arrive at Quince's house. "So do you know what my birth mom's second clue is talking about?"

"Yes and no, like I said." A violin concerto starts up as he thinks and I stew in my impatience. "So the lines

113

go, 'At the center of the lake with no waves, look for the jewel in the sunken caves.' I know where the lake is. It's called Crystal Lake, and it's completely frozen through, but I've never heard of any sunken caves filled with jewels in it."

"Oh." I try to hide my disappointment as I turn off the highway and onto a side street.

He lets out almost the exact same long-suffering sigh as before, by the Mage Stone. "I know someone, two people, actually, who'd probably know, though."

"Well, that's good, right?" Four minutes left.

He shakes his head. "It's my cousins, Sean and Shannon. They live near the lake the clue is referencing. But they're a little," he hesitates, "out there."

"Would they help us?"

"Oh, yes. No question there. They love a good mystery as much as the next fae. Just–consider yourself warned."

"Noted," I say.

I pull into his driveway. Quince's home, like mine, is outside the main part of Duluth and is surrounded by trees.

He moves to get out, then looks at his sweatshirt, which is currently doing its best to flood the floor on the passenger side of the car. "Can I leave my sweatshirt with you? I can't think of a good way to conceal the truth about why it's wet without lying to my parents. I'd rather tell them I let you borrow it." His grin is crooked. "Still practicing the whole 'telling the truth to conceal the truth' thing."

In ten months of dating Damian, I'd never once been allowed to borrow his sweatshirts. "Babe, this sweatshirt is name brand, I can't let just anyone wear it," he'd always say. "You might spill something on it." At the time, I'd been satisfied when he'd follow this up with wrapping his arms around me. Now, I think how ridiculous it was he didn't trust me to wear his precious name brand clothing.

Quince's sweatshirt is a department store zip-up hoodie, with no brand in sight.

"Sure," I say. "I'll wash it tonight and get it back to you tomorrow."

"No rush," he replies. "I'll try and get in contact with my cousins. Hopefully this next clue brings us closer to finding your birth parents."

He closes the door and I wait in the driveway until I see him go inside.

Chapter 14

Maggie Knows Too Much (Also I Hate Keeping Secrets)

Mrs. Field, my science teacher, is talking about some project where we have to interview family members to track our genetically inherited traits. It's meant to help us get a better understanding of genetics for our unit on DNA.

I hate projects like this.

I know what she'll tell me if I mention I'm adopted–to track inherited traits in my adopted parents and their families, as much as I'm able. I'm not sure what she'd say if I mentioned that tracking my adopted parents and their genetic traits may be interesting, but what I'm really curious about is learning who I inherited my orange wings or flower markings from.

She hands out packets for the projects and launches into her lecture on DNA. Pencils scratch at notebook paper around me, and I follow the crowd, penciling down notes as slides illuminate the front of the class. Soon my mind is wandering from Mrs. Field to the fields and forests in the fae realm. She switches to another slide, and I relive sitting next to the Mage Stone with a black-winged Quince by my side, the summery breezes wafting across the grasses.

Finding Fae

Looking down at my notes, I see I've written exactly two bullet points on DNA, followed by the two clues I've found so far.

I draw question marks around the clues. How many are there? What do they lead to? Will I find my birth parents at the end and finally get some answers?

To help my jumbled brain, I turn to a fresh sheet of paper and create a table with two columns.

<u>Finding My Fae Family</u>

<u>What I Know</u>	<u>What I Don't Know</u>
• Clue #1: "The Mage Stone, they call it, rests on the plains. Take note of its western face when it rains."	• How many clues there are
• Clue #2: "At the center of the lake with no waves, look for the jewel in the sunken caves."	• What kind of fae my birth dad is
• Birth mom and birth dad are both fae.	• Where my birth parents are living
• Birth mom uses blood magic–most likely high up in Unseelie Court	• IF my birth parents are living
• Possible fae traits– hearing, possibly hiding (Q's comment in library when I was trying not to be	• What all my fae traits are
	• Why Folsom acted so weird when he saw me?? And what he did to get demoted??
	• Why Folsom and

117

noticed), anger?? Or maybe that's just me and not a fae trait haha...

- Q is also fae

- Folsom-frog-creature thing, Unseelie Court member, demoted for some reason

- My fae appearance: orange butterfly wings, orange flowers on temples, glowing eyes

other fae keep staring at me...like, am I just paranoid? Or is it something else?

By the time biology is over, I've written as much about fae as I have about DNA, but as I gather up my books I rationalize that in a way, I'm trying to fulfill Mrs. Field's DNA project by following the clues to find my birth parents. In theory, it will lead me to learn more about my genetic heritage. But I doubt I could include "glowing eyes from birth father's side of the family" on my project without raising a question or two.

*****

The din of the lunch room–students talking, forks clattering, trays slamming–echoes around me as I flop down at the table where Cam and Maggie are sitting. My backpack thumps to the floor. I hadn't had time to get to my locker and the smell of fried chicken was too enticing. The top unzips on impact and a few books slide out.

"Here, let me help." Maggie kneels down next to me and picks up W. B. Evans-Wentz's *The Fairy-Faith in Celtic Countries*, as well as one of my notebooks where I had doodled a picture of the fairy on the cover during my second period today. She hands them to me without a word, but I can see her analytical brain already at work trying to figure out why, in the past week, I've suddenly shown an interest in fairies outside of *A Midsummer Night's Dream*.

"Sweatshirts tied around the waist are fine if you're out hiking, E," she says as we both sit back down to eat, "but as a fashion statement, I'm not sure it's working for you."

I spoon some corn into my mouth, and my stomach gurgles in appreciation. "It's Quince's. I didn't want to forget to give it to him today," I explain around my mouthful of food.

Cam tucks their now vibrant purple hair behind their ear. "How was the date?" they ask casually, taking a sip of their chocolate milk and exchanging a look with Maggie.

"Yeah, E, how was it?"

I shoot them both a mock-venomous stare. I'd obviously made a mistake telling them who I was eating burgers with last night.

"It wasn't a date," I say.

"Look at her blush!" Maggie crows to Cam, who grins at me. "Gotta say, E, I didn't think theater-guy was your type, not after Damian and that certain someone I'm not ever supposed to mention who you were totally hot for in eighth grade."

I groan. "Can you not bring up my stupid eighth grade crush every time we talk relationships?"

"So there is a relationship to talk about," Cam interjects while taking an innocent bite of the salad they'd brought for lunch.

"No, there isn't."

"Why shouldn't I bring it up?" Maggie asks with a smirk, adjusting her yellow headband which matches the flowers on her bright knot-front blouse. "I think it's hilarious you liked my big brother. He says hi, by the way–I was chatting with him last night." She elbows me and laughs. Even Cam's chuckling. I scowl at them both and set to work on finishing my lunch.

Of course, it's at the exact moment my cheeks resemble a chipmunk's that Quince "really-needs-to-work-on-his-timing" Florentz sits down next to Cam on the bench right across from me.

I choke on my mouthful of mashed potatoes, which I didn't think was possible, and Maggie thumps me on the back.

"I–have–your–sweatshirt," I cough.

"Saw that," Quince remarks. "You really don't have to return it right away, you know."

Maggie gives me a knowing look.

"No, it's fine," I say, ignoring Maggie and untying the sweatshirt from my waist. "I have plenty of my own, and if I don't give it to you now I'm going to forget about it for an indeterminable amount of time." I toss the sweatshirt across the table to him and wince when it hits Cam in the face instead.

As Cam hands the sweatshirt to a chuckling Quince, my face flames and I mumble something about my sporting ability or lack thereof.

"It's all good, E," Maggie says, throwing an arm around my shoulder. "We love you anyway, girl."

I somehow make it through the rest of lunch without disappearing into a puddle of embarrassment on the floor.

"See you in study hall," Quince says when the warning bell rings.

"Wait. What?"

"I talked to Principal Lowell this morning about it and she agreed to switch me into it. I didn't really need another elective class, and I can use the time to work on my AP Chem and other research."

Two things stick out to me about this. One, that I hadn't considered Quince to be an AP Chemistry guy, and two, that he's without a doubt practicing the whole "saying something true to cloud the truth" thing. Other research could mean for other classes, if you didn't know that he's fae, and I'm fae, and he wants more time with me to help me figure out the clues to my past. The self-satisfied grin on his face more than confirms it.

"I'll save you a seat at the computers. They get taken fast."

With that, he's maneuvering the crowded cafeteria like a seasoned pro and is soon out of sight.

"Not a date, huh?" Cam asks. "What a coincidence that he's switched into the same study hall as you the day after you eat burgers together." Their eyes twinkle gleefully as I do my best to act like I haven't heard a word they've said.

*****

Sure enough, when I get to study hall, there's Quince at the computers, a stack of books on the seat to his left, and his friend Jim, who I recognize from the Instagram photos, in the chair to his right.

Quince waves me over, but I gesture at him to wait and head over to the checkout desk to return my books. Whatever I still need to learn about the fae realm isn't going to be found in the pages of the library books. I discovered that soon enough after another fruitless hour last night poring over them when I'd gotten home from dropping off Quince.

I'm almost to the desk when someone strides right in front of my path. I don't stop quickly enough and feel the man's foot crunch beneath my own. To add insult to injury, my books slide out of my arms and land on the same foot I'd just stepped on as he's moving away.

"Ohmigosh I'm so sorry!" I exclaim, scrambling to pick up my books. I look up at him and my stomach contracts in fear at the anger I see. His ratlike face is breaking out in blotchy red spots. When he notices me staring, he flashes a feral smile which exudes no warmth.

"Next time, watch where you're going, missy," he drawls, limping behind the desk and sitting down in Ms. Bates' seat.

"Right," I mumble, anger sparking in my chest. Depositing the books in the book drop, I retreat to the computer seat next to Quince. He and Jim are both snickering.

"I see you've met the sub, Mr. Abscons," Quince whispers.

I make a "you think?" face at him. "Yeah, first impressions are my specialty, as you can see." I keep my voice quiet, too, Mr. Abscons' angry, blotchy face still vividly seared in my brain.

Jim snorts at this, and Quince starts upright. "Oh! Eevee, this is my buddy, Jim. We go way back. Jim, this is Eevee. I somehow didn't know she attended this school until last week, but she claims she's gone here her whole life."

"You were in Ms. Johnson's third grade class, right?" Jim asks me.

I blink in surprise. "Good memory."

"Her story checks out, dude."

Quince shrugs. "I guess it's unlucky of me that I just met you last week."

"You were too busy being in a show or dating someone you'd met while doing a show," Jim reminds him.

I notice Quince doesn't deny this.

"Do you do theater too?" I ask Jim when I see the tips of Quince's ears resemble the color of strawberries.

"Kinda. I do the tech stuff. Lighting, sound, special effects. Lighting design is my favorite, though."

"Cool!"

He beams at me. "I enjoy it." His expression dims. "I want to do it professionally, but my dad says I should go into a more practical career."

"What does he know?" Quince asks as he pulls up a tab on atomic structures and properties. "He's never come to any of the shows you've worked on. Your lighting design for last year's show was brilliant."

Jim glows at Quince's praise, but ducks his head.

"Less talking, more working!" Mr. Abscons admonishes us from the checkout desk.

The rest of the class period passes with the sounds of keyboards clacking and book pages turning.

I'm getting ready to head out when Quince puts his computer to sleep and turns to me.

"So it's your birthday on Saturday!" he says, his voice carrying an extra "I know what turning eighteen really means for you" tone to it.

"You're taking this birthday guessing gig a step far, aren't you?"

He follows me to the hall. "I had help. Maggie told me."

"I didn't know you two were friends."

"She added me on Instagram last night."

"That traitor," I grumble.

"She invited me to her house on Friday night to celebrate your birthday, said I could bring Jim."

And just this morning she'd told me it'd only be the three of us on Friday. I make a mental note to send her some choice words later.

"We usually just hang out and watch movies on Netflix," I say. "And eat cake."

"Sounds good to me," says Jim, who's caught up to us in the hall.

"Gotta help you celebrate your eighteenth birthday in style."

Quince's face is crinkled in a grin, which widens when I mumble, "I'm gonna kill Maggie."

*****

E: *WHY DID U INVITE QUINCE & JIM TO HANG OUT WITH US ON FRIDAY??*
E: *FOR *MY* BDAY???*
M: 😄🤐😄
E: *seriously Mags wtf*

M: 🧚💬 *didn't think u would mind*

M: *plus i think Jim is adorable*

E: ...

E: *ur a jerk*

I absentmindedly flip through my science textbook. The reading for tonight isn't sticking in my brain, but I pause and write a few notes. My phone dings; Maggie is either done with her homework or avoiding it.

M: *you'll thank me later* 😊

M: *so why the books and art about fairies, E?*

M: *is this gonna be ur new agate thing?*

I spend one summer combing the beaches of Lake Superior for agates and she won't let it go.

M: *bc u still have like literally multiple jars of agates u never do anything with*

M: *i just gotta be prepared for an intervention*

M: *u kno, for the fairy obsession*

E: 😊 *i was just doing research*

M: *4 what? DH has ZERO projects that'd require u to research fairies*

Of course Maggie would know that. She makes it her job to know everything about everything at school. My secret identity wells up in my mind and a desire to tell her and Cam everything floods through me. Even the images of me in mental institutions with a straitjacket don't have as much strength as they had before. Can I convince them without picture evidence, though? If I don't say something soon, knowing Maggie, she'll start coming to her own conclusions.

I look out my bedroom window. The sun glows red through the pine trees in our backyard, and the branches are aflame with its light. A thought forms, and I sent a text in the group chat to Cam and Maggie.

E: *can u guys come over 4 a bonfire 2nite?*

As I wait for them to respond I realize I forgot one important step in my plan. I pad down the stairs and find dad on the couch eating crackers and cheese and watching a nature documentary about chimpanzees with Jess, who's snuggled next to him under a fuzzy blanket. They look cozy. I love watching movies with Jess. She's the only one in the family who will watch murder mystery documentaries with me.

"Fine by me, but ask your mom," dad says, his attention glued to the chimps on the screen.

Making my way through the house, I end up hearing mom before seeing her and turn toward Greg and Charlie's room on the second floor, down the hall from my room.

Greg and Charlie are in various stages of undress and mom is wrangling a crying Charlie into his pajama shirt.

"We do this every night, Charles Adam, you can't wear the same shirt five days in a row!"

Over his wails of mom's unfair stance on clothing, I shout my question about having Cam and Maggie over for a bonfire.

Charlie's crying stops immediately and she's able to slip his pajama shirt over his stomach. He tugs on mom's sleeve and she holds up a finger to me to wait while he whispers in her ear.

His whispers are no match for my super-hearing, though, and I hear every word.

"Can we roast marshmallows with Eevee? Please? I'll wear my pjs at night all week without crying!"

Mom straightens and folds her arms across her chest. "What did your father say?"

"That it was okay with him but I should ask you."

She sighs. "Fine. But start the fire now, it's already getting late and your brothers have school pictures tomorrow. I don't want them up too much past their bedtime."

Greg and Charlie are bouncing off the walls.

"And you're in charge of helping your brothers with their marshmallows," she calls after me. "Send them in as soon as they're done, you hear?"

I'm followed out to the backyard by two whooping, pajama-clad, marshmallow-loving monsters.

After I stack the firewood and stoke the fire until it's got a healthy flame, I send Cam and Maggie, who have notified me they are on their way over, a picture of Greg and Charlie roasting marshmallows with the caption: *better hurry before all the marshmallows are gone*

Chapter 15

Embers and Proof

Slinky stalks at the edge of the pines, a black hole shaped as a cat amongst the shadows. I skewer the last marshmallow on my stick and thrust it above the dying embers.

"Eevee, your friends have to leave soon, it's a school night!" mom calls through the kitchen window.

"Okay!" Maggie, Cam, and I all shout back.

My marshmallow erupts into flames and I pull it away from the fire, blowing it out with a grimace.

"I'll take it," Maggie says, grabbing my stick and removing the marshmallow with the tips of her fingers. "I like 'em burnt."

I wrinkle my nose at her as she pops the whole charred mess of a marshmallow in her mouth.

Amelia's sitting to my left, engrossed in her phone. Probably Snapchatting the guy with the shoulders from her math class.

I clear my throat. "Did you hear mom?"

"Yeah," she replies without looking up. "We gotta go in soon."

Cam, who's been on their phone almost as much as Amelia tonight, looks up and sees the look of frustration on my face. They lean over and tap on Maggie's arm.

Maggie knows me well enough to see I'm bursting to talk about something. "You know," she says, reclining in her plastic lawn chair, "I hear Trent's gonna be working out in the school weight room tomorrow after school with some of the other guys on the wrestling team."

Amelia lights up with this knowledge. "Thanks for the tip, Maggie," she bubbles, locking her phone and stretching. "I gotta go figure out a cute workout outfit I could pack for tomorrow. And ask mom if I can stay after. I bet Phoebe could give me a ride home…" She zooms back to the house.

I swat at a mosquito buzzing around my head. "So there's something I wanted to tell you guys, but I don't know how to say it."

"Cam and I have been talking," Maggie says at the same time.

We both stop.

"You go," I say. Maybe they'll finally tell me why Cam's been on-and-off weird with me this week. "What's up?"

Cam gulps and acts interested in their hands, which are clasped in their lap. As I wait for one of them to respond, crickets chirp to each other in their nightly chorus.

"Cam?"

Cam shakes their head and Maggie pulls out her phone, scrolling through it. She hands it to me. Lit up on the screen is an article titled "Childhood Regression in Adopted Adults" by the Reverend Doctor Wolfking.

I scan it, my jaw tightening and a wild laughter claws its way up my throat, but I swallow it down.

"Cam and I are concerned about your sudden interest in fairies," Maggie says as I finish skimming the article and hand her back her phone. "And we looked up some stuff online this afternoon and it brought us to that article."

"Your interest in fairies has kind of come out of nowhere," Cam adds. "Maggie just told me about the library books and whatnot today. How she saw you hiding them at the Java Jive and at lunch." They tuck one of their knees up to their chest and avoid my gaze, looking at what's left of the fire instead. "It makes me feel like I don't know you anymore. I know that sounds like an overreaction, but you're one of my only friends and," they fiddle with the ragged ends of their oversized sweatshirt, "you've never been into that fantasy stuff before, even when I've tried to get you interested in it."

It's true. I can't begin to list all the movies Cam's made me watch over the years, or the books and TV shows they've recommended, or the sci-fi and fantasy conventions they've dragged me to with them. The closest I get to enjoying fantasy is Shakespeare. Titania and Oberon and Puck. Even then, the play ends with an invitation back to reality, as well as a not-so-subtle call to applause: "Give me your hands, if we be friends, And Robin shall restore amends." I'd much rather read Shakespeare, or an article about animal care, than a fanfiction about made up creatures like vampires or werewolves. Though, given what I've seen in the last week, they may not be as made up as I originally thought.

"I haven't changed, not really-"

"There's something else I need to tell you, kind of unrelated," Cam interrupts.

"You go first," we say in unison.

Maggie groans. "Okay, enough of this or Mrs. Acker's gonna be kicking us out before anything's said. Eevee, you go first since your birthday's on Saturday, and because I invited Quince and Jim to your birthday party tomorrow without asking you first. Then Cam can go."

They're both looking at me and I wonder if they can hear my heartbeat because all I can hear in my ears right now is a frantic thump-thump-thumping.

"I'm not suddenly interested in fairies because of childhood regression or whatever," I start, then pause.

They wait in silence and my breathing is so shaky it rattles in my chest.

"I'm interested in it because I am a fairy."

Crickets, literally and figuratively.

After what feels like forever, Cam asks, "You mean you identify as a fairy?"

Maggie's on her phone. "Wow, there's a whole ton of people out there who think they're fairies." Her phone's light illuminates her face as she reads.

"I don't *identify* as a fairy, I don't *think* I'm a fairy, I *am* a fairy."

Maggie looks up from her phone, a wary-but-curious expression playing across her face. "Explain."

I tell them about my birth mom's note, my first trip to the fae realm when I met Folsom, and my second where I tracked down the Mage Stone. I leave out Quince's role in it, though. That's his secret, not mine to tell.

By the end of my explanation, which spills out of me like most of my former secrets–all at once, with no warning–Maggie and Cam are both slack-jawed and glassy-eyed.

"So, that's about it," I conclude. They stare in silence, so I add, "Welcome to my week."

"I was way off with childhood regression," Maggie mutters, unlocking her phone and typing. "This is full-blown, bat-shit crazy."

Images of me in a straitjacket dance across my vision. "Cam?"

"You've been going through a lot," they hedge. "What with Damian, and that info about your birth parents."

"Good thinking, Cam. You think stress-induced hallucinations maybe? I'm reading about them now, they're totally a thing."

I check my phone. Mom is going to come out and tell us to break it up soon. I hadn't planned any more than getting Maggie and Cam alone so I could tell them about everything, but seeing is believing, after all.

"I can prove it to you." Swatting another mosquito, I stand. "I can take you there right now."

The glowing embers of the fire play across Cam's pale face, but Maggie strides over to me and crosses her arms. "This I gotta see." I can hear the challenge in her voice, the unsaid "Prove it, then."

"Cam?"

They don't answer at first, and when they look up at me, their eyes are like a terrified deer's. "I'm really worried for you, Eevee." They shift in their chair to face Maggie directly. "And I don't like that you're encouraging…" Cam gestures at me. "Whatever this is."

Maggie and Cam lock into a silent battle of wills. Cam deflates after only a few moments.

"Fine," they say, standing and tucking their hands into the front pocket of their sweatshirt. "But once it's clear Eevee's suffering from stress hallucinations or whatever, we go to her parents."

My poor parents, who adopted a fairy baby without realizing it.

"If I prove it to you guys, that what I'm saying is the truth, you tell no one."

"But-" Maggie starts. I hold up a hand.

"No one."

She chews the inside of her cheek. "Fine."

"If it's true, I promise I won't tell," Cam responds, their voice hard to hear over the competing frogs and crickets. "But if it isn't," they pause, and I watch them shift from one foot to the other, "don't be too mad if I tell your parents."

"Deal."

Cam looks equal parts taken aback and worried by the confidence in my voice.

"You both need to hold my hands," I instruct them. Maggie places her left hand in my right at once. Cam trudges around the bonfire, their head down, purple hair hiding their face, but they take my hand as well.

"Here we go," I say, then close my eyes and think of Elfaeme, where fairy folk who look like me live and where there are magical forests that change from spring to autumn with the rising and setting of the sun.

I know it's worked when I hear a sharp inhale of breath to my left and Maggie hollering "What the fudge?!" on my right.

I open my eyes on a moonlit scene, dizzy from the effort of bringing two people to Elfaeme with me. We're in a clearing in a forest, but it doesn't appear to be the same one I visited on my first trip here, which is good. I have no desire to run into Folsom again if I can help it.

A waterfall cascades somewhere beyond the line of trees, which glow under the moon's pale light. Their branches are bare, skeletal in an otherworldly way. The ground is coated in a fine layer of frost which sparkles like diamonds.

"No telling anyone," I say, my voice cracking. I'm so relieved nothing went wrong with getting here it takes a moment to register that Maggie and Cam are both gawking at me.

"Holy shit," Maggie says with a laugh. "You have wings, E! What the fudge?!"

"Yeah, I do." I'm smiling so wide my cheeks hurt. I hadn't realized how much my secret had been weighing me down over the last week. But now? I am light as air. My two best friends in the world are here, in the fae realm, with me. Suddenly, anything seems possible.

"Watch this."

They're looking around curiously, Maggie's face shining with excitement, Cam slack-jawed with awe.

I wait until their attention is turned toward me, then crouch down like I remember Quince doing last night next to the Mage Stone. Reckless confidence courses through me as I launch myself into the air.

Freedom. As if they've been waiting for this, my wings flex, then flap, beating against the crisp air until I'm above the topmost branches. Above me, the stars glitter in the inky sky, and part of me wants to keep flying until I can catch one.

An owl glides by, stealth on the wind with its silent wings. I look over my shoulder at my own wings and gasp. They're beautiful. I can see the stars through them, and their edges catch and reflect the light of the moon.

My elation is punctured when I hear a startled grunt from below and Maggie's voice shouting, "What the hell?"

Flying upward is easier than descending, I discover, and I crash down toward my friends in a shower of twigs which scratch at my face and arms.

Once my feet are back on the frosty ground, I fight my way toward Maggie and Cam through a tangle of branches. I stop short, panting, confused. When I had launched into the air only moments ago, I'd left them in a bare clearing. Now, the trees are bending toward where Maggie and Cam are huddled, and their limbs creak and crack as they intertwine. If I don't stop it somehow, my friends will soon be out of sight.

"Hold on!" I shout to them, the panic in my voice mirroring the terror I see in their faces.

At the sound of my voice, the trees surrounding the clearing straighten and disentangle their limbs. Maggie and Cam rush over to me. A woman emerges out of the tree in front of us. She has eyes the color of the night sky and markings of vines decorate her bare arms, much like the orange flowers on my temples. There's a misty quality to her skin, as if she's made of the fog that furls around haunted forests.

"I did not know they were with you." Her voice is the sound of branches swaying and scraping together in a frost wind. She offers no apology or explanation.

"Yeah, we're with her, didn't you see her come here with us?" Maggie says, all defiance, though her eyes betray her fear.

Cam shakes like a quaking leaf.

The woman ignores Maggie's outburst and says to me, "The forest can take care of these humans quickly, if that is your desire."

"They're my friends."

I've said the wrong thing. Her face twists. "Humans are not friends to the fae. They all deserve to die for what they've done."

"Eevee?" Cam whispers, tugging at my sleeve.

"And any fae who protects humans, no matter who they are, is a traitor to our kind."

I'm transfixed by the seething hatred in her voice. It speaks of thousands of years of festering and rotting.

"Eevee, the trees!" Maggie hisses, jabbing my side with her elbow.

The woman fades back into the tree behind her and I look to where Maggie is pointing.

We're completely enclosed in a twisting, writhing mass of trees and branches. I turn, sweat trickling down my temple.

There's no way out.

Cam whimpers and cowers as the branches tighten and crack, closing together so tightly we're cut off from the moonlight.

"Take my hands," I whisper in the darkness, groping until I feel Maggie and Cam. Twigs snap and boughs groan. I get the sense, though I can't see them closing in on us, that our space is dwindling fast.

My hands are clammy but I cling to Maggie and Cam as tight as I can. It's so dark I don't have to close my eyes.

I picture home, the dying embers of the fire, the plastic lawn chairs in a circle around it, the empty marshmallow bag tossed on the ground next to the roasting sticks.

I hear the frogs singing their calls of love and sway on the spot.

I did it.

Cam staggers to their chair and collapses into it, breathing in panicked gasps.

Maggie props me up where I stand and I lean into her warm strength.

"Holy shit, E," she whispers to me.

I bark out a nervous laugh. "Told you so."

"We believe you." She guides me to my chair and I sit, my legs shaking, and watch as she paces.

"So you're legit a fairy."

"Yes."

"With wings and everything."

"Also yes."

"And your birth parents, who are also fae, are hiding somewhere in the fae realm, hoping you'll find them someday?"

"Well, my birth mom wants me to, anyway. I don't know if my birth dad knows she left me those clues with her blood magic."

"I don't want to go back there." Cam's voice quavers. "I don't think you should either, Eevee. That tree woman had no problem trapping you with us, even though you're fae too." They stuff their hands into their sweatshirt pocket. "It's dangerous."

"But Eevee wants answers, don't you, E?"

"Well, yeah."

"And we'll help you as much as we can," Maggie concludes, her face hardening into the look of pure determination I recognize from the beginning of all of her big investigative projects for the school podcast.

"We will?"

Cam's still shaking and their skin has an unhealthy sheen to it, like I remember seeing on Amelia before she threw up all over the Christmas presents when she was six.

"From here," Maggie reassures them. The going-to-throw-up look fades, but they still look uneasy. "No offense, E, but I'm with Cam on that one. I don't want to go back there either."

"None taken."

"But what can we do from here?" Cam asks.

Maggie's pacing faster now. "Loads. E, you've got that envelope with everything in it, right?"

"Wrap it up!" mom shouts. The back door creaks shut and we all wince at the sound of wood on wood.

"Bring it to my house tomorrow," she says.

"But Quince and Jim are going to be there too-"

"Not all night."

Maggie and Cam gather up their stuff and I walk them to Cam's family van. In the dark of the evening the rust is hard to see and it looks new, not like it's on its last legs.

It grumbles to life like an old man being asked to move when he doesn't want to as Cam turns the key in the ignition.

"Promise you won't go back there?" they ask as Maggie clambers into the front seat.

I swallow. "I promise," I say aloud.

They don't look entirely convinced as they back the van out of the driveway.

Loophole, I think. *You were too vague, Cam. I promise to not go back to that exact spot if I can help it.*

Chapter 16

Math Test, Interrupted

Our strategy for dealing with me being fae but not wanting anyone else to know appears to be "pretend like last night never happened."

Even in the van on the way to school, Cam didn't hint once at our sojourn to Elfaeme. Of course, we had Amelia riding with us, so we hadn't been entirely alone, though with how much she had been on her phone, we may as well have been. As soon as Cam had parked the car, she opened the door and shot toward school like an arrow.

"Phoebe's giving me a ride home, see you tomorrow, Eevee, have fun at Maggie's tonight, byeeee!"

In fact, most of the day has passed in a blur, with not a single mention of anything fae, not even during my study period with Quince, who had seemed more interested in joking around with Jim than talking to me or doing any of the studying he'd promised Principal Lowell he'd do if he switched into study hall.

"Everything off your desks except writing utensils and calculators."

I run through a list of profanities in my head. I'd completely forgotten about the math test today.

Everyone shuffles in their seats and books slam to the ground. Cam looks back at me from their seat and mouths, "Good luck," as Mr. Jenkins passes out the tests.

"Keep the tests face down until I say you can start."

Brandi, a junior who works on the school podcast with Maggie and is known for her witty episodes on the girl's volleyball and basketball teams, hands me the test and I cringe. It's three pages, front to back.

"You have until the end of the hour. If you finish early, you may deposit your test on my desk. No homework this weekend. Try not to be too disappointed."

With all the tests distributed, Mr. Jenkins returns to his desk and lowers himself into his seat. "Begin."

Papers flip, pencils scratch. I start in on question one, trying my best to remember everything we've learned over the last couple of weeks. I'm halfway down the first page and losing confidence in my recall ability when there's a knock at the door, a hesitant tap-tap.

A few students look at the door, then to Mr. Jenkins, who adjusts his sweater vest as he stands.

"I got it, Mr. J!" says Mark, a front row seater I've never talked to as I'm a strictly "back row" kind of student. He hops out of his plastic desk chair and bounds to the door with enthusiasm. I can't tell if he's trying to suck up to Mr. Jenkins or avoid the test. Maybe both.

Ms. Bates' sub, Mr. Abscons, comes in with a stack of papers in his arms. He scans the room, and I see recognition in his beady eyes when he catches sight of me in the back.

Yes, it's me, the one who stomped on your foot and dropped books on it seconds later, I think.

His gaze shifts from me to Mr. Jenkins. "Saw these on the copier, Harv. Thought I'd bring them to you, save you the trip."

"How thoughtful. Cordelia usually leaves our copies in stacks next to the machine for us to grab when we can. Sometimes she'd put sticky notes with our names on them on the top. But she'd never do room deliveries."

A small, satisfied smile plays across Mr. Abscons' face.

"Mark, can you…?"

Before Mr. Jenkins can finish asking, Mark yanks the papers from Mr. Abscons' hands and delivers them to Mr. Jenkins, who straightens them as he places them on his desk. Most students hunch over their tests once again, but I watch Mark scurry back to his seat and notice Mr. Abscons hovering in the doorway.

"Was there something else?" Mr. Jenkins asks, a hint of irritation in his voice.

Mr. Abscons scans the classroom again before replying, "No, that's all. Have a nice weekend, Harv." He exits in a furtive manner, as if trying to cause as little commotion as possible, and closes the door with a quiet click behind him.

The room fills with the frantic sounds of pencils scratching paper and calculator keys clicking.

I guess my way through a couple questions and am on the last page when there's another knock at the door, this one like the peck-peck-pecking of a persistent woodpecker.

Mr. Jenkins lets out an audible sigh of annoyance as Mark springs up again and opens the door with a flourish to reveal Marjorie Lewiston, a senior who's involved in so many clubs I don't know how she keeps track of it all, but somehow she does it all with energy to spare. She bounces on her heels in the doorway with a miniature tower of packets clutched to her chest.

"Hi!" she squeaks, tossing her blond ponytail over her shoulder and thrusting the top packet at Mark. "Homecoming info! I'm on the committee. Can you get that passed out to everyone? It's got all the pride week days on there and info on the dance. The theme this year is a night in Paris, eee!"

A night in Paris is the theme about every other year, so the only one who is excited about this news is Marjorie. She pokes her head around a dazed-looking Mark and waves enthusiastically. "Hey Ruth! Good luck on your test!"

Mr. Jenkins has this look of concentration on his face like he's trying not to roll his eyes. "Speaking of the test-"

"Do you want these handed out now or later?" Mark interrupts. He's torn into the packet and has half-pulled out the contents, slips of paper a shocking, neon yellow.

Mr. Jenkins' right temple pulses. "Now, I suppose, since we're already sidetracked."

"Oh, super!" Marjorie beams. "Gotta run, lots more packets to deliver!"

As she dashes out of sight, Mark takes it upon himself to personally deliver a sheet of paper to each student in the class, all twenty-six of us.

Both of Mr. Jenkins' temples are pulsing by the time Mark is done, and his long, basset hound face is pinched tight.

"You have until the bell rings to finish your tests," he barks at us.

I finish with a few minutes to spare and drop off my test on the top of the pile on Mr. Jenkins' desk. He's grading someone else's test and gives me the barest of nods. It's probably because he's busy, but I swear he's been avoiding interacting with me ever since our altercation last week.

Resisting the ridiculous urge to wave my hand in front of his face, I retreat to my seat and gather my belongings so I'm ready to bolt when the bell rings. Needing something to do to pass the next few minutes, I skim the blinding yellow paper for the Homecoming Week information.

Duluth High Homecoming Week

Spirit Week
Monday: PJ Day
Tuesday: Twin Day
Wednesday: Superhero Day
Thursday: Dress to Impress Day
Friday: School Spirit Day

Homecoming Game
Friday, October 5 @7pm.
Come cheer on the Duluth Foghorns as they take on the Barnum East Bullfrogs!

Homecoming Dance
A Night in Paris
Saturday, October 6 from 8-11pm
Come dance the night away in the City of Love!
Cost: $10/ticket (couples $15)
Sign up by Wednesday, October 3 to get your name entered into a drawing to win a Foghorn drawstring bag packed with goodies!

Note: all attendees who want to bring visitors must register separately. See Mr. Jives in the office for the visitor form.

As I read it, I'm transported back to last year's homecoming dance. The theme was A Night at the Disco (another repeat theme), and I had spent hours with Maggie the afternoon of the dance making sure every strand of hair and thread of fabric were perfect.

For the first time ever, I had a date to the dance, and he had been an older guy: Damian. Maggie, who never has trouble wrangling someone to go to dances with her, had gone with Pete, another member of the football team.

We'd eaten out at a Chinese restaurant before the dance as a group with the varsity football players and their dates. Our poor server had spent the evening dashing from one end of the table to the other with a harried look on her face.

I barely ate, I was so nervous. When we arrived at the dance amidst applause (the Foghorns had won their homecoming game last year), Damian wrapped his arm around me as he steered us through the crowd. As soon as we entered the school gymnasium, which was transformed into a discotheque with glittering disco balls and multicolored lights, he had dropped his arm and my shoulders were cold in its absence.

"Gotta make the rounds, you understand, right, babe?" he asked.

I understood. He'd made the winning touchdown, he deserved to soak in some of the glory.

Later that night, when he made his way back to me, he greeted me as if we'd been separated for months: hands all over my body, his mouth on mine.

I hadn't realized then that this would become a pattern for our dates: go somewhere with a group, get ignored most of the evening while Damian chats with friends, then engage in a heated makeout session for a while before I'm dropped off back at home.

The paper crinkles in my hands. I'm not going, of course. Not this year.

On my way out of the classroom I toss the crumpled flyer in the recycling.

Chapter 17

Birthday Party

I'm running late, as usual, so as I crash through Maggie's front door I shout, "It's my birthday we're celebrating, the party doesn't officially start until I say so!"

"Seems reasonable," Maggie's brother says, leaning in the doorway between the entryway and the living room.

Pretty sure my face matches the pink crop top I've changed into for the night. He is so tall his head almost touches the top of the door frame. If I stand on my tiptoes next to him, the top of my head might reach his shoulders.

"Oh, hey, Zach." I ruffle my hair with my fingers, conscious of all the inches I'd chopped off almost a month ago now. It's grown long enough that the ends of my bangs, which I'd left longer, now feather out in front of my eyes unless I style them back. "Didn't know you were home this weekend."

The short sleeves of his shirt tighten around his biceps as he crosses his arms. "Maggie seemed to really want me home. Besides, some buddies of mine will be around this weekend and we're getting together tonight to play a game or two at Stebner Park."

I've turned a shade darker than my shirt. After Maggie and I had become friends and I had that stupid crush on Zach, I spent hours learning everything I could about soccer, and the rest of my free time begging mom and dad to bring me to games, where I'd stand awkwardly on the sidelines watching Zach play. I never dared to cheer for him at risk of seeming uncool. He'd played in a local league, and to my eighth grade self's knowledge, there had been no better soccer player on the field.

"Anyway," he continues while I grapple with crippling mortification brought on by embarrassing eighth grade flashbacks, "I gotta run, my buddies are waiting. Good to see ya, and happy birthday a day early, E."

"Thanks," I manage to eke out as I step out of his way.

"Oh, and I like the haircut," he adds on his way out. The screen door shuts with a snap. "Very edgy." He flashes me a grin identical to Maggie's, but somehow hotter (in my unbiased opinion), and saunters down the driveway to his car. I hear some chatter floating up from the basement and decide to head down.

"Seems like a nice guy," Quince says from behind me before I can turn, and I trip over my own feet, landing in the arms of Quince "too-sneaky-for-my-liking" Florentz.

He holds me upright, smiling. "I'm surprised you didn't hear me coming." When he tilts his head, the overhead light in the entryway illuminates half his face, casting the other half in shadow.

"Guess I wasn't paying attention."

The headlights from Zach's car shine through the screen door and Quince and I break apart.

"E, you finally made it!" Maggie comes skidding into the entryway, barefooted and wearing a cute plaid dress that shows off her long legs. Her Afro is dotted with these little white flower clips I'd given her for her birthday last year. She's clutching two plastic cups, one in each of her hands, which she's somehow managed not to spill. "Zach hooked us UP for tonight!" she hollers, pushing one of the cups at me. I sniff it and blink, my eyes watering. "Come on, E, we've been waiting for you to get here to start this board game Jim's brought! Here, I'll take your stuff to my room." She separates me from my backpack and dashes up the stairs.

I take a sip of the unholy concoction she's given me and try not to cough as I follow Quince into the basement.

Cam's by the stereo, hooking up their phone to it and thumbing through their playlists. At the coffee table, Jim sits on the floor, arranging pieces of the board game he's brought.

Maggie thunders down the stairs. "Okay, y'all, mom's working the overnight shift at the hospital tonight and this is dad's weekend to be out on the roads. As far as either of them knows, Zach was here keeping an eye on us tonight, got it?"

"I can certainly attest he was here," Quince says. He and I share a look. Loophole.

"Great." Some upbeat pop music plays through the speakers. It's not Cam's favorite music, but they know I dislike all the punk bands they listen to.

"Made this for your birthday," they say when I flash them a surprised smile.

"Let's get this party started!" Maggie flops down on the floor next to Jim, who looks at her from under his lashes, his neck all red and blotchy.

Poor guy doesn't stand a chance, I think. I sit down across from Jim and catch Maggie's eye. She hides a giggle behind her hand.

I've never played this particular board game before, but I'm a naturally competitive person, so when I'm down to my last card and only a turn or two away from losing, I have to fight not to overturn the board.

The game is like a card game with levels you have to beat, mixed with a tabletop world-building game, with a dash of dragons and wizards, and the only cards I have left are resources. I've completely run out of wizards.

"I am sick when I do look on thee," I say with a scowl to Jim. He's prevented me from using my resources by laying down a knight on top of the marketplace.

"*Midsummer Night's Dream*," I hear Cam whisper to Quince.

"Yeah, I got that," he replies to them.

Jim cocks an eyebrow at me. "You never stood a chance against me. Your brain is as dry as the remainder biscuit after voyage."

"Oh damn!" Maggie hoots. "E, you're caught at your own game!"

"*As You Like It*," I mutter. "Good one."

The corner of Cam's mouth quirks upward as they look at me. "Throw all the insults you want at each other," they throw their cards down on the table in triumph, "I've just won." On top of the pile is a card titled "Ring of Power," which means they just acquired all the goods in the marketplace.

I toss my cards on the table too and Jim packs up the game as Maggie refills everyone's empty cups. A cool wind blows through the window, which Maggie cracked open after she had lost all her cards in a duel with Quince.

"C'mon, E," she says, teetering toward the stairs. "Let's go make some popcorn. Cam, wanna get the movie set up?"

"Sure." They beam up at me. "I know which one."

"*Crouching Tiger, Hidden Mongoose*!" Cam, Maggie, and I all shout in unison.

"Never seen it," Jim remarks.

"Jim!" I exclaim. "Your life has held no meaning until now. How could you not have seen *Crouching Tiger, Hidden Mongoose*?"

"Or any of the four sequels?" Maggie adds.

Jim lifts his shoulders. "My family's not big into movies?"

"Jim, Jim, Jim," I say, shaking my head at him. Maggie's dragging me up the stairs. "Your life's about to change!" I proclaim to him while Maggie giggles.

"Come ON, E! Popcorn!"

We pad into the kitchen. Over the sound of popping kernels, Maggie says, "So I took a quick look at the letter you brought over, the one your birth parents wrote?"

My brain's foggy, and I blink at Maggie for a moment before what she says sets in. "Wait. You were going through my stuff?"

"I just wanted to take a quick look!" she protests. "Anyway, I've been thinking about your birth mom using blood magic. Do you think your birth father would have known about it?"

"I'm not sure," I say. "I get the feeling he didn't know about her postscript for me, anyway."

"Right." She taps her chin. "Next time you're there, in the fae realm, you should find out more about blood magic and let me know what you find." With a shudder, she adds, "You couldn't drag me, or Cam, for that matter, back there again if you tried."

The microwave beeps and Maggie pulls out the bag of popcorn and opens it, upending the contents into a red plastic bowl. "I think it could answer a lot of questions you have about who exactly your birth mom was. I mean-"

"Hold on." This time, I do hear him before I see him. I hold a finger up to my lips.

Quince enters the kitchen. "Movie's ready. Cam said they wanted water, so I thought I'd get a glass for myself, too. Tap, or…?"

"Fridge," Maggie says.

As Quince passes me, he hisses out of the corner of his mouth, "We need to talk."

I focus on his face, which blurs a little before my eyes. Even blurry, I can see he's angry. Maybe water isn't the worst idea. I grab a glass as well and fill it up at the fridge after Quince has filled the glasses for himself and Cam.

When I turn to him, there's no sign of the usual mischievous glint in his eyes, and the water in my glass ripples as my hand shakes. "When?" I ask. "Now, or…?"

"It can wait," Maggie interrupts. "We need to introduce Jim to *Crouching Tiger, Hidden Mongoose.* Priorities, Quince!" Maggie grabs the popcorn bowl in one hand and loops her other through Quince's arm. Water from the two glasses he's holding sloshes onto the kitchen floor, but Maggie doesn't notice as she drags him to the basement.

By the time I rejoin everyone, Maggie's situated herself between Jim and Cam on the couch and is tossing popcorn in her mouth. Quince is sitting on the plush loveseat, his arms crossed. I hesitate. There's not really room on the couch, which leaves the loveseat or the floor.

Honestly, with the stormy look on Quince's face, the floor is the most tempting of the two options. I go to sit on the floor in front of Maggie, but Quince shifts over as I pass, making more room on the loveseat for me.

Cam gives me a knowing look as I sit next to Quince, and Maggie starts the film with a flourish of the remote.

I spend the next hour and a half contemplating what Quince could want to talk about while he sits like a marble statue next to me and doesn't even laugh at any of the funniest parts.

Quince has officially ruined *Crouching Tiger, Hidden Mongoose* for me.

While the credits roll, Maggie starts grilling Jim on all things *Crouching Tiger, Hidden Mongoose* like he's a contestant on a game show. Cam's on their phone, a slight frown creasing their face.

"Upstairs," Quince mutters, stalking away before I can answer.

I catch Maggie's eyes as I turn to follow him, and am not surprised to feel my phone buzz in the side pocket of my leggings.

M: *he's totally asking u out*
M: *callin it now*

I put it away without answering her. I can disappoint her with the news later, when she's not as busy with Jim.

Entering the kitchen, I find Quince waiting, face still stony, foot tapping on the marble-patterned linoleum.

"What?" I ask, bristling.

"You told Maggie and Cam about you being fae."

"I wasn't aware my secrets and who I tell them to were any of your business," I say through bared teeth. "I didn't tell them about you, if that's what you're worried about."

"It's not, but thank you." His eyes soften, but his mouth remains in a grim line.

"What is it then?"

He lowers his voice and his foot-tapping stops. "You brought them with you to Elfaeme?!"

I take a step back from him, wary of the nervous energy crackling around his body. "They didn't believe me. About being fae. I thought it'd be easier showing them. Besides, what's the big deal? We weren't there that long."

Quince isn't satisfied with my explanation. "They didn't eat anything while you were there, did they? Were you seen by anyone? Where did you take them, to the Mage Stone?"

"Why does it matter where we went or if they ate anything? You're acting like this is a big deal. It's not. We went, they saw I was telling the truth, we came back."

"Eevee, this *is* a big deal! Humans can get lost in the fae realm and end up wandering it forever. If they eat anything when they're in Elfaeme, they're fae-marked, and any fae, Seelie, Unseelie, or neither, can find them. And that's if they're allowed to leave after they've eaten. Most humans are entranced enough by the food that they willingly choose to stay and rot."

I've backed up so far my legs bump into the kitchen table by the door to the hall. Quince reaches out, as if to place his hands on my shoulders, then balls them into fists as his sides.

"Just–answer my questions," he says, his voice strained.

"No, they didn't eat anything." I watch as a little tension leaves his face. "I don't know where we were, though. Some forest with frost covering the ground. And we weren't seen by another person while we were there."

He narrows his eyes. "Loophole. You were seen, but not by a person. Who saw you?"

I sigh. I should've figured it wouldn't work, trying to cloud the truth by saying something true. I give him a quick run-down of the tree woman, downplaying the danger as much as possible, and emphasizing my flying and our successful escape. "So, as you can see, it turned out alright, and they don't want to go back anyway."

"Smart friends."

I'm about to reply when Cam enters. "Maggie sent me to get the cake, but I think she wanted a chance to make out with Jim," they state blandly, crossing to the counter where the cake box sits.

Quince coughs out a laugh. "Jim and Maggie, huh?"

"What's so funny?" Cam asks as they rummage in the silverware drawer.

"Jim's...painfully shy. He's a great guy, he just clams up when it comes to girls he likes."

"I think Maggie's extrovertedness more than makes up for it," I say.

A crack appears in Quince's agitated veneer; I'm happy to see him smile.

"Hey, Cam, let me help with some of that." I grab the paper plates and plastic forks off the top of the cake box before they fall. "Don't want my birthday cake to end up on the floor."

Cam shoots me a grateful smile and heads toward the basement, stepping louder than they need to on the steps, probably to give Maggie and Jim time to disentangle themselves.

"Are we good?" I ask Quince.

The mischievous look is back in his eyes. "I can't stay mad at you on your birthday,"

The tennis ball-sized knot in between my shoulders loosens. He steps past me in the hall, his hand brushing my arm as he reaches for a fork.

"Especially not when cake's involved."

Chapter 18

Emotions Are Confusing

My stomach is stuffed to bursting with birthday cake. Quince and Jim left a while ago, and Cam and I have made our way to Maggie's room where I'm cocooned in a mass of blankets and pillows. Between the warmth of the blankets and my full stomach, I'm already half asleep.

Maggie's tramping around the room, toothbrush hanging out of her mouth. She's on her phone, probably texting Jim, who seemed reluctant to leave for some reason.

"Thanks for the party, guys," I say, snuggling deeper into the blankets.

"Party may be over, but you're not allowed to go to sleep yet!" Maggie garbles. To emphasize her point in case I couldn't understand her through her mouthful of toothpaste, she prods me in the side with her toe.

"It's my party, I'll do what I want," I say, covering my head with a fluffy fleece blanket.

"Have it your way, we don't have to talk about the letter tonight," she says around her toothbrush.

I can tell she's dying to talk about it. Her tone, even distorted as it is with the toothpaste, is too casual.

"Will you spit already?" Cam asks, making a disgusted face at Maggie, who gargles loudly on her way to the bathroom. "We really don't have to look at it tonight if you don't want to, you know," Cam says quietly to me when she's out of earshot.

"No, it's okay." I sit up and reach for my backpack, trying to brush off the cobwebs of sleepiness stretching across my brain.

When Maggie returns sans toothbrush, I take out the contents of the adoption packet, all the information my birth parents left for me on display for Cam and Maggie to look through and analyze.

Even though they're my best friends, it feels weird, like they're scientists and I'm the alien species under the bright light on the exam table. I pick up the card as they go through some of the other documents and run my fingers over the heart-shaped red balloon and the fuzzy-looking teddy bear.

"I could take these physical descriptions in the medical records and make some sketches," Cam says. They're already pulling their sketch pad out of their backpack. I don't think they go anywhere without it. "If you want?" They pause and look at me, pencil poised above a blank page.

"That's a great idea," Maggie says before I can answer. "It'll give us a basic idea of what your parents might look like, E."

"Birth parents," I remind her. "Not my parents."

"Right. My bad. Todd and Penny are the best, you know I'd totally let them adopt me if my mom and dad wouldn't take offense to that."

"You're pretty much an honorary Acker," I tell her, waving away her apology. "Same with you, Cam."

"So, what do you think, E? About Cam doing the pictures?"

"You really think you could come up with some sketches?" I ask them, dubious. I'm not an artistic person in the slightest, but even knowing Cam's skills, I am not sure if there's enough information in the medical records to come up with anything that might look like my birth parents.

They nod. "If that's okay. It'll give me an opportunity to practice my portrait work at the very least."

I tell them to go for it and they start copying down my birth parents' descriptions into their sketch pad.

Maggie is looking at the letterhead on the first page of the records, which has the name of the adoption agency on it. "I bet I could do some digging at the agency, see if I can find and interview some employees who would've been working there when you were adopted. They might have some insight into your birth parents, too."

I wrap my arms around them both, pulling them into a hug. "You guys are the best. You know that, right?"

"Tell me something I don't know," Maggie jokes. Cam and I can't help but laugh along with her.

It's comfortable, this feeling; sharing my fae identity with Maggie and Cam is the best decision I think I've made in a while, despite what Quince may think.

*****

Three hours of sleep is barely enough to function. I pour myself a cup of fresh-brewed coffee when I arrive at Gramp's, a few minutes late because I forgot it takes a little longer to drive there from Maggie's house.

"You didn't take your birthday off?" Mike asks from his spot by the grill as I make my way to the dish washing machine, coffee clutched in my hands like it's my only hope of survival for the next couple hours. He flips fried eggs into the air and onto a plate in a smooth, practiced motion. "Figured I wouldn't see ya this weekend since it's your birthday today."

"Couldn't find anyone to cover for me."

I yawn and set to work on the dishes, starting with my now empty coffee cup.

The hours pass in a haze. Coffee's made me jittery but has done nothing for the fog clouding my brain. A couple times I drop the clean plates. I'm thankful; thus far I haven't broken any.

With ten minutes left in my shift, Harriet, the manager, steps into the kitchen.

"Happy birthday, Eevee." She holds out a cranberry nut muffin, which I take after wiping my hands on my pants. Even so, they're still damp, and my fingers are wrinkled from being in the dishwater. "Now get outta here. Dontcha got better things to do on your birthday than wash dishes?"

"Yeah. Sleep," I say around a mouthful of muffin. It's warm, she must have zapped it in the microwave before bringing it to me.

"Well, scoot!"

It's only ten minutes, but I take it. I'm most of the way through my muffin when I sense a pang of hunger at the edges of my consciousness. The thing is, the hunger pains I feel now are not my own.

"Scamp," I whisper. I don't see him, but I can sense him, lurking nearby. And I almost forgot his scraps for a second Saturday in a row. He'd never forgive me.

I push my way back into the kitchen and grab a napkin, loading it up with some bits of egg and an unfinished sausage link.

When I exit again, he's there, bushy ashen tail swishing back and forth and green eyes staring hungrily at the napkin in my hand.

I set the napkin on the ground and lightly pet him on his back right above his bony shoulders.

"You like the sausage a lot huh?" He's not talking to me, of course, he's a cat. But I feel a surge of excitement when he chews on the link and gobbles it down. "I'll have to save those more often for you if I can."

This connection with Scamp has to be one of my fae abilities I've grown into now that I'm eighteen. While Scamp scarfs down food, I wonder if it's from either of my birth parents. Can my birth father also feel animal emotions? Does my birth mother talk to cats in her spare time?

Scamp is purring like a buzzsaw by the time the napkin's empty, and rubs along my legs like we've been best friends forever and his love isn't bought with food. Tossing the napkin in the dumpster, I sense satisfaction where hunger had crouched at the edge of my consciousness only a minute ago.

Now the food is gone, his interest in me has waned and he trots away.

"All men call thee fickle," I call after him. Not that Scamp appreciates the *Romeo and Juliet* reference, but still.

I take out my phone and meander to my car, not in any particular hurry to get anywhere. Birthday messages from family and friends take up most of my newsfeeds and texts, and I make a mental note to check and reply to them all later.

First, I have someone I need to talk to. I pull up my Instagram messages between me and Quince.

E: *i think my abilities r kicking in*

E: *also sry again 4 u kno what. im not bringing them again, promise*

Already dreaming of my bed with its feathery soft pillows and cozy blankets, I set my phone down and start the car.

*****

When I arrive home, I realize two things. One, sleep is a long time coming because, two, the driveway is packed with my relatives' cars.

I groan inwardly as I step out of the car. If I had remembered the fall birthday party extravaganza was actually on my birthday this year, I wouldn't have stayed up so late with Cam and Maggie last night. For some reason I thought it was supposed to be tomorrow, not today.

I'm swept up in a swarm of family, all of them asking variations of the same questions: how's senior year going? Have you applied to any colleges yet? What do you want to do when you graduate? How's that nice guy you're dating, Damian, isn't that his name?

That last question is the most painful. It's easy enough to say my senior year is going fine, grandma, and no, I haven't applied to colleges yet, but I'm planning to go to one in Duluth and pursue a career as a vet tech.

But the question about Damian rips open a wound which hasn't fully healed. It's only been about a month since we broke up and I blocked him on all social media. I can't deny I've been wondering, too, how he's doing lately.

I'm answering the question about Damian for a fifth time, this time for my great aunt Franny, and wishing to myself that more of my family would use social media so they'd know I was single (then again, maybe not). She gives the same sympathetic shake of her head I've seen from my grandma and my aunt Patricia, and I think maybe I've discovered an inherited behavioral trait I can discuss for Mrs. Field's DNA project.

Amelia rescues me with a can of pop and starts talking to great aunt Franny about how her freshman year is going while Franny nods along, looking lost at Amelia's rapid delivery.

I take a quick moment to check if Quince has responded, and almost choke on my mouthful of pop when I see his second message.

Q: *that's great. can't wait to hear about it. remember, you're bound to the rules of the fae now, too.*

Q: *hey, want to go to the fall equinox celebration with me?*

I stare at my phone. Is Quince Florentz asking me on a date to a party in the fae realm?

Not sure how to answer, I slip my phone in my pocket. Greg and Charlie run by with a couple of our cousins. Over the din of overlapping voices, I hear my dad shout, "Who wants hot dogs?"

It's comical how quickly Greg and Charlie do an about-face and zoom back the way they'd come from, on their quest to find dad and the food.

I'm about to follow them when I feel my phone buzz.

It's probably Quince. He sent that message about the equinox party a few hours ago and I haven't responded yet due to recounting my painful breakup and post-graduation plans with family members.

I frown down at my phone. The message isn't from Quince. In fact, I have no idea who it's from; the number isn't saved in my phone.

Unknown Number (UN): *hey! happy bday* 😊
E: *thx. who's this? don't have the # saved, sry*

I go grab some food and sense fear, not mine, cowering in the back of my mind. Thinking back to Scamp, I take a bite of the hot dog covered in ketchup and wander through the house until the sense of fear intensifies when I'm just outside my room. When I enter, I find Slinky trembling under my bed.

"Hey there, Slink. Want a bite of hot dog?" I coax Slinky out from under the bed by tearing some hot dog bits and placing them on the rug.

He creeps out from under the bed and I brush some dust bunnies off his sleek black fur.

"I know, I don't like crowds either," I tell him.

The hot dog consumed, he rolls onto his back and meows. With one hand I scratch his belly, and with the other I check my phone.

I should respond to Quince. A fae party sounds like a lot of fun. But Quince is hard to read. I can't tell if he's asking me because I'm fae and he feels it's his duty to introduce me to fae culture, or if he's asking me because he likes me and wants to spend time with me. I chew on my lip. He's different from my other guy friends. When I'm with him, it's easy to get caught up in the moment, like when we walked to the stream in the In Between. I was so enthralled by everything I hadn't realized we'd been walking hand in hand until we were a good way to the stream. But what about when he gets over the excitement of me being another fae at Duluth High? When that fades away, would there be enough chemistry, enough staying power?

I'm not sure. And given his track record of a new girlfriend with each show he's in, the likelihood of us lasting as a couple until the winter solstice are slim to none.

No, better to stay friends so he can date someone like Laura. She's nice, and seems really into him.

I'll just have to make it clear to him when I respond that I'd love to go to the equinox party as friends.

I'm thinking of how exactly I want to word my response when a message appears from the unknown number, turning my stomach to icy knots.

UN: *its Damian. been thinking of u lately*
UN: *think we can talk? i feel really bad about how we left things*

Frigid tendrils snake out from my stomach and course through my veins until my whole body feels like it's been encased in a snowbank.

Damian. I've talked about him so much today, and now here he is, texting me. And he remembered my birthday, which is...well, it's something. But remembering my birthday in no way makes up for breaking up with me after I'd helped him move into college.

E: *thx for the bday wishes. idk if i want 2 talk tho*
UN: *i get it. i was a dick. i should've told u i wasn't sure about doing distance b4 u came to 'nona w/me*
E: *u think?*

I'm pleasantly surprised by his response, and my fingers thaw enough to grab at my bedspread, so I pull myself up and flop onto my bed, leaving my paper plate with its half-eaten food on the rug.

This is more introspection in one text than I'm used to seeing in Damian. Could college have changed him so much in a month?

UN: *im @ home this weekend. we could meet up @ our usual spot 2nite if ur free?*

I should say no. I don't know why I hesitate. Part of me would love to see him, get a chance to tell him all the ways he'd hurt me. But I know me, and I know Damian. We've had our fair share of talks which ended with our arms around each other and our lips locked. No, that won't do. But I do have a few things I want to say to him.

E: *im free later. like 9? but i can't meet long. maybe meet @ Northern Creamery 4 ice cream?*

He takes a moment to respond, and in that moment I have a ping-pong match in my head between the Eevee who thinks it was really stupid to invite him to go out for ice cream and the Eevee who wants nothing more than to see Damian and...what? Shove an ice cream cone in his face? Waste of ice cream. Recite Shakespeare at him? Waste of good quotes.

UN: *k. see u then.*

Slinky sneaks out from under the bed and starts licking the ketchup off the remainder of my hot dog, but I don't care. I don't think I could eat it anymore anyway.

*****

Damian looks no different, though I'm not sure what I expected. It's only been a month, after all. His blond hair is gelled back, and he's wearing a form-fitting polo which emphasizes the blue of his eyes.

I can't deny he looks sexy, and when he gets up from the booth to hug me, I don't exactly protest when the hug is a little longer than a hug between friends.

"It's so good to see you," he says after I've ordered a bowl of ice cream and sit down opposite him. "I almost didn't recognize you without your hair."

I touch my head. I've styled it to give it some volume and love how it turned out with the way it frames my face. "Yeah, it was kind of an impulse decision," I say. I leave off the fact it was inspired by our breakup. How cliché.

The next half hour passes with stories of Damian's college exploits. He asked me at first about my senior year, but what could I say? "Turns out I'm fae and not human at all, isn't that crazy?" Easier to tell him my year's going fine and let him talk.

And that's when I realize it. I'm letting us fall into our old patterns, slipping them on like a form-fitting glove. He dominates the conversation with a hand on my arm, his fingers tracing some of the freckles that dot my forearms, while I let him talk and I nod in all the right places.

"I'm sorry," I interrupt, pulling my arms away. "What are we doing here?"

Damian stops his story about the pizza eating contest he and Chet had won. "What do you mean? We're having ice cream, like you requested. It's your birthday, can't say no if the birthday girl asks for ice cream." His smile is all innocent confusion.

"And then what? You're going back to Winona. And you said you weren't sure about doing distance, which you definitely could've said before I traveled to Winona with you, but you know…"

"That again?" He shakes his head. "I'm sorry, Eevee. I didn't know how to tell you. But we're here now. And I'm not going back to Winona until tomorrow." He wraps my hands in his and tries lacing our fingers together, but I don't move.

He frowns and removes his hands from mine. "I just thought we could have some fun, celebrate your birthday, while I was home. Nothing serious, you know?"

I can't help it. I laugh. "Do you even know how to be in a serious relationship?"

He sits back and crosses his arms, all lines of his body on the defense. "You and I dated almost a year. Before that, I was with Stacy for half a year and Lexi for two."

My arms are crossed now too. "I can't speak for Stacy and Lexi." Though if Maggie's to be believed, and I consider her to be a reliable news source for all things Duluth High, there was some overlap between Damian's time with Stacy and Lexi. "But in our ten months of being together, a whole two months shy of a year, by the way, I was in a relationship with a guy who was in a relationship with himself."

I get up and he looks up at me, his face blank. "Maybe when you understand what I mean, we can talk again."

As I turn to leave, he asks, "What, no Shakespeare insult to hurl at me this time?"

His voice is low, and I turn to see him looking down at what's left of his waffle bowl. To the melting ice cream in the waffle bowl, he says, "I probably deserve it."

Damnit. I hate seeing people upset, even Damian. I sit back down and keep my voice light. "Maybe I was having a hard time deciding which one to use."

"I know it sounds ridiculous, but I actually have missed your weird Shakespeare references since I've been at college."

I didn't know he listened to my Shakespeare references.

For a while, I regard him while he stares at his waffle bowl. Maybe, just maybe, he isn't looking to hook up for fun. Or, maybe he doesn't know what he wants. I can understand that.

"I can't jump right back into anything," I tell him. "But we can talk again, see what happens? Maybe grab ice cream when you're back next time."

He looks up at me with a hungry expression and a look in his eyes that would've made the Eevee of a month ago melt into his arms like the chocolate ice cream pooling in the bottom of his waffle bowl.

I steel myself, but somehow end up enveloped in his embrace, breathing in his expensive cologne.

"I'll message you," he whispers in my hair before pulling away.

His scent lingers with me and I'm dazed, my emotions all over the place, but I walk out to the parking lot with him.

"I'm parked over there." I indicate my mom's car, and he walks me to it. I'm rummaging in my purse for the keys when I feel his hands on my arms.

His voice is husky when he says, "Seriously, Eevee, it was really great catching up with you."

And I don't know if he leaned in or if I pulled him toward me, but my back is pressed up against the hard glass of the driver's side window of the car and my hands are everywhere, under his shirt, running through his hair. His skin is warm to the touch, and we explore each others' lips with our tongues like it's been years since we last kissed, not weeks.

Whichever one of us started it, I know I have to be the one to end it. I drop back, and my voice is husky too when I say, "We'll have to get ice cream again when you're in town."

I slip into my mom's car and wave, grateful for the glass separating us. I want to punch him still for how he broke up with me, and kiss him again, but I force myself to put the car into drive instead. When I'm a few roads away, I press my fingers to my lips, which are still swollen.

*****

Sleeping in is my only plan for Sunday. I think it sounds like a great way to spend the day after my eighteenth birthday. What with being able to sense the feelings of animals (hello, new fae ability), Quince maybe possibly asking me out, a typically hectic family gathering, and ending the night making out with Damian, all after next to zero sleep the night before, I'm emotionally and mentally drained.

Unfortunately, Greg and Charlie think Sunday mornings are best spent roaring at each other like dinosaurs.

I flop over and drag my pillow over my head, but it's no use, I'm awake. My eyes burn and I have a headache, but I'm alert enough to process the blinking light on my phone letting me know I have unread notifications.

Probably more birthday wishes. But then, slowly, my brain forms the thought that it might be Damian and I unplug my phone and unlock the screen.

D: *2nite was fun. should i txt u next time im in town to get ice cream again?* 😋

Should he? Last night was fun, he's not wrong about that. Well, at least, parts of it were. Maybe Damian in small doses isn't the worst idea.

E: *yeah sure* 😊

I scroll through birthday wishes and send a quick message to Cam and Maggie.

E: *guess who i saw last nite??*

Greg and Charlie's dinosaur roars have diminished, probably thanks to mom telling them to keep it down. I send a mental thank you to mom. Before sleep takes me, I log into my Instagram to respond to Quince and see he's sent a follow-up message.

Q: *i'm asking bc u should go, it's a lot of fun. and my cousins said we could come over before the party to get ready at their place*

His cousins? Why would we want to get ready at their place? I'm too tired for this. My brain laboriously puts the pieces together and it dawns on me. His cousins! The ones who can help with the next clue.

I should have figured. Yet again, I've misjudged Quince "not-actually-asking-Eevee-out" Florentz. He wants to find more clues to the mystery, and inviting me to the equinox celebration provides a good cover story.

E: *sounds fun. gotta check with mom & dad, but i should be able to come as long as we're not back 2 late (school night, ugh). ur parents are ok with us going 2 ur cousins?*

He responds almost immediately.

Q: *yep. they love my cousins. i told my parents, if you said yes, we'd go to their house after school that day to get ready and meet them at the party afterward*
E: *sounds like a plan 2 me*
E: *good night*
Q: *it's 11am??*
Q: *Eevee?*
E: *i said what i said. Good night, good night! Parting is such sweet sorrow, That I shall say good night till it be morrow*

Maybe Quince will appreciate a *Romeo and Juliet* reference more than Scamp.

Chapter 19

A Bit of Trouble

I haven't been able to sit still all day. In every class I've found some excuse to get up: bathroom breaks, sharpening pencils, even volunteering to pass out papers.

Tonight's the equinox party, and in a few minutes, when the bell rings, I'll be heading to the fae realm early to meet Quince's cousins and get help with the clue we'd found on the Mage Stone.

I open my yellow notebook, the one with the fairy I've drawn on the cover, and jot down the homework pages for math, then flip to the page with my table of what I know and don't know about my birth parents and my fae identity. After my birthday last Saturday I've added "can sense animal emotions" to my list of abilities. If any other new abilities unlocked on my eighteenth birthday, I haven't figured out what they are yet. When we were talking about it in study hall this week (as much as we could with Jim there–talking in code when he was sitting by us or in short bursts when he'd get up to find books or print assignments), Quince said some of my abilities might be latent until I return to Elfaeme.

I haven't gone back to the fae realm since I'd taken Maggie and Cam; not by myself or with anyone.

Not that Cam wants me to go back. And besides, Maggie and Cam are both upset with me for talking to Damian again. Cam's been really quiet and has barely talked to me all week. I glance up from my notebook to where they're sitting, jotting down notes as Mr. Jenkins talks. They haven't looked back at me all period. Tomorrow I'm considering taking the bus, even though it's Friday, rather than sitting through an uncomfortably silent van ride.

I circle the bullet point "How many clues there are" with a red gel pen.

The first clue, on the back of the letter, led me to the Mage Stone at the edge of Seelie territory near the In Between. The second one is located at some lake in the Unseelie lands, near where Quince's cousins live. How many trips to different parts of Elfaeme am I going to have to take before I reach what my birth mother wanted me to find?

Quince thinks we're getting close.

"She can't have had time to place too many clues. And the fae are partial to the rule of three," he'd said in an undertone while Jim was at the printer with Mr. Abscons.

If he's right, the clue at the lake is the last one.

No wonder my body can't stop moving. I'm bursting with nervous energy.

Today could be the day I meet my birth parents.

The bell rings and I dump all my belongings into my backpack and bolt for the door, reaching it before Mark who's sitting in the desk closest to it.

I weave through the hall until I reach Quince's locker. I've already crammed everything I need into my backpack, including the sweatshirt Quince told me to pack.

Quince isn't at his locker yet, but Laura's at hers. I say hi, a little out of breath from speed walking the whole way here, but she acts as if she can't hear me and continues putting her textbooks away.

I know her hearing isn't the problem because when Quince arrives and says hi, she's all smiles and they chat about the fall musical, which I discover, thanks to my exceptional fae hearing, is to be a production of *My Fair Lady*. I tap my foot while they chat and Quince grabs his backpack, slinging it over one shoulder.

"I just think we should rehearse the flower market scene a bit more, you know? Really get the overall mood right. Some of the cast are just going through the motions and it shows," Laura's saying. "I don't know why Ms. Wilson's been having us do the scene with the servants, we've got that down already."

"Totally. Oh, that reminds me. Laura, can you tell Ms. Wilson I won't be at rehearsal today? I already let her know, but you know how she forgets things."

"You're missing rehearsal today? But we're doing the choreography for the big scene at the end of Act I!"

That shimmer in the air around Quince shines almost as brightly as the smile he directs at Laura. "Guess you're going to have to go over it with me."

"It'll mean staying late with me after a few rehearsals, it's a big number," she says, looking delighted at the prospect.

They square out details for their rehearsals while my foot works on tapping out a hole in the floor.

"You ready?" I interrupt when it's clear Laura's not going to be done talking anytime soon.

Her smile dims when she realizes that the reason Quince is missing rehearsal has something to do with me.

"I thought you said you had a family thing?"

"I do. Kind of a twice-a-year tradition."

"Oh."

He doesn't explain why I'm coming along to the "family thing," and I can see Laura struggling with whether she should ask or not.

"Come on," Quince says, tugging on my elbow. "See you, Laura. Have fun at rehearsal!"

She gapes after us as we turn to head down the hall. In our haste, we almost run into Mr. Abscons, who's talking to Mr. Nelson, the business ed teacher. Mr. Nelson keeps on talking, but Mr. Abscsons' lips press into a thin line.

"Sorry!" I call over my shoulder. I let Quince drag me down the hall and out the door. There's still a sizable crowd of students milling about on the sidewalk.

"We're not leaving right from here are we?" I ask, wondering what the other students would think if they noticed Quince and I disappear into thin air.

He laughs and shakes his head. "You crack me up. No, I thought we could head to the nearby park. There's some semi-secluded paths we can walk on there. It's easiest to travel to Elfaeme when you're in nature. Besides, we don't want to alarm the fireflies." He gestures to the other students around us.

I catch up to him on the sidewalk. "You've said fireflies before. What do you mean by that?"

Lowering his voice, he says, "This is still so weird to me, how much you...What do you know about our life span, the life span of the fae?"

I think back to what I'd read on the innumerable websites since I found out I was fae. "Are fae immortal?"

Now that's an aspect of my fae life I hadn't considered: a long, possibly eternal, life span. The years stretch before me, endless, marching on like relentless soldiers whose mission and purpose are as resolute and consistent as their steps. Left, left. Left, right, left.

My thoughts stray to my family and I feel a pang of premature loss. If I don't age at a normal rate, if I can never die, how many of my friends and family will I have to watch as they grow old and die while I remain mostly unchanged?

It's a dizzying, depressing notion.

We're at the edge of the park and stroll by a soccer field, heading toward a paved path which winds into a small grove of trees.

"No, fae aren't immortal. But we can live hundreds, even thousands of years, as long as we aren't killed by illness or unnatural means like murder. Compared to humans, whose lives are short and burn bright, like fireflies."

Not immortal, then, but close enough.

I survey him out of the corner of my eyes, wondering how old some of his relatives are, like the cousins we're about to visit.

"Compared to a lot of the fae, we're practically babies," he's saying. "I can't wait for my abilities to kick in when I turn eighteen. My mom's Seelie and has the ability to enhance plant growth. Her garden is better than any professional displays. I've always hoped I get that green touch from her. Guess I'll see in a few months."

He stops. "I think we've got enough cover here."

I can hear some kids playing on the soccer field, but he's right, I can't see anyone.

"My cousins should be expecting us. If they remember that we're coming. I've warned you they're a bit out there, right?"

"A few times, yeah," I say, crinkling my nose at him. "If they can help us with the next clue, I don't care."

"Then let's go pay them a visit."

He reaches out to me and I think he's going to grab my hand, but he tugs at one of the straps of my backpack, sliding it off my shoulder.

"Travel tip," he says, slipping one of the straps of his backpack to a single shoulder as well, "when going from the human realm to Elfaeme, your clothes will change to fit your wings, but backpacks won't. It can get a little uncomfortable, to say the least."

I leave my backpack dangling from one shoulder and let Quince take my hand. As our hands connect, I feel a shift, difficult to describe. It's been a week since my last hurried trip to Elfaeme with Maggie and Cam, and I'd forgotten the moment of disorientation that occurs from traveling between the fabric of one world to the next.

This time, I keep my eyes open and watch as the sparse grove of trees fades, leaving a winter wonderland in its place. We're surrounded by a world which exists in a permanent winter. Icicles sparkle off branches and a blanket of pure white snow covers the ground. Through the trees I can see jagged mountains breaking up the horizon in front of me.

I shiver and release Quince's hand so I can retrieve my sweatshirt from my backpack. There are two slits in the back of it that weren't there before, and I pull it over my head, then promptly get tangled in my attempt to fit it over my wings.

"How do you get dressed with these?" I ask, my sweatshirt over my head.

Quince is laughing. "I forget how new you are to being fae." He tugs my sweatshirt off my head so I can see him. I scowl at the way his eyes sparkle with amusement. "You can make your wings non-corp."

I stare at him blankly.

"Non-corporeal."

At my shrug, he explains, "You can make it so your wings have no physical form–so you can see them but they can just go right through things. Like this." He tugs his arms through the sleeves of his sweatshirt, then takes a deep breath and releases his shoulders. His black, feathered wings turn shimmery, and he quickly slips his sweatshirt over his head and yanks it down over his waist. He turns his back to me so I can watch as it passes through his wings. As soon as it's on, they lose the glistening quality. I reach out and run my hands over one of them, my fingers sliding over the silky feathers.

"Hey, that tickles." His wings shift and he turns back to face me.

It takes me a couple of times to get the breathing and shoulder relaxing just right, and then another two times to perfect the timing of pulling my sweatshirt over my head before my wings go back to their normal state, but I finally manage to get my sweatshirt over my head. With all the effort I've exerted, my cheeks are red and the sweatshirt is almost pointless, I'm so warm.

"My cousins' house is just over that hill," he points to a hill over my right shoulder. "About a five minute walk. Shouldn't take us too long to get there."

"Why didn't we just materialize in their house?"

He slows, tilting his head to look back at me as I work to catch up. "That's a little rude, don't you think?"

My already red cheeks flush even more.

"Besides," he says, ignoring my embarrassment, "I wanted to arrive a little ways away to show you the land a bit since you've never been here before. The Unseelie lands are beautiful, don't you think?"

"In a cold way, yeah."

My breath puffs out in front of my face in a misty cloud. The crisp air doesn't bother me as much as I thought it would, and I bring this up with Quince.

"It's your Unseelie blood. The cold is their natural element. I bet you've always been the kind of person who isn't bothered by the cold temperatures when everyone else is bundling up."

I am, but I'd always chalked this up to my Midwestern hardiness.

We trudge through the snow, and I find myself wishing I could've brought my winter boots. The cold air doesn't bother me so much, but I don't like how my wet socks cling to my feet in my shoes. Mom would've asked me why I was looking for my winter boots in September, though, and then there's the issue of finding somewhere to put them during the school day, so I didn't even bother trying to locate them.

Quince isn't wearing boots either, but he does put on a set of gloves as he walks and points out the features of the landscape.

Crack. Crack.

I look behind us, my eyes narrowing as I try and see through the snow-laden pines.

"I could have sworn I heard something moving behind us," I explain when I see Quince's curious look.

"Lots of animals around," he reasons. "I heard it, too. Still, we can hurry it up a bit."

We reach an intricate gate made of weathered wood, which opens at our approach.

"Good, they remembered," Quince says in obvious relief.

"Are they like you?" I ask. "Both Seelie and Unseelie?"

The gate clunks shut behind us and we both jump a few inches in the air.

"No," Quince says when we resume walking up the long drive. "They're true Unseelie. My aunt and uncle are pretty high up in the Court. Not as high as my dad was before he was banished for marrying my mom, but closer than most Unseelie are to the Unseelie throne."

I'm blown away by what Quince doesn't say. "That means you're even closer than they are to the throne. Like, you could inherit it?"

Quince shrugs as if this is no big deal. "Yes and no. Theoretically, yes. But I'm part Seelie through my mom, and my dad was banished from his spot at the Court, so it's a tenuous claim at best. Fae have long lives and longer memories. It's been ages since the Seelie and Unseelie have agreed on much of anything."

"Not all of them."

"No." He looks sidelong at me. "Not all."

The road up to the house is lined with stone statues: fantasy creatures, fae with wings, fae in battle, all guarding the road with empty eyes and stern faces. As we crest the top of the small hill, I get a better view of his cousin's house.

It's not a house at all. In front of us, nestled among a pine forest, is an ice castle out of imagination. As we near it, I realize it's not actually made of ice. Its sides are all covered in icy sheets, and it reflects the cold light of the afternoon sun in glittering facets. Even the windows have icicles growing down over them, giving them the appearance of bars on a frozen cage. I shiver.

"It's the Kings and Queens who refuse to work together," Quince explains. "Well, Queen. The Seelie King Oakspirit and Queen Hibiscus won't have anything to do with King Nightglade, and the feeling's mutual."

I want to ask him what happened to drive the two Courts apart, because this isn't the first time he's mentioned the tension between the Courts, but he's holding a finger to his lips.

"What?" I whisper. We aren't yet to the front door of his cousins' ice castle–I disagree with Quince classifying the frozen mansion in front of us as a house.

Then I hear it, too. Branches crack behind us, and there's a wrenching smash as the gate at the end of the road is splintered to pieces by a creature at least twice my size.

"Get down. Behind the dryad statue. Quick!"

Quince's voice is deadly serious, so I don't even think, just do as I'm told and dash behind the statue he's pointing to and drop to the ground.

The snow melts beneath the warmth of my palms and I strain my ears. What is that thing at the gate?

Crouching next to me, Quince drops his backpack on the ground and launches himself into the air, his feathered black wings extending outward as he flies back down the drive the way we came.

His shadow is small on the snowy ground. I lift my head and risk peering around the statue to get a better look at the creature.

Whatever it is, it's lumbering up the drive on two legs and its shape is vaguely humanoid, but its blue skin and beard of icicles are distinctly fae. What kind of fae,

I'm not sure. But given Quince's reaction, I'm guessing a dangerous one.

"Over here, you big brute!" Quince flies just out of the creature's reach and smiles down at it. "You're just a big ol' ice troll, aren't you? I bet you're really strong."

I can see the air around Quince glimmering, like when he talked with Laura and Ms. Bates, and I realize he's trying to charm the ten-foot-tall ice troll.

The ice troll, however, is impervious to Quince's charms, and it roars, brandishing a stone club at him. They enter into a dance of cat and mouse, and I find myself crossing my fingers from where I hide behind the statue.

A wide swing connects with one of the statues, and chunks of stone fly through the air. I hear the dull thud of one of them connecting with the side of Quince's leg and watch as he drops a few feet in the air before recovering.

"Quince!" I shout, then clap my hands to my mouth as the ice troll lowers its club and grunts, looking in my direction and scratching at its icicle beard.

"I'm fine, Eevee, just stay down!" Quince yells.

The ice troll turns its attention back to Quince, and I feel anger burning like an ember in my chest–at the ice troll for attacking us for no reason, and at Quince for thinking he can tell me what to do.

"Hey!" I step out from behind the statue. "Blue guy!"

Mid-air, Quince slaps a hand to his forehead.

His flinty eyes on me, the ice troll stomps in my direction. At least he's slow-moving. When he gets closer, I can see old scars criss-crossing his arms and legs. He's barefoot, but is wearing pelts for a rudimentary loincloth, more for show than to keep him warm, I think.

I let him close in, then I zigzag out of his way. He swings the club and it smashes into the statue I'd been hiding behind, knocking off the dryad's head. He roars in frustration and turns, but I'm already moving away.

In the air, Quince continues to alternate between yelling at me for disobeying him and at the ice troll to try and distract it. He's given up all attempts to charm it.

I don't think I can keep this pace up for long. The troll may be slow, but it's used to moving through snow. As for me, I may have grown up in Minnesota where it's winter for more of the year than I'd like, but it's been more than six months since I last put on boots.

Dashing out of his way, I run in a circle around it, forcing it to spin on the spot. It keeps spinning until it sways and clutches at its head. I use my wings to half-jump, half-fly to the top of the headless dryad statue.

"What are you doing?" Quince shouts. "Let me handle this! It's not my first ice troll!"

The ice troll in question stops shaking its head and heads straight toward the statue I'm standing on.

My anger pounds through me like a drum beat and I let the sound of my heartbeat fill my ears.

"Bring it, troll guy!" I shout, beckoning it to keep running at me.

The invitation to come get me only serves to enrage and confuse it, and I see its sharp teeth gnashing as it nears.

It'll be within striking range in a few seconds, and I have only the vaguest of ideas of what to do next. I crouch, then leap out of the way, right over its shoulder.

When its club doesn't connect with anything, the force of the swing sends it sprawling to the ground.

Quince lands just out of the troll's reach. "Keep back, Eevee."

The troll snarls. With surprising agility for a creature its size, it stands and lurches toward Quince, who stumbles as his weight comes down on his injured leg. I watch, helpless and terrified Quince is about to be eaten by an ice troll. He takes a few more stumbling steps, then flies upward, away from the troll's swinging club.

Seeing Quince limp sends my anger over the boiling point. I run up to the troll, whose back is to me as it tracks Quince's position in the air, and direct a hook at its unguarded side, hoping my aim is true; the spot I've zeroed in on looks softer in comparison to the thick, grayish skin of the troll's knees and elbows.

I'm not the strongest person, so I'm surprised when it lets out a roar of pain like a wounded animal. My brain catches up with my body and I stumble backward.

"Holy shit."

I stare down at my fist. Flames are crackling around it. Actual, real live fire. On my fists. As my anger diminishes, replaced with surprise, the flames lessen too.

The ice troll is clutching its side and whimpering.

"Go on, get out of here!" Quince says, shooing it with his hands as he descends.

It doesn't move at first, but when I raise my fist to examine the last of the flames, it scrambles away, disappearing in the direction of the nearby mountains.

The spot I'd punched may have been soft in comparison to other parts of the troll's anatomy, but it was definitely not soft. Now the flames have abated, I'm left with a hand that tingles. Bruises are already forming over some of the knuckles and joints.

"I think we just discovered another one of your abilities," Quince says, warring tones of awe and jealousy in his voice. "Come on, let's get inside before anything else happens."

"What about you?" I ask as we go grab our backpacks out from under the rubble. He's still limping.

"The statue chunk glanced off me. It's probably just a bad bruise."

My skepticism shows in my face, because he adds, "I'll be fine until we get inside. My cousins have good healing salves for this kind of stuff."

I worry every second of the minute it takes us to reach the door, but the ice troll doesn't return.

"Ready to meet my cousins and find the next clue?"

"I just hit an ice troll with a flaming fist. I'm ready for anything," I answer.

Chapter 20

Meeting the Cousins

Quince's knocks are met with silence. My nerves, already frayed from punching an ice troll with a fiery left hook, jangle inside me like loose change in a piggy bank.

"They're here, right?" I ask as Quince steps over to a window to peer inside.

"Oh, they're here." Oddly, Quince sounds annoyed. I give him a quizzical look, but he shakes his head at me and opens the door.

I accompany him inside to an interior the exact opposite of the cold exterior. We walk through an inviting entrance hall and into what appears to be a sitting room. A fire crackles merrily in a large hearth at the far side of the room. Plush couches and chairs take up much of the space around it, but they are in disarray, as if someone had torn through the room. Or had been fighting in it.

When we walk around the furniture, I gasp.

Two bodies lie facedown on the floor with knives between their batlike wings. Blood seeps from the wounds, pooling between their shoulders.

"What's happened?" I whisper, horrified. I watch as Quince limps over to one of the bodies. I think he's going to check vitals or something, but instead, he rears back with his good leg and gives the immobile body a swift kick in its side.

"Quince! What are you doing?"

The body on the ground lets out a small groan.

"Get up." Quince is irritated, his arms folded across his chest and his eyes narrowed. "This is no time to be playing dead body. Didn't you hear us fighting that ice troll? We could've used your help!"

"You seemed to be handling it fine," says the other body in a muffled voice, its face pressed into the area rug.

"Not the point," Quince retorts, exasperated. "Will you get up? I need some of that healing salve you've got, and we're running out of time to check out that clue for Eevee before the equinox celebration."

This rouses them. They both roll onto their sides and stand, stretching. They take turns pulling out the knives and wiping each other's backs of the fake blood with handkerchiefs. Even from where I stand, holding onto a couch for support, I can see the knives are props now. They had looked so real when stuck between their wings.

"How long was that?" the one closest to me asks the other.

"At least twelve hours," the other replies after checking his pocket watch.

"Not our longest game of dead body, then." The first sighs, then turns to me. "Oh, goodness! You look just like-"

"-someone we once knew," finishes the other, placing a hand on his brother's arm as he steps up next to him. They exchange a look, then he faces me again. "Welcome, Eevee. We have been looking forward to meeting the mysterious fae our cousin has been telling us about."

"We do love a good mystery."

"And secrets."

187

Their eyes, the pale blue of a winter sky, gleam like ice.

"I'll just go help myself to the salve, then," Quince says. "Be right back." He limps away, leaving me in the sitting room with his cousins.

We stare at each other.

"So, who's Sean? And Shannon?" I ask awkwardly. Apparently Quince hadn't thought it necessary to introduce us formally before getting the salve.

"I'm Shannon," the one on the left says. He brushes his snowy white hair out of his face with both hands, and I notice there's a streak of black hair framing the left side of his face. Gesturing to his brother, he says, "and that is Sean."

Sean smiles in a way that's both reassuring and feral, an unsettling combination.

I study them. They're hard to tell apart. Same elbow-length snowy hair and icy blue eyes, same leathery wings on their backs. But then I see that while Shannon has a black streak of hair on the left side of his face, Sean has a black streak framing the right side of his.

I make a mental note of this, then Sean asks me about the clue, so I take the notebook out of my backpack.

The twins are poring over my notes when Quince returns, no longer limping.

"This is most certainly referring to Crystal Lake," Shannon says to him. "You were right to bring the clue to us."

"So you can help me?" I ask.

"Yes," they both reply.

"We love mysteries and secrets, remember?" Sean asks. He turns to Shannon. "I'm thinking the jewel-"

"-isn't an actual jewel. My thoughts exactly."
Shannon finishes. "But we'll have to go into the ice caves
to get an idea of what it might be referring to. You know,
this reminds me of that treasure hunt we did when we were
twelve, back in the eighties. Remember that, Sean?"

"No."

"Really? Because I remember everything. You got
lost in the human realm, and when we found you, you
were sucking your thumb and-"

"Perhaps we should focus on Eevee's clue, yes?"
Sean interrupts, his smile frigid. Quince is snickering
behind his hands.

"You guys were kids back in the 1980s?" I ask,
mentally trying to calculate their age. "That would make
you both in your forties?"

They look maybe in their late twenties, early
thirties, if I had to guess.

"He meant the 1780s," Sean says shortly.

My mind reels. They're hundreds of years old.
That means they were alive when the United States
declared its independence.

"So you do remember!" Shannon says, delighted.

"Let's just go to the lake," Sean answers.

We exit out of one of the back doors at Quince's
insistence. He doesn't say it, but I think he wants to avoid
the front door in case the ice troll is still hanging around.

I gaze around at the thick pine forest that takes up
most of the backyard. "How far is the lake?"

"A day away as the crow flies," Shannon answers.

Confusion clouds my mind and I slow down. "But
then, how...?"

"She's still really new to Elfaeme," Quince says to
Sean and Shannon, who nod knowingly. "There's a couple

189

ways to get there quickly. We could return to the human realm, then travel to the lake from there, but that would sap a lot of our energy. You haven't gone back and forth a lot in one day yet, but it's not something you can keep doing without consequence."

"It's how Sean got stuck in the human realm in the eighties," Shannon says. We pass into the pine forest, and the thick layer of snow diminishes to maybe an inch. I can feel a bed of pine needles under my feet as I walk. "He'd gone back and forth from the human realm to Elfaeme too much in one day and exhausted his fae powers. By the time we found him sucking his thumb, he was sitting in the middle of a mushroom circle and asking why it wasn't working and-"

"I think Eevee gets the idea," Quince interrupts.

Sean's face is a stony mask. "Good thing I don't get angry anymore," he says lightly, his voice like thin ice over a tempestuous sea.

"Okay, so if we can't travel to the human realm and then to the lake, how are we getting there? Doesn't the equinox celebration start in a couple hours?"

According to the clock on my phone, it's almost five.

"Oh, no one ever arrives on time, Eevee," Shannon says, laughing good-naturedly. "The start time is more of a guideline than anything else."

"The other reason I asked my cousins to help us is they have a moonstone on their property."

"A moonstone? Like the Mage Stone?" I ask.

"Yes, but unlike that one, this one is active," Quince says.

We reach a clearing where a smooth boulder sits, a layer of snow atop it.

Sean brushes off the snow with his sleeve, revealing a gray stone. Unlike the Mage Stone, which is a dull gray, this moonstone has light dancing across its surface. I realize I've seen moonstones before, a whole circle of them, in fact, the first time I visited the fae realm.

"That's how you can tell an active moonstone from an inactive one," Quince explains quietly, pointing at the light undulating across its top and sides. "The active ones have magic shining in them. When they're dormant, they look like ordinary rocks."

"We'll all take turns using it to travel to the lake," Shannon says. "I'll go first." He reaches out, touches it with his bare hand, and vanishes.

Sean does the same. I turn a panicked face to Quince. "I've never–I can't-"

"We can travel together," he reassures me. "It does mean holding my hand again, though."

I grip his hand without hesitation, hoping he doesn't mind how sweaty my palms are.

"Alright, here we go."

Leaning forward, Quince touches the moonstone and the quiet pine forest around us disappears.

Chapter 21

Beneath Crystal Lake

Traveling by moonstone is not at all like traveling between the fae and human realms. That can be disorienting momentarily, sure, but the first time I'd traveled to the fae realm I hadn't known I'd done it until I looked around. The disorientation fades quickly, like the slight dizziness which comes when spinning too many cartwheels in the grass.

But traveling by moonstone? It's as shocking to my body as the time I fell backward off the swing at school in the third grade and had the air knocked out of me.

When we appear on a small peninsula, what would be a beach if it weren't covered by snow, I'm gasping for air and clutching at my chest with my free hand.

Quince keeps a hold of my other hand despite it being hot and sweaty. He doesn't have much of a choice; I've got his hand in a death grip.

My heart rate finally slows and I inhale, releasing my grip on Quince's hand. "So," I say, trying not to sound like I've just completed a thirty minute intense cardio workout, "this is Crystal Lake?"

I don't think I've succeeded at sounding unfazed by the moonstone trip because Shannon comes up behind me and thumps me on the back.

"The first time traveling by moonstone is a bit of a shock, isn't it?" he asks sympathetically. "I remember my first time-"

"You were eighteen months old," Sean interrupts. "Mother remembers. You remember her story."

"No, I remember," Shannon counters placidly. "I thought I'd never breathe again. It was terrifying."

Sean looks like he wants to say more, but restrains himself. He paces at the edge of the lake, his eyes taking in the silent frozen expanse and the empty sky. "Shall we?"

Quince lets go of my hand and rubs his hands together. "I've been wanting to explore the ice caves for years." He rushes toward the lake, but Sean throws out an arm to stop him.

"Not so fast. We need to proceed with caution."

"Why?" I ask. The place looks deserted to me, unlike the Mage Stone, which boasted a fair number of fae folk milling around it.

Instead of answering me, Sean takes to the sky, his batlike wings moving as if he were using them to swim through the air.

"What's he doing?" I watch as Sean circles above us and out over the lake.

"Looking for any wyverns," Shannon answers.

"Wyverns?" I exclaim.

Quince smiles sheepishly at me and scuffs his foot in the snow at the edge of the lake. "There's a reason my parents don't want me exploring the caves with Sean and Shannon. It's...dangerous. They don't even come out here that often, do you?"

"Oh, definitely not. For a lark every decade or so, sure. But fae are not immortal, you know. We dare not risk our lives too often," Shannon answers.

"Why would my birth mother leave a clue where wyverns live?" I squeak. Before they can answer, I add, "Also, what are wyverns?"

I should've been paying attention during all those fantasy movies Cam made me watch.

"Think dragons, but the size of a horse," Quince says.

I think he meant to reassure me with his answer, but I've seen a Clydesdale in person and that's big enough to cause real damage, especially if it has any special dragon powers.

An image of a horse galloping toward me breathing fire rises unbidden in my mind. I bite the inside of my cheeks to keep myself from telling them we should just abandon the whole thing. *Focus, Eevee. You might get to meet your birth parents soon.*

"And Crystal Lake is home to an entire quiver of wyverns," Shannon says cheerfully. "The key is to visit the caves when they are out hunting or when they're sleeping."

Sean lands silent as a bat next to me in the snow. "They're asleep. I estimate we have another hour or so before they begin to rouse."

"They're nocturnal," explains Quince.

"I saw a large cave entrance at the middle of the lake," Sean says, pointing behind him with his thumb. "It's as good a place to start as any, given the riddle said to look in the ice caves in the middle of the lake."

"How exciting," Shannon says. "We've never explored the caverns in the middle. We usually only explore the outer caverns." Lowering his voice, he says to me, "Less likely to run into wyverns away from their main nesting place." His tone is conspiratorial, as if we're sharing a delicious secret.

I'm seriously questioning my birth mother's sanity. Why couldn't she have left the clue for me to find somewhere I'd be less likely to run into a whole group of horse-sized dragon things?

"If we want time to explore, we'd better go now," Sean says, his voice tense.

"Wait," Quince says. He pauses, and his cheeks flush. "You guys won't tell my parents what we're doing before the equinox party, right? I told them I was bringing Eevee to meet you both and get ready for the party with you, but they never would've let me come if they knew I had planned for us all to go to Crystal Lake. They don't know about Eevee either, except that she's fae and raised by humans."

"And get ready we shall!" Shannon exclaims, brushing his hair back from his face and striking a dramatic pose. He drops the pose and beams rapturously. "After facing possible danger in the wyvern caves, of course."

"If they ask, we had a delightful visit at the manor and enjoyed getting to know your friend Eevee. Eventually, we got ready for the party," Sean adds. "Plain and simple."

Quince's shoulders loosen and he smiles. "Thank you."

Sean nods, then takes to the air again. Shannon follows, flying next to Sean. I'm determined to show Quince that I've at least got this part of being fae down, so I crouch and launch myself upward, feeling the rush of freedom like the first time I'd flown. I peek backward at my orange wings, so much like a butterfly's, and smile at Quince, who's hurrying to catch up.

He flies up next to me. "Check it out," he says, pointing below us. "Like an ant farm, isn't it?"

I look down at the lake. It's entirely frozen through, and from our vantage point above it, I see what Quince means. The wyverns have dug through the ice, creating burrows and tunnels criss-crossing the expanse of the lake in a dizzying pattern. Holes dot the surface where the wyverns have made entrances and exits to their icy home. I can't make out any wyverns sleeping below us in the tunnels, the frozen surface is too thick, but knowing they're down there, sleeping, fills me with unease.

"I'd get so lost in there," I joke, trying to cover up my nervousness.

Quince laughs and shakes his head at me. "Let's hope not."

We follow Sean and Shannon to the large opening Sean had spotted in the middle of the lake and circle above it like hawks.

"I think one of us should stay near the entrance to keep watch in case any wyverns happen to be out hunting," Sean says. "It's unlikely, but I don't want to take any chances."

"By 'one of us,' he means himself," Shannon informs me.

A plan in place, we descend slowly, alighting on the surface of the ice at the lip of the tunnel's mouth. I peer down into it, seeing if I can discern any shapes. It slopes downward at a gradual angle, and though it's larger than the other holes I'd seen, I judge it to only be about ten feet across and maybe seven feet tall.

Shannon steps up next to me. We'll have to be as quiet as we can when we head down," he says. "Don't want to wake any of them."

Quince is already stepping down into the tunnel. Slipping a little on the ice, he places a hand on the wall, catching himself.

"Contact me immediately if something goes awry down there," Sean whispers to Shannon.

"What could possibly go wrong? The wyverns are sleeping," Shannon responds with an impish quirk of his lips. He follows after Quince, who is nearly out of sight at the end of the tunnel.

Sean nods to me as I pass by him to step into the wyvern tunnels.

"You really think this is where my birth mother hid the clue?" I ask him, hesitating just inside the tunnel.

"Oh, yes." He's taken a knife out of his pocket and is playing with it, twirling it in his fingers. "Your birth mother, if I were to venture an educated guess…" He pauses to focus on the knife, throwing it in the air, then looking me dead in the eyes. "I'd say your birth mother had a *very* good reason for hiding the clue where few would dare to look." Without breaking eye contact, he reaches out and catches his knife. "Think about it." He glances behind me at Quince and Shannon, who have walked back up the tunnel to see what the hold up could be.

"Sean is right. Your birth mother obviously planned to lay clues for you to find before she wrote the first one on your letter. They're not just random. They're a trail, one she and your birth father had followed to throw off pursuers," says Shannon, folding his arms calmly in front of him, as if discussing riddles at the mouth of a wyvern tunnel was just a normal day for him.

"Pursuers?" I ask.

Sean shoots him a warning look.

"So the clues are like breadcrumbs she left for Eevee," Quince says, scratching at his horn as he thinks. He lets out a low whistle. "But instead of bread-"

"-she used her blood magic." I finish. I turn to Sean, who is glaring at an innocently smiling Shannon. "You're saying my birth mother didn't just hide a clue here randomly, but that she actually hid here with my birth father to keep away from pursuers? Why? What were they hiding from?"

Neither Sean nor Shannon answer.

"If we keep following the clues, we could ask her and find out, rather than speculate," Quince says.

This settles it. I'm still uneasy as I walk into the tunnels and descend into the frozen waters of Crystal Lake, but there's a rod of determination in me keeping my spine straight and my shoulders proud as I walk. If my birth parents could brave the wyvern colony in Crystal Lake, so can I.

The tunnels are eerily quiet, all sounds deadened by the walls of ice around us. It's cold down here, but then again, it's cold everywhere in this part of Elfaeme. I'm reminded of when my family did a cave tour on one of our summer camping trips. We'd signed up for the tour on one of those Midwestern summer days where it's so hot and humid the air feels like hot bath water around you and you no longer know if you're sweating or if the air is just making your skin continually damp. Descending into the cave that day was bliss.

The longer we investigate the tunnels and caves below Crystal Lake, the more I'm unable to get my birth parents off my mind. Who or what could have posed such a threat to them that they decided it would be safer to have me adopted by humans than live with them? It has to be a threat they didn't anticipate would go away anytime soon. Otherwise, why bother with the convoluted escape plan? First to the Mage Stone in Seelie territory, and now below the ice of Crystal Lake in Unseelie lands.

Amongst wyverns.

We pass by a number of openings which lead into caves with groups of the beasts sleeping piled on top of one another.

The lighting down here is diluted and dim after passing through feet of ice, but it's enough to make out their serpentine forms and their scaled wings. In one hollow, there's a large wyvern curled around a collection of eggs.

"Oh, a nest!" Shannon exclaims in a whisper. He tiptoes inside and Quince and I have a silent, gesture-filled battle over who should go in after him.

Looking paler than usual, Quince steps up to Shannon, who is bent over the eggs, and taps him on the shoulder.

"Focus," I hear him mutter.

Shannon straightens and sighs, casting a wistful look at the eggs before returning to the tunnel.

"Of course, it'd be risky," he whispers to me a few minutes later as we turn down another passage.

"What would be risky?"

"Stealing a wyvern egg." He blinks in mild surprise, as if I should've known what he was talking about. "If the mother had woken up, we might not have made it out. They're fiercely protective. Still," he muses, "it would be fun to have a wyvern as a pet. I'd name it Fearghas."

Quince and I steer Shannon away from another clutch of eggs when we notice him dawdling by it. As we descend deeper into the lake, I start to smell something like a mixture of urine and rotten fish. We turn one corner and the smell is so strong it makes my eyes water.

"Looks like we've found where they're storing some food," Shannon says. In front of us are piles of fish in various states of decay.

"I thought the whole lake was frozen?" I ask. "How are they getting the fish?"

"It is frozen," Quince says. He jabs at a fish with his shoe and it flops over.

"Mostly frozen," Shannon corrects him. I follow his gaze into a smaller side tunnel and at first I don't see what he's referring to. There are a couple of wyverns asleep in the space, their legs entwined. But then I see it– what looked at first like a dark patch of ice in the center of the small cave is actually open water.

"They must have wells like this melted out throughout the lake with their fire breath so they have a source of water in their home," Quince says. At his voice, the diamond-tipped tail of one of the wyverns twitches and we quietly back away from that tunnel.

The more tunnels and caves we explore, the less hopeful I become at finding my birth mother's clue. What if Shannon doesn't have as good a sense of direction as he claims and we're stuck wandering these tunnels until a wyvern decides we'd make a good breakfast?

"What if it was destroyed by the wyverns years ago?" I ask Quince after a few more minutes of walking in silence.

"No way," he says, shaking his head. "Your birth mother wouldn't have left the clue somewhere it could be destroyed."

"But then where could it be?" I'm frustrated, I know, and I immediately feel bad for snapping at him.

"I don't know."

"I think I do!" Shannon says from ahead of us, a hint of glee in his voice. He's out of sight, just around a bend in the tunnel.

Quince has already forgiven me for my outburst, apparently. He flashes me an excited smile. "This could be it!" he whispers to me, and we hurry around the corner to find Shannon pointing at a crevice in the ice at the end of the short tunnel.

Hope wells up in my throat, making it hard to breathe.

The crevice is too small for the horse-sized wyverns, but just big enough for someone roughly human-sized to fit through.

There's also a wyvern laying sprawled in our path, fast asleep. If we want to get through the hole in the ice to explore it, we'll first have to step over a wyvern without waking it.

It's not as big as the two we saw by the pool of water, but it's big enough to pose a problem, taking up most of the passageway. Going around it will be impossible, and its body is a good three feet high and at least that wide, so simply stepping over it would be difficult. It curls its lip back in its sleep, and I see it's missing a couple teeth. I shift my eyes away from its teeth–even missing some, the rest are still sharp and worryingly dangerous–and back to the problem at hand: how to get around it. There's maybe only four feet between its body and the ceiling of the tunnel, so flying over it is out.

Or so I think.

"Watch this," Quince says. He dashes toward the wyvern on tiptoe, then, when he's right up next to it, his wings expand and he hop-flies over its body, landing silently on the other side and spinning toward us, a wide smile lighting up his face.

"Come on!" he mouths.

Shannon doesn't need any further coaxing. As silent as Quince had been, he runs to the wyvern, his long, white-blond hair flying out behind him, and sails over it with a flap of his leathery wings. Hovering for a moment, he lands on the other side with ease.

Come on, Eevee, how hard can it be? I ask myself, bouncing on the balls of my feet.

Quince and Shannon are both watching me expectantly. I take a deep breath and flex my wings, reassured when I feel them opening and closing behind me.

I keep my eyes on Quince and Shannon on the other side of the wyvern as I break into a soft run, painfully aware of how loud my footfalls are in comparison to their nearly silent ones.

Ten feet away. Five. Three.

I launch off my right leg and clear the wyvern's body, then flap my wings hard to make sure I don't scrape my feet on its wings.

A moment of elation fills me as I'm mid-air. I've done it!

But then my head hits the top of the tunnel with a loud crack.

I plummet downward, crashing into Quince and knocking us both to the cold ground.

"Quick, into the hole!" Shannon hisses to us. His gaze is on the wyvern. "I just saw it move."

My head is ringing. I feel Quince's arms wrap around me as he sits us both up.

"Are you okay?" he asks, touching my head with gentle fingers.

"Let's get into the protected cave first, then we can worry about Eevee's head," Shannon says, pulling himself through the hole. I watch as his wings turn translucent and they pass through the ice.

Behind us, the wyvern snuffles in its sleep. My antics have definitely roused it from its deep sleep, but it isn't fully awake yet.

"You made your wings non-corp earlier to put on your sweatshirt. Think you can do it again?" Quince asks. His inky eyes, only inches from mine, are filled with worry and fear.

"I think so," I say.

He helps me to my feet and stars twinkle before my vision.

"I'll go after you," he says, shifting so he can keep an eye on me and the wyvern at the same time.

My head is throbbing, but I try to focus on the motion of releasing my shoulders as I pull myself up and through the hole after Shannon.

When a scab peels off and leaves new skin in its place, the new skin is always more sensitive than the old, and even the smallest of scratches across it can be enough to make me clench my teeth with the pain.

That's how it feels when my wings scrape against the jagged edges of the hole.

I try hard not to cry out, but a whimper escapes my lips.

Quince's hand is on my shoulder. "You got this, Eevee," he says in a low voice. "You can do it."

I shake my head to clear it, which is a mistake. The spot where I'd hit it on the top of the tunnel pounds.

I look into the cave and see Shannon walking around, investigating the space.

The cave where my birth parents had stayed while on the run. The place which might have my birth mother's next clue for me.

I take a deep breath and relax my shoulders again.

"You're doing it!" Quince whispers. Before my wings can become corporeal again, I pull myself the rest of the way through the hole and into the room.

Quince clambers up after me. "Wow, I can't believe we found it!"

"Your birth parents were most certainly here, Eevee," Shannon says, striding toward us. His face is tense. "But we should search quickly. I just heard from Sean." He wrings his hands. "He said he's been flying above the lake and noticed some movement in the tunnels. The wyverns are waking."

Chapter 22

Where the Wyverns Are

There's a tense moment where we're all holding our breath and the only thing we hear is the gentle snores of the wyvern outside our hideout–the hideout my birth parents used nearly twenty years ago.

Quince breaks the silence first. He clears his throat, and I can see him shaking. "We'd better hurry, then, if we don't want to be stuck in here until the wyverns fall asleep again," he says in a voice fighting to remain calm. His face, usually alight with mischievous charm, is grim.

Shannon seems unperturbed by this prospect. "It is a cozy little grotto. I would not mind staying a night here." At a look from both of us he adds, "But yes, let's hurry."

We fan out across the icy cave. Even though we don't have much time, I linger by the remains of an old fire pit. Charred wood and ashes are surrounded by a circle of stones.

How long did my birth parents stay here, hiding among the wyverns, before moving onto somewhere else–possibly their final destination?

Shannon is rummaging in the far edge of the cavern by a place where the ice juts out just a bit and is partially hidden from view. "Looks like they had stored food back here," he says, emerging from behind the ice holding up a nub of a frozen carrot.

The small cave yields little else of interest.

"We're going to have to go soon," Quince says to me. He's standing near the hole to the wyvern tunnels. "Our wyvern friend out there is getting restless. He's twitching in his sleep like my old dog used to do when he'd dream of chasing squirrels."

I cast a desperate glance around the cavern, looking for something, anything, in the sparse surroundings that could be the jewel my birth mother refers to in her clue. "At the center of the lake with no waves, look for the jewel in the sunken caves," I whisper to myself.

"Sean says we have forty-five minutes at most to get out before the wyverns are fully awake, based on what he sees from above," Shannon informs us. "I suggest if we don't find it in the next few minutes, we make our retreat."

Pacing like a caged animal, I peer into every crack in the ice in vain. The lighting, already weak when we had started our journey, is dimmer still. Outside, above the ice, the sun must be setting.

Shannon kneels by the fire pit and examines the stones. "Look at this one," he says, indicating one of them.

Quince and I join him by the fire pit. The one Shannon is pointing at looks like a normal rock to me, and it's not until Quince whispers "dormant moonstone" to me that I realize why Shannon pointed it out. A moonstone is a crystal, and sometimes people refer to crystals as...

"Could that be the jewel?" I ask in a hush.

Shannon picks it up and moves to hand it to me. "Possibly. Do you see anything on it?" he asks.

I take it from him. It's cold as the ice it had been resting on, and heavy, even though it's only the size of a baseball, but I don't see any message written on it in blood like on the letter or the Mage Stone.

Quince kneels down next to the fire pit and shifts the other stones. "Shannon, your knife."

"What is it?" I ask as Shannon hands him a knife he's pulled out of seemingly nowhere.

"Hold on."

I wait while Quince uses the knife to chip at the ice. "Almost got it–it's a little iced over in places, but it looks like someone made a hole and stuck this in it, then covered it up with those stones. Here," he says in an excited whisper.

He deposits in my hands a black box about the size of a shoe box. On the top of the lid is a glittering, blood-red jewel.

"Look at that, the clue actually is a jewel," Shannon murmurs, leaning forward to peer at it over my shoulder. He goes quiet, and when I glance at him, he's got a far-off look on his face.

"Open it, Eevee!" Quince urges me.

Looking down at the box, I stall, anxiety and excitement tangling together in my chest. I'm holding proof my birth mother didn't forget about me, proof she thought about me even when hiding from danger.

Inside could be the next (and hopefully final) clue.

I lower my fingers to the latch when Shannon interrupts me, tapping on my shoulder.

"I just told Sean about the box. He's as surprised as I am about the clue leading to an actual jewel as well. He also said we'd better get out now we've got the clue. He's seen more movement in the tunnels."

"I'll open it later, then," I say, tucking the box under my arm.

One by one, we exit the secluded cave. In the time it took Quince to chip the box out of the ice, the wyvern who had been sleeping nearby had apparently awoken.

It's nowhere to be seen.

I'm suddenly hyper aware of my breathing and the way my feet clunk on the icy ground no matter how much I try to mimic Quince and Shannon's silent steps.

"Use your wings," Quince murmurs to me.

We fall behind Shannon, who is leading us at a brisk pace back through the tunnels; no more stops to study sleeping wyvern nests. Quince points to Shannon's wings, which are flapping slowly as he walks.

"He's using his wings to lift himself off the ground a little bit as he walks," Quince explains when I raise my eyebrows at him. Jabbing over his shoulder at his own wings, he adds, "So am I."

I experiment as we race through the passages, flapping my wings ever so slightly. It feels kind of how I imagine it would be like to walk on the moon. Each time I take a step and flap my wings simultaneously, I launch forward in the air. I'm definitely bouncier than Quince or Shannon, who look more like human-shaped hovercrafts ahead of me. At the very least, my steps are quieter now.

The box weighs in my hands as we flee, and I wonder what's in it. Ahead of me, Shannon stops at a fork in the tunnel, looking to the left and the right.

As he and Quince argue under their breath about which direction leads us back the way we came, I run my index finger along the jewel on the box.

"We turned left here, which means we turn right to go back," Quince hisses.

"I'm fairly certain we need to go left," Shannon argues.

My fingertip slides off the jewel and along the top edge of the box, then down to the latch. It's simple, made of the same black wood as the box, and it's unlocked.

"We'll go your way," Shannon says to Quince. "But we need to speed it up. Sean says he's run into some trouble at the entrance."

I flip the wooden latch and crack open the lid. Just one little peek at what's inside won't hurt.

A melancholy melody echoes throughout the tunnel. I snap the lid shut, but the damage is done.

Quince and Shannon are looking back at me with shock on their faces.

"I'm sorry," I whisper. "I-"

Shannon holds a finger up to his lips, his icy blue eyes wild.

Somewhere in the tunnels, we hear a snuffle and some low grunts.

We run down the passages, no longer careful of the noise we're making. I grip the box to my chest and mentally berate myself for my impatience. Why couldn't I have waited to see what was inside when we were safely back at Sean and Shannon's ice mansion?

I round the corner after Quince and smash into him. We both stumble, and the box falls from my hands. It drops to the ground and the lid flips open. The melancholy music fills the tunnel again and a doll tumbles out, rolling a couple times before coming to a stop. My hands fly to my mouth. The doll isn't just any baby doll; it's the same one that was next to me in the baby picture my birth parents had left for me in my adoption packet. It's even wearing the same orange dress with little blue flowers.

Lowering my hands, I rush to the doll and the box, which is still playing its sad melody. "Crap, crap, crap," I say as Quince helps me put the doll back in the box and close the lid. "Why'd you stop?" I ask him.

He points ahead of us, where the wyvern we had woken grunts and paws at the icy ground with one of its two legs. It's mouth is open, revealing the gaps in its teeth.

My own legs turn to water beneath me and my hands go numb. I drop the box and Quince catches it before it hits the ground.

At Quince's movement, the wyvern lets out a hiss and its diamond-tipped tail swishes angrily, thumping against the sides of the tunnel.

"Maybe I'd better hold this for now," Quince says in a low voice to me, tucking the box close to his chest.

I don't argue; I've dropped it enough in the last couple minutes, and I'd like to get out of these icy caves alive if I can help it.

Shannon stands in front of the wyvern, his body rigid, his arms held out stiffly on either side of him. He mutters words in a language I don't recognize under his breath.

"What's he doing?" I whisper.

One of Shannon's arms points toward the wyvern, and a white light emanates from him until it surrounds him and the wyvern. When the light fades, Shannon steps back and slumps against the side of the passage.

"Freezing time," he says to me, his voice exhausted. For the first time since I met him, he sounds as old as he really is. "Or, more specifically, freezing the wyvern's perception of time momentarily. We have a minute to get out of here. When the minute is up, it will think a second has passed. I'd like to be out of the tunnels by then, wouldn't you?"

He doesn't wait for us to answer, just pushes himself upright and breaks into a stumbling run.

As we near the main entrance where we'd come into the tunnels, I hear the scraping sounds of claws raking against ice.

"Don't look behind us," Quince whispers after he looks over his shoulder.

I can't help it. I peer over my shoulder, too, and my heart rate, already high from running, spikes.

A whole group of wyverns is hot on our trail. I can see them in the distance, at the end of the tunnel, but they'll catch up to us soon enough.

We exit the main tunnel and resurface on top of Crystal Lake.

"Over here!" Ahead, we see Sean, knife in hand, holding three wyverns at bay. His knife is glowing, and I see one of the wyverns has an iced over cut on its shoulder.

The wyverns snap at him and he brandishes the knife at them as they circle around him.

"When I say the word, start flying to the moonstone," Sean says. "Wyverns are slow to get flying after waking."

The way they slither their serpentine bodies around Sean, weaving around each other in a dizzying pattern, I think they look speedy enough.

Sean's free hand glows white, and a ball of ice appears in it. He tosses it in the air and the three wyverns all stop and watch its ascent.

"Now!" he shouts.

We all spring into the air.

I don't know if I'll be able to keep up with the three of them, but I push all doubt from my mind and

211

focus on Quince's back, watching his black feathers flutter madly as he beats his wings against the bone-chilling wind.

Shannon, Quince, and I make it back to the shore and land by the moonstone. I look to the sky and see Sean, pursued by what looks to be the whole quiver of wyverns.

"Eevee, this moonstone isn't big enough to allow us all to use it at once!" Quince yells, shaking me and drawing my attention from Sean, who looks as if he's now trying to draw the wyverns away from the moonstone. When I look at him, he says, "We have to go."

"But Sean-"

"Will be fine," Shannon says. He sounds worried, though, and his attention is already back on his brother. "I'll stay here and help him. He and I will use the moonstone together as soon as we can. Go!"

Quince drags me to the moonstone.

The last thing I see is Sean descending on the beach with the cloud of hissing wyverns behind him, and Shannon, facing the horde. Both of their hands glow white.

Chapter 23

Party Preparations

I'm still gasping for breath as we let ourselves into Sean and Shannon's ice mansion. Traveling by moonstone is definitely not my preferred mode of transportation in the fae realm.

We no sooner settle down in the sitting room when the owners of the mansion slip in through the door.

"You're bleeding!" I blurt out.

Sean holds a hand up to his temple. His fingers are red when he pulls them away.

"Just a scratch," he says with seeming indifference.

"I'll get the salve." Quince jogs out of the room.

"We should add it to our list for the next time we're at the market," Shannon says. His right hand is pressed against his left side just below his ribcage, and he wheezes a little as he speaks.

"Must be some salve," I comment. The sight of the two of them hurt sends waves of guilt through me. They wouldn't be hurt if it weren't for me wanting to track down my birth mother's clue.

"Made by the best healers," Shannon says, then grimaces and rests on the arm of one of the couches. "It costs a pretty penny, though."

Sean returns and they tend to their wounds, filling us in on what happened after we'd used the moonstone.

"And let me tell you, it is no easy feat to travel by moonstone while simultaneously fighting off a quiver of cranky wyverns who are upset you woke them up!" Shannon finishes. He lowers his cream-colored tunic shirt over the wound in his side, which is covered in a layer of new, pink skin beneath a shiny layer of the healing salve.

"It's not something I'd like to repeat anytime soon," Sean says. "Maybe ten or twenty years from now, when I'm feeling restless."

Under Shannon's watchful eye, Quince adds another log to the fire. After spending the last couple hours in these wintry lands (and in an icy lake), the fire's warmth is welcome.

Sean lounges on the couch nearest the fire and holds his hands toward it, warming them.

"Was it worth it at least?" he asks me.

I'm not sure if I'm imagining the menacing undercurrent of "it better have been worth it." Sean's smile is innocent enough, but when he glances at me with those icy blue eyes, they're calculating.

I look down at the box in my hands. I had taken it back from Quince as soon as we were in Sean and Shannon's backyard and have been holding it ever since, running my fingers along the jewel and the smooth wood. I haven't opened it again, though, not even to examine the doll again. The music it plays when it's open is still winding its haunting melody through my head, and I'm not sure I'm ready to hear it echoed in reality.

"I think so," I answer. "I mean, I don't see anything on the jewel, but I think the clue is in this box, I just haven't had time to look at what's inside yet. You guys got back pretty much right after us, and there was a lot of blood distracting me. You know. Real blood this time."

Sean stands and makes his way toward me, his hands outstretched toward the box as if to take it, but Shannon stops him with a hand on his arm.

"The clue has waited eighteen years for Eevee to find it–I think it can wait another couple hours." Shannon sweeps his hair back with a flourish. "Right now, we must prepare for the Equinox celebration!"

Disappointment must darken my face, because Quince leans in and whispers, "We can always open it later tonight together. I don't think you want to feel rushed looking through it, right?"

I nod. A small part of me is relieved I don't have to listen to that music again for another couple hours.

"Fine." Sean's smile is flinty. "I suppose since we have less than an hour to prepare for the party, it makes sense to wait."

Shannon drags me and Quince up a winding stone staircase and into a room dedicated entirely to clothes.

Eyes sparkling, Quince says, "I've always thought Ms. Wilson would be green with envy if she could see all these outfits my cousins have acquired over the years. Think of all the shows she could costume with just a quarter of this room!"

"I didn't know the equinox celebration was a costume party," I say, running my fingers over the corner of a crushed velvet jacket.

"It isn't," Sean says from behind a rack of clothes. He emerges with an indigo mask which covers the right half of his face. The sapphires dotting its surface glint as he moves and grins.

"But Sean and I are of the opinion it is better to be overdressed than underdressed," Shannon says. He's changed into a flowing white robe made of satin; intricate designs are embroidered on the cuffs and hem.

Quince and I peruse the shelves with the guidance and suggestions of Sean and Shannon. My cheeks flush when Quince takes off his own plain t-shirt in the middle of the room.

I'm not sure if Amelia's math class crush with the shoulders has anything on Quince Florentz. He typically wears looser t-shirts with jeans, and the one play I saw him in he was clothed in either loose peasant blouses or bulky jackets.

But with no fabric in the way, there's nothing to hide the lean muscles or the way they shift with him as he pulls a ruffled red cotton blouse over his head and relaxes his wings, turning them non-corp.

I quickly bury my head in the rack of clothes I've been flicking through so Quince can't see how my face now bears a striking resemblance to a tomato.

Already dressed, Sean and Shannon turn their attention to me, and I'm thrown a variety of masks and outfits to try on.

Quince holds up a decadent, floor-length silk ballgown. It's beautiful, starting as a light periwinkle on the bodice and slowly deepening to a midnight blue at the bottom. The top of the bodice is decorated with white diamonds, and the train is covered in opalescent jewels. I panic and shake my head at the sight of it, thinking of how the silk would cling to me.

"Absolutely not," I retort.

Eventually I settle on a simple cotton dress in a pale yellow. A pattern of vines and leaves play across the bottom, which is edged in lace. Sean helps me tie on a mask he's found; its green color almost perfectly matches the embroidery on the dress. Unlike his mask, which leaves part of his face uncovered, my mask hides my whole face.

I emerge from the room and head downstairs with Sean to join Shannon and Quince, who are waiting in the sitting room and eating from a platter of food Shannon must have put together while waiting for me to finish picking out an outfit. Quince looks like a masked pirate with his frilly red blouse and knee-high boots; oddly enough, the look works for him with his dark hair and wings.

When the platter has been emptied of its fruit, cheese, and crackers, we trek out to the moonstone, all decked out in our party attire. I've stuffed my regular clothes in my backpack on top of the black music box and my schoolwork. At this point, I've resigned myself to the fact I'm not getting any math done tonight.

The snow crunches beneath our feet, and I try not to shiver. Quince has assured me that the equinox party, which is always held at a clearing in the In Between, will be warmer than it is here in the Unseelie lands.

I'm struck, as we pass below the whispering pines, by how much has happened in the last few hours. Honestly, it feels like years have passed since Quince and I left school together and traveled to Elfaeme to track down my birth mother's clue, not hours.

"So, what's the equinox celebration like?" I ask as we near the moonstone.

"Eevee." Shannon turns and places his hands on my shoulders. His voice is grave, but his eyes are dancing with merriment. "This is your first equinox party. It must be experienced!"

He twirls to join Sean at the moonstone. Sean nods to me. "Shannon is right. See you there." He touches the stone and disappears, quickly followed by Shannon, leaving me and Quince alone in the quiet, dusky forest.

Chapter 24

The Equinox Celebration

"My parents can't wait to meet you," Quince says, holding a hand out to me.

I look up at him, studying what I can see of his face, which is his eyes and the lower half, for any clues that he might be harboring feelings for me, but I only see anticipation.

If I've misjudged him, if this is a date and he isn't just helping me because it's exciting to know another fae at his school, especially one with a mystery tied to her, well...it's certainly been a unique date. I can't say I've ever fought ice trolls or escaped from wyverns on any of my past dates.

Also, if this is a date, things just got a lot more complicated between me and Quince "the-masked-pirate" Florentz.

I may be fae, but I've been raised by Todd and Penny Acker who believe in the importance of being polite, and though I'm more nervous than when I had punched the ice troll, I smile and say, "I'm looking forward to meeting them, too," and take his hand.

For the third time today I fight through the uncomfortable after-effects of moonstone travel, but this time my suffering is on display for the plethora of fae folk already at the celebration.

El Holly

Luckily, my reaction to moonstone travel goes largely unnoticed except for Quince, who squeezes my hand and smiles sympathetically.

"I swear you get used to it after a while," he says.

While I gasp and try to catch my breath, I let go of his hand and adjust my backpack, turning to take it all in.

Immediately, I'm struck by a sense of belonging, of familiarity. There are booths set up haphazardly around the clearing, and wooden stages where some fae are performing for cheering crowds. Here and there are tables where elderly fae rest, young children running in circles around them.

It reminds me of an outdoor festival, or of the state fair in Minnesota. Music, laughter, and excitement all buzz through the air.

The clearing we're in is large; the leaves carpeting the ground a resplendent array of fall colors, a sure sign we're in the In Between somewhere. I don't see any landmarks I recognize around me, though. How big is Elfaeme? I make a mental note to ask Quince for a map.

It's certainly more populated than the secluded corner of the forest where I met Folsom on my first trip to the fae realm. Will he make an appearance at the celebration? I reach up and fidget with my mask, grateful for its full coverage of my face. Something about my encounter with Folsom still feels off to me, and after finding out a little of his backstory from Quince, I'm even more certain he had ill intentions.

A group of small creatures, no more than knee high, and the color of mud, appear at a moonstone next to us.

"Brownies," Quince whispers to me. "A lot of fae races come together tonight to celebrate the changing of the seasons."

He points to a raucous group, their laughter like the braying of horses. "Satyrs!" I answer before he can say anything. Their hooved lower halves are a giveaway.

"Of course," Quince explains as we weave through the crowd, "none of the fae folk appear as their true selves in the human realm. Some fae, fairy folk like you and me, look like humans. But others-" he points to a horned, devilish-looking creature- "like that goblin? They appear as animals."

My future career as a vet tech may have become more interesting.

A fae, her long hair flowing behind her like an ethereal waterfall, appears out of nowhere in front of us. She twirls and capers away across the field barefoot, singing of the leaves.

"Are we meeting any of your friends tonight?" I'm excited at the prospect of meeting other fae, at getting to know the side of Quince he can't show at Duluth High.

"Maybe."

"Maybe?"

He lowers his voice and brings his face closer to mine. Behind his mask, his eyes are twinkling. "I may have told them I was on a date tonight."

I punch him lightly in the arm. "Shut up, no you didn't."

He pulls back, laughs. "Some of my friends will definitely be here, which is good, because Sean and Shannon have already abandoned us." He points to two white-blonde heads in the crowd near one of the stages where a fae is playing raucous music on a guitar.

221

Many of the fae in the clearing are garbed in fancy attire, though some, I see, wear little to nothing. I avert my eyes, my cheeks burning. I guess being raised in the Midwest, where for many months of the year our bodies are covered in layers upon layers of clothing, has not entirely prepared me for the fae who prefer to lounge about on top of wooden tables in nothing but their own skins. Will Quince's friends be similarly clad?

Even though the dress I'm wearing is fancier than a majority of the clothes in my closet back home, I feel underdressed in comparison to most of those around me, and I understand now why Sean and Shannon had been pushing me toward the satins and silks. Pair that with the backpack I have slung over one shoulder, and I feel the sense of familiarity I'd felt before shrinking, replaced with a sense of being more like an outsider, a tourist.

Quince waves to a pair of fae in the crowd, who turn and make their way toward us. They look about our age, but considering Sean and Shannon are hundreds of years old, I've given up guessing fae ages at the moment. They are also just as clothed as we are, which I have to admit, is a bit of a relief to see.

"Carl, Mindy, this is the fae girl I was telling you about, the one who was raised by humans and only just figured out she was fae!"

Carl sticks out a hand and I shake it. "Pleased ter meet yeh," he says, his high-pitched voice in direct contrast to his bulky shoulders and horns.

"You're a goblin!" I say.

"Am not!" he exclaims indignantly, a hand to his chest.

"Oh, stop being so dramatic," Mindy says. She brushes a strand of her hair, which is the green of a spring leaf, out of her eyes. "The girl just learned she's fae, she can't be expected to keep all the races straight." She blows a big, pink bubble and pops it, eyeing me. "Poor thing."

"I suppose," Carl says.

"He's a gnome," Quince explains. "Quite similar in appearance to goblins, like the one I'd pointed out earlier, but-"

"But gnomes are earthier." Carl grins, and points to his horns. "Made of rock. No goblin has rock-horns."

We walk around with Carl and Mindy, who are just as excited as Quince is to show me around.

"Your ears will grow in, you know," Mindy says next to me.

"What?"

She points to her ears, which are pointed at the tip. "All fae have pointed ears once they're of age, but they get more pointed with time."

I reach up to my own ears and feel the tips of them, which do have a small point I hadn't noticed before.

"You must be over eighteen then?"

She nods. "Just turned nineteen. Me'n'Carl have grown up with Quince. Our families tend to stick together, meeting at places in the In Between."

"Oh, are you…?"

"Little bit of both, yeah." She looks both proud and defiant, as if willing me to say anything against being a child of both the Seelie and Unseelie Courts.

"I'm not," Carl says before I can ask. "My family is one of the many fae who ain't affiliated with either Court. We're alright with everyone, so long as no one's causin' any trouble."

"Why're you two wearing masks, anyway?" Mindy asks, raising one of her willowy arms and touching my mask. "Fashion statement?"

Behind my mask, I frown, then turn to Quince, who is watching a fae juggle balls of fire. I tug on his frilly sleeve. When I have his attention, I whisper, "Hardly anyone else is wearing a mask. Did you notice that?"

Quince cranes his neck, looking around. "You're right. I wondered why Sean and Shannon had insisted it was a masquerade. In all my years of coming to the equinox celebration, I've never heard of it having a theme."

"Not a fashion statement, then?" asks Mindy.

"Believe me, I would've chosen something different if it were for fashion," Quince answers. He reaches up and removes his mask, stuffing it in his backpack and making a silly expression at me once his face is free.

I wrinkle my nose at him, not that he can see it, and reach up to remove my mask, too, but a hand stops me.

"Leave it," Sean-or-Shannon whispers in my ear, their breath cold like a winter breeze. I turn and see the indigo mask covering half his face–Sean. "It makes you more mysterious," he says.

"But-"

"I agree with Sean. You should leave it," Shannon says when I don't lower my hands. He spins to the music on his way toward us, deftly maneuvering past a rabbit-like fae couple. "Everyone loves a good mystery, Eevee."

Quince shrugs when I look to him for advice. "It does make you more mysterious, I guess," he says.

"I don't know. It's getting kind of warm."

Sean's hands tighten on my shoulders, and his voice is so quiet I can barely hear it. "Believe me. It is in your best interest to keep that mask on tonight. Now laugh like I just told you a joke."

A shiver runs through me. What could he mean? Why would it be in my best interest? What does he know that I don't? I lower my hands and let out a strained giggle. "Well, as Shakespeare says in *As You Like It*, 'one man in his time plays many parts.' Perhaps my part tonight will be the mysterious maiden."

Sean removes his hands from my shoulders, leaving behind a feeling of ice where they had touched me.

"I do love a good mystery," Quince murmurs, and the look in his eyes speaks of secrets told in the dark; I find I can't look away. But then the moment is broken and he laughs and gestures toward Sean and Shannon's receding figures. "Guess it runs in the family."

We wander away from the fireball jugglers and head toward the outer edge of the large clearing in search of Quince's parents. I had wanted to ask Carl and Mindy more questions about what Quince was like when he was younger and what it was like growing up in Elfaeme, but Carl had to help his family with their gadgets exhibit and we lost Mindy somewhere near the weightlifting competition.

The edges of the clearing where Quince and I are wandering now are less congested than the middle, and some of the noises from the forest can be heard over the music and hum of the crowd.

Ahead of us, a goblin (or gnome, I still can't quite tell them apart) with large, curved horns and a snoutlike nose passes out pamphlets. He shoves one in my hands, and I'm overcome with the smell of grease and sweat pouring off of him. "Join the cause, fight for what the fae deserve," he growls in a voice as greasy as his smell.

"What? What fight?" I ask, but Quince steers me away from the goblin-or-gnome, who passes out more pamphlets to some fae behind us.

I look down at the pamphlet in my hand.

FREEDOM
Fae Reclaiming the Earth, End Dominion Of Men

Join the just and righteous fight against the usurpers,
the vile humans!
Together, we can reclaim the earth and end mankind's
destruction of its beauty.

Power in numbers!

Fight for FREEDOM!

For information on the next meeting, write "tell me more"
on this paper within 24 hours of receiving it.

"Freedom?"

Quince makes a disgusted sound and takes the pamphlet from me. "Fae who want to kill humans."

"You mean–all of them?"

He crushes the pamphlet. "Yes. Of course, few of the members actually live in the human realm. They let their warped perceptions of humans fuel their hatred."

"I mean, I get that humans aren't perfect, but eliminating all of us?" I catch myself when Quince quirks an eyebrow. "I mean, all of them? That seems a bit extreme."

"It's because those who are in FREEDOM think all humans hate nature and litter all the time and spend their free time killing animals and plotting how to turn the whole world into a metropolis," Quince says. He smooths out the pamphlet and starts tearing it into pieces.

Paper falls to the ground like confetti, and Quince catches my "you-hypocrite-you're-littering-right-now" look. "It's a type of fae paper, used for secret messages. It'll turn into dirt by tomorrow night."

"Do a lot of fae want to kill us–I mean, kill humans?" I whisper. The fae folk around me, so merry and full of life, now have a menacing edge to their smiles and a brash tone to their laughter. How stupid I was to have brought Cam and Maggie here. We're lucky that tree-woman didn't kill us all on sight. Now Quince's reaction in Maggie's kitchen makes sense to me.

"Most of the fae think killing all humans is not feasible or necessary," he says, his voice lowered to match mine. "There's even a group of mostly Seelie fae who live in the human realm full time and try to help the humans take care of the earth. They're part of an organization run by the Seelie King Oakspirit and Queen Hibiscus." He opens his hands and lets the rest of the pamphlet pieces fall to the ground. "I wish I could say all the fae followed that philosophy."

"The organization has mostly Seelie fae in it? What about the fae who aren't part of either Court? Or the Unseelie?"

His face darkens. "King Nightglade, the Unseelie King, has no part in the organization, though the Seelie King and Queen have asked him to join many times. His approach is the opposite of theirs. Not only does he refuse to help their efforts, he's been known to allow the Unseelie fae in his Court to hurt and even kill humans."

"That's awful!"

"Yes. As long as they can justify their actions by saying they saw the human harming the earth, King Nightglade turns a blind eye to what the members of his Court do."

"And nothing is solved." My insides seethe with the pointlessness of those deaths.

"No, nothing changes. And the changes wrought by the Seelie-led organization are too slow for most fae. They don't think humans will improve their ways anytime soon. Thus, the appeal of FREEDOM."

"There has to be another way to help the earth so the fae are happy without killing all the humans on it."

Our conversation is cut off by a middle-aged fae couple waving us over to the picnic table they've commandeered. No question who they are–the man looks exactly like Quince, if Quince were middle-aged with a mustache and a gut. He has the same black wings and horns and dark, glittering eyes.

His mom is hard not to love. She reminds me of a mouse with wings–brown hair, warm brown eyes, and an affinity for cheese.

The long, thin tail protruding out behind her only helps cement the image in my mind.

She hands me a cube of herbed cheese.

"Quince has told me about your unique circumstances," she says cautiously, nibbling on her cheese. "Jerry and I are quite as stumped as you are, of course. And to be raised by humans, not even knowing you were fae-"

"My parents did alright," I say, feeling defensive of Todd and Penny Acker, who are still in the dark about my true self and think I'm studying at Quince's house tonight.

"Oh, of course, that's not what I meant, I just, oh dear."

"Are you putting your foot where your mouth is again, Myska?" Jerry asks, smiling at her with warm affection.

"Yes, as usual!"

"It's really okay, I know what you meant," I say, wanting to smooth out the worry lines crisscrossing her forehead.

She pats me on the arm and turns to Quince. "You have half an hour, Quincent, and then we need to head home. It's a school night."

"Quincent," I whisper when Quince catches my eye.

He flushes and grumbles at her use of his full name. My smile remains hidden in the shadows of my mask.

"Want to walk around a bit more before we go?" he asks me.

We promise his parents we'll meet them back at the picnic bench in thirty minutes or less, and Quince leads me on another loop of the packed clearing, which is now overflowing with fae of all kinds.

Lights twinkle merrily in the trees surrounding the clearing as we walk. Quince heads for a boulder near a stage where a trio of fae are throwing knives and freezing them in blocks of ice conjured out of midair. I can see the white-blond hair of either Sean or Shannon in the crowd.

When I point Sean-or-Shannon out to Quince, he says it's probably one of them, "but they usually hang with their own crowd."

He sits down on the boulder and I lower myself next to him, adjusting my mask and setting my backpack on the dewy grass. We're both silent, watching the show, but it feels comfortable, this silence.

Now that I'm not moving, the cold of the night settles on my skin, easily sneaking through the light cotton of my dress, and my arms erupt in goosebumps.

Deciding to go for comfort over fashion, I tug my sweatshirt out of my backpack and pull it on, relaxing my shoulders as Quince showed me so I can pull it down while my wings are non-corp.

"You're getting the hang of that," Quince observes. Something in the proud, happy smile he flashes me awakens butterflies in my stomach I hadn't known had been there until now.

"Thanks."

"Today's been fun."

"Which part, getting attacked by an ice troll or escaping from wyvern tunnels with your cousins?"

"Both." He's looking up at the stars, and the same ridiculous desire I'd had to run my fingers over his jawline when I'd seen him in the principal's office comes over me again. I shove my hands in the front pocket of my sweatshirt. I don't know what's going on with me and

Damian, but until I figure that out, I'd better not give in, no matter how much I may want to.

"Seriously, though," he adds, leaning back onto his elbows and flexing his wings, "Even with all of that, I can't think of the last time I had such a fun day."

"It was eventful," I hedge, the butterflies now a fluttering mass.

His foot taps the ground. "You know, we could spend more time together in the human realm, too. Like at the Homecoming Dance? It'd be less dangerous than what we've been doing in Elfaeme today, most likely."

I stop breathing and my whole body freezes, except for the stupid butterflies in my stomach.

Glancing at my still figure, he adds, "No, yeah, you're right, the Homecoming Dance would totally be more dangerous than what we've faced today." When I still don't answer, because breathing has become an issue, he says hesitantly, "Want to go anyway?"

Nervous hot energy thaws me out enough to force out a hoarse, "Sorry, probably not. It's not you, it's just– it's complicated."

I can't stay and watch his face break into a million pieces so I pick up my backpack and run into the woods.

"Eevee, wait!"

I look over my shoulder. He's quick.

But I'm fae, too.

I stop moving and close my eyes.

"Eevee!"

When I open them again, I see the fire pit in my backyard. Slinky's sitting on our back porch watching for mice, his eyes wide and his tail twitching.

My phone starts dinging from the front pocket of my backpack where I've stashed it, filling up with all the notifications I've missed while in Elfaeme. I take my mask off and head to my house, ignoring my phone for now.

Chapter 25

The Final Clue

I'm relieved and saddened when Quince doesn't follow me, but I don't have much time to figure out what that means because the kitchen light is on and I can hear my mom moving around in there.

"Eevee, is that you?" she asks in a whisper, and I wince, closing the back door behind me with a click.

She peeks her head through the kitchen and into the living room, where I'm kicking off my shoes onto the rug by the door, my legs aching after all the running from wyverns and walking around at the Equinox celebration.

"I don't remember you leaving for school wearing that dress," she says with a you-better-explain-yourself tone humming beneath her pleasant words.

I look down at the dress, admiring again the way the vines and leaves intertwine along the bottom hem, right above the lace. I'm not much of a dress person, but this one is comfortable, and not altogether horrible.

"That's because I didn't," I say truthfully.

Fae rule number one–fae can't lie–is the only rule I really know. I should ask Quince–

My heart constricts. No, I guess I can't go ask Quince about the other fae rules, not after the way I ran off at the end of our maybe-date.

Mom's still waiting for an answer, her lips pursed and her arms crossed.

"You know how Quince is into theater?"

"I know you told me you were going to be studying with him tonight."

Technically true. I just didn't tell her the thing we'd be studying was my birth mom's clues.

"We did study!" Just not as much as I'd hoped. The box in my backpack begs to be opened. *Soon*, I think.

"And then you played dress up?"

She looks skeptical. I can't blame her. Two high school seniors playing dress up? It's ludicrous.

"Come on, mom," I say, lacing my voice with copious amounts of sarcasm. "No. There were just these racks of clothes Quince showed me and I borrowed this because I liked it."

I can tell mom knows I'm leaving out details, but her head is also tilting toward the kitchen. The smell of baking bread wafts toward us.

"I better get outta this dress and head to bed. School night," I say.

Mom's torn, but then the kitchen timer beeps. I give her a quick hug and head up to my room.

Somehow I need to find a way to tell her and dad, and even my sisters and brothers, about me being fae. "We're the Ackers," dad always says. "We stick together through it all." Maybe my worries about getting shipped off in a straitjacket are unfounded. I'm just not sure I'm ready to test that theory yet.

I get to my room and deposit the backpack on the ground, then slump against the wall, leaning against a poster Cam drew for me of the scene with Titania and Bottom with his donkey ears from *A Midsummer Night's Dream*. My whole body feels twice as heavy as normal as I peel off the dress and get into my pajamas–fuzzy pants with hearts and a large t-shirt–much better for lounging in than the dress had been.

Though it's late, I can't wait a second longer. I unzip my backpack and grab the box. It's cool in my hands, as though made out of the ice where it had rested for the last eighteen years.

I set it down in front of me on the bed and sit cross-legged on my pillows, excitement making my heart skip in an erratic rhythm. In my peripheral vision, I see a puddle of yellow on the floor where I'd left the dress. Seeing it all balled up on the ground doesn't feel right, though, so I tear myself away from the box and my comfy bed and grab a hanger out of my closet.

Once it's properly hung up next to the three other dresses in my closet, I sit back down on my bed, staring at the box.

This is it. I reach for the latch, then stop. I'll have to be quick, if I don't want to wake anyone with the music. Walking through the house isn't usually enough to wake my family, I can move quietly when I want, but if they were to hear strange music coming from my room, they might wake. And ask questions. Like where I had gotten the box, and why.

Satisfaction. But not mine. I look up to my door, which I had left cracked open. It's wider than it had been a moment before. On my rug, Slinky spits out a mouse, which squeaks feebly and scrabbles a few inches toward the door before Slinky bats it with his paws. When the mouse has been pinned, he blinks up at me, his eyes orblike, as if to judge how proud I am of him.

"Slinky, no!" I hiss. He never eats them, just plays with them mercilessly.

Slinky's confusion floods the back of my mind when I pick up the mouse and bring it down to the porch. It runs away into the trees and Slinky meows.

"It's just cruel, to play with them like that," I scold him.

I swear he shrugs his little kitty shoulders at me. Self-important indifference rolls off him.

"Just don't catch anymore tonight," I tell him.

"Mouse?" mom asks as I come back in.

I nod.

"Oh, Slink," she says with a sigh.

"Yeah, he's a dork."

Mom laughs. "We all are. It's on the Acker family crest, I think."

After washing my hands under scalding hot water, careful not to rub my bruised knuckles too hard, I close my door all the way and flop onto my bed.

Deep breath in. *This could be it.* As quick as I'm able, I open the latch, flip the lid, and grab the doll out of the box.

The eerie music only plays a total of three haunting notes before I'm able to close the lid, but I wait, holding my breath, clutching the doll to my chest.

I don't hear anything except the dishwasher running in the kitchen downstairs. Since I hadn't woken anyone with my mouse rescue operation, I hadn't thought it likely a few musical notes would wake them either, but as dad always says, it's better to be safe than sorry.

Slowly, I lower my arms until the doll rests on the bed in front of my crossed legs.

Its orange dress with the blue flowers looks handmade, now that I have a closer look at it. I wonder who made it? The doll itself isn't anything unique; it has painted on brown hair and blue eyes which close when it lays down.

If this is the clue, I don't get it.

I pick it up and turn it over, feeling the soft, stuffing-filled body. Squeezing it experimentally leads to disappointment. I don't feel anything hard hidden inside.

Its plastic feet are bare, so there are no shoes to hide anything in either.

What if this is it? What if my search ends here, with a baby doll and a jeweled music box?

Despondency burns in my chest and pricks at my eyes. I feel like I'm so close to finding answers to questions I've wondered about my whole life. Can I go on with my life from here not ever knowing those answers?

I'm not sure. Before getting the packet with my adoption information, I would have said "yes" without hesitation.

But to have found some of the answers, and then have my search cut short?

It feels coldly unfair.

I realize, as I stare at the doll in my hands, I'm jealous of Quince. He's known his whole life that he's fae. His parents hadn't thought it necessary to hide him from the truth, had been willing to make adjustments in their lives and leave the Courts, to be a family.

They hadn't abandoned him.

As soon as I think that, the anger, resentment, and rejection I've felt on and off my whole life rises to the surface like a monster coming up to drag me down to the depths with it.

When I was younger, about eight or nine, I had come home from school crying because some kid in my class asked me if there was something wrong with me, if that was why my birth parents had given me up for adoption.

So I had asked my mom and dad. We hadn't discussed it before, that I could remember.

"Evelyn, you were not given up for adoption," dad said. "Your birth parents made the choice to have you adopted. Saying that you were given up implies you weren't wanted. That is far from the truth."

"But how can you know?" I remember asking. My face had been shiny with tears and snot.

They couldn't answer why my birth parents had decided to have me adopted, of course. But I remember their arms enveloping me.

"All that matters is you're here, now. And we are so proud to have you as a daughter." Mom's voice had been trembling, but in their arms, I felt loved and safe.

I hadn't asked them again.

But I want to ask my birth parents, if I can. I want to look them in the eyes and ask them why. Why did they decide to have me adopted? Why did they keep my identity from me? Why did they choose to have me raised by humans? Then I want to look at my birth mother and ask her why she left me these clues, when the letter she wrote with my birth father says explicitly I should not try to find them.

The doll tips forward listlessly in my hands, and that's when I see it, at the crack in the neck where the head has been attached to the body. A corner of folded up paper.

There's no way that can be part of the doll. I try and pinch at it with my fingernails, but they are too short and stubby to get any kind of grip, and end up pushing the paper up into the neck further.

I sneak to the bathroom, my heart thudding in my ears, and grab a tweezers. Careful not to push the paper where I can't get it, I bend the doll's neck forward and stick the tweezers into the gap.

Some cautious tugging and seesawing pays off. After a few minutes, I've got enough of the paper free to grab it with my fingers and draw it out the rest of the way.

It's folded into a small square. As I unfold it, I see on one side is a map. I turn it over to the other side.

Just like the previous clues, this one is two lines long, though it's not a perfect rhyming couplet like at the end of Shakespeare's sonnets; its lines form a near rhyme. I mentally shove my random Shakespearean factoids to the back of my mind and focus on the clue written in blood, the clue only I can read.

> *In the circle of moonstones in the wood*
> *One will bring you to me with your blood.*

I flip back over to the map, and my breath catches in my throat. On the map, a few places are labeled. Like Dragonfly Falls, and Satyr Grove.

I know where the circle of moonstones is that the clue is referencing. It's where I had met Folsom the first time I had traveled to the fae realm.

Chapter 26

Run-ins

"So that's it? You've found the last clue?" Maggie squeals.

"Shh! Yes!" I look around quickly, but none of the Duluth High students crowding the halls this Friday morning pay any attention to the three of us.

The coffee in my hands is lukewarm at this point, but I drink it anyway. No amount of makeup can hide the dark circles under my eyes this morning. After finding the map and clue, sleep had been hard to find, and I think I dozed off around two in the morning.

"And you said you're planning to go back there by yourself soon?" Cam can't hide the worry from their voice. They tuck their fading purple hair behind their ear. "I don't know how I feel about that, Eevee. I didn't like that place."

Cam has been less chilly to me today, probably because I haven't mentioned Damian at all this morning. On the ride to school in their rusty family van, I updated them on everything from last night, and we've just finished catching up Maggie.

"It's Eevee's birth parents, though, Cam," Maggie says. She hands my notebook back to me, open to the page where I had written all of what I know so far on the fae and my past. On the ride to school I had written the most recent clue at the bottom of the "What I Know" column.

"What about you guys?" I ask. "I know you've probably been busy with school and work, but have you made any headway on the adoption agency lead, Mags?"

"I wish." Maggie's shoulders slump. "I haven't found anything yet, E." Her mouth thins to a determined line. "But I'll keep looking. Someone out there has to know something about your birth parents. Names, more detailed physical descriptions, something."

"I'm still working on the drawings," Cam says. "Sorry, Eevee."

"The real question," Maggie says as I drain my coffee, "is what Eevee is going to say to Quince today in study hall."

I toss the empty coffee cup into the trash. My insides tangle up when I think of Quince. I secretly hope he won't be at study hall today, but my current plan is to arrive early and hide in the bookshelves the whole time.

I know. Super cowardly of me.

I tell them I'll meet them at lunch and enter the throng of students navigating the halls. Though I'm heading toward my first period class, my mind is a realm away, thinking of Quince, and clues, and maybe-dates involving trolls and wyverns.

Reality crashes down around me when I slam directly into someone in the hall. Books and papers go flying.

"Ohmigosh, I'm so-"

The person I've run into is crouching down to pick up the jumbled mess on the floor. He looks up at me, and I stop mid-sentence. Ugh. Just my luck.

"You have to start paying attention to your surroundings, missy," Mr. Abscons says, his tone severe.

He's sorted through our books and papers and hands me what I've dropped, glaring at me with his sharp, beady eyes.

"Sure, Mr. Abscons." He's not wrong, but I'm not going to tell him that.

He huffs and scurries away toward the library, scowling at me as he turns the corner. When he disappears from view, I roll my eyes.

I have got to stop physically running into that guy. Hopefully Ms. Bates isn't out for the whole school year. She's strict, but I doubt she'd hold a grudge over a few accidental, klutzy moments.

"Away, you three-inch fool!" I mutter under my breath. I know he can't hear me, but that's probably for the better. I imagine Mr. Abscons would react to a Shakespearean insult just as well as, if not better than, Mr. Jenkins. Then again, he's a librarian, even if he's just a substitute. Maybe he'd appreciate the reference to *The Taming of the Shrew* before throwing me into detention.

At the very least, quoting Shakespeare has cheered me up, and I manage to slip into my small animal care class just as the bell rings.

*****

"Eevee?"

I set my phone down guiltily.

"Sorry, Damian. What were you saying about your...English class?"

"Economics." He spoons some chocolate swirl ice cream into his mouth and licks his spoon.

"Right. And your test went...badly?"

Swallowing his ice cream, he surveys me. "Okay, what's up? You've been distant all night. I didn't drive all the way up from Winona to Duluth to spend time with you when you're a million miles away."

I bite back a snappy response. Because how could he know what's up with me? Our text conversations have been brief, and I don't think anything I've gone through the last few days would be easy to explain.

Ice trolls. Wyverns. A box containing a doll and a clue from my birth mother. A celebration with goblins, brownies, gnomes named Carl and a fae named Mindy. Twins who are hundreds of years old.

Not that Damian would believe me if I told him all of it. But let's say, for whatever reason, Damian was the kind of guy who'd be open to believing in fairies if his ex-girlfriend/currently-complicated-status-person told him she was fae.

All of those events and people involve Quince, who I haven't talked to since I disappeared in front of his eyes in the In Between in response to him asking me to the Homecoming Dance. I succeeded in avoiding him in study hall yesterday, and when I saw him in the halls, he'd been talking to Laura and Jim.

I have no idea what to do. Hiding in the bookshelves during study hall is not exactly the best long-term plan.

"Lots on my mind, sorry." I put my phone in my pocket. Luckily, this is enough explanation for Damian.

This time, he's driven both of us to Northern Creamery. To say my parents were cool toward him when he came to pick me up is an understatement. I don't think I've seen my mom that icy to anyone ever. Damian didn't seem to notice or care about their chilly attitudes, though.

"Don't be late," mom had said as Damian revved up the car.

"I will text you every minute you're late," dad warned. A truly terrifying notion, as my dad never texts.

"I'll be home before curfew, promise," I said, hugging them both.

Between their arctic attitudes and Cam and Maggie's disapproval of Damian after our break-up last month, I've found my own excitement about tonight dwindling with each second that passes.

Seeing Damian slowed that a little; the way his hand found mine as we walked into the Northern Creamery felt natural. The little jolt I always get when our skin touches didn't hurt, either.

I let him talk, and stare at the neon pink ice cream cone in the window above his left shoulder. Maybe we should go to our spot tonight, like he wants. There's a secluded beach alongside Lake Superior, where we had spent many dates walking, or picnicking, and even more dates just laying on a blanket, making out. It'd be a little chilly tonight, but chilly nights are good for cuddling.

"Hey, Damian-" I start, before the blood drains from my face.

No. It can't be.

Moving toward the door are the figures of Quince, Jim, Laura, and a few other theater kids.

I sink lower in the booth.

"What?" Damian asks. He frowns. "You okay? You're paler than usual."

"Want to…" I can't ask about the spot, not with Quince so close. "Want to go see a movie or something?" I ask instead.

244

The door opens, inviting in a draft of cool air with the group of laughing teens.

At Damian's hesitation, I hiss, "I'll pay."

"Alright, sure."

I gather up my purse and jacket. When Damian finally finishes his last bite of ice cream, I slide out of the booth and come face-to-face with Quince, who's holding a strawberry ice cream cone to his mouth.

To my horror, Damian throws an arm around my shoulder. "Ready when you are, babe."

Quince looks at Damian's arm draped possessively around my shoulder, then at my face.

"It's complicated, huh?"

I wince.

"What's complicated?" Damian demands.

"Quince! Hurry, I don't know how much longer I can save this spot for you!" Laura sits at a booth already filled to double capacity, her back against Jim's shoulder and her feet up on the booth seat, giggling.

I want to grab Quince, close my eyes, and transport the both of us to Elfaeme, away from Northern Creamery and Laura's giggles and Damian's arm over my shoulder. Somewhere we can be alone, so we can talk, and I can assure him it's not what it looks like. Probably.

Instead, I watch as he lets out a disappointed huff under Damian's flinty gaze and shakes his head at me imperceptibly. He sidesteps past me and sits at the booth of raucous theater kids.

Damian leads me out to the parking lot. Through the window I can see Quince has put an arm over Laura's shoulders. She looks delighted, her cheeks flushed a pretty pink.

I tell myself it's stupid to be jealous of her, but I'm jealous nonetheless.

The movie goes pretty much how I expect it to–a little bit of popcorn, a lot of making out. I lose myself to the dark of the theater and the sensation of Damian's mouth on mine. I can't even remember the name of the movie; some action flick Damian had wanted to see.

When we get in the car, I can tell he wants to continue what we started in the theater. He looks sidelong at me. "What about checking out our spot?"

"I can't," I say. "My dad'll be texting me every minute I'm late."

"So turn your phone off."

"I want to go home, Damian," I say.

The ride home is filled with silence.

"Thanks, this was fun," I say when he parks in the driveway.

His laugh is hollow. "What, running into your other boyfriend at the ice cream place, or the awkward as hell car ride just now?"

"Quince isn't my boyfriend, and neither are you," I retort.

"Then what was the point of tonight? I drove all the way from Winona so I could see you, you know." His voice is loud. I look to the house, worried someone might hear us.

"I know. You already made sure to tell me that multiple times." I open the door. "Besides, you did see me! Plus got to see a movie, which I paid for, if you remember."

"I got us the popcorn," he says, scowling.

I close the door, but he opens the window.

"Eevee," he says, his voice soft.

"What?"

"What do I have to do to get you to trust me again?"

"I need time, Damian."

This isn't the answer he wants; Damian isn't known for his patience. He throws the car into reverse.

"I can only wait so long!" he yells.

"Good thing I'm worth the wait!" I shout back. I clench my hands at my sides, anger at Damian intermingling with satisfaction at getting in the last word.

"We'll see about that!" Damian calls before peeling away.

I shout wordlessly, shaking my fists at his receding tail lights.

"What's going on with your hands?"

I whirl around and tuck my fists behind my back, panicking at the sight of flames flickering along my knuckles. I had thought since my wings don't appear in the human realm that the flames wouldn't, either, but I guess I was wrong.

"What are you doing out here, Jess?"

She rubs her eyes and yawns. "Mom and dad heard yelling." She points up to the house, where I see our parents hovering in the doorway.

"So they sent you out?" I raise my eyebrow at her.

"No, I wanted to make sure you were okay so I went out the back door. So what's up with your hands?"

Jess has always had a bit of a one track mind. Once she has her mind fixed on something, it takes monumental effort to get it to focus on something else.

"Good question." I peek over my shoulder. The knuckles are still flaming, but the fire is dying out. "I'm-"

I want to make up a lie, but the words dry up and turn to ash in my mouth.

Jess sidles over, trying to get a look at my hands, and I turn.

"Girls, come inside!" mom calls. "Jess, it's past your bedtime!"

Thinking of Quince is painful, especially after seeing him with Laura at the Northern Creamery, but his words pop into my head unbidden. "There are lots of ways of saying something true in a way that clouds the truth...Loophole."

Jess looks at me. Even though I'm five years older, she's already taller than me, all legs and elbows. "It definitely looked like my hands were on fire, didn't it?" I check over my shoulder. The flames have moved to my fingertips, and are faint, almost imperceptible. I shake my hands a little and grin innocently at Jess. "Weird. But look," I hold them up, "no flames, see?"

She eyes them with intensity. "I could have thought...where'd the fire go?"

"I don't know," I answer truthfully. I pull out my phone and check the time; nearly eleven. I've made it back before my curfew, at least, so no texts from dad. "Are you sure you even saw fire on my hands?"

She blinks and doubt flits across her face. I feel a little guilty at asking this deceptive question, but I'm still ready to tell my family about my fae side.

"C'mon, let's go in," I say, looping my arm through hers and turning her toward the house. Her skin is cool to the touch, like porcelain. "You've got to be cold out here in your PJs."

She doesn't protest, but I catch her looking at my hand on her arm a couple times as we walk up to the house.

Chapter 27

Convos at the Java Jive

Something about the smell of coffee is inherently comforting to me. I hold my mug up to my face and breathe in. Today's mug has a group of kittens on it with the phrase "Cat Mom" below it. Maggie's not on break for another ten minutes and Cam's running late, so it's just me and my thoughts, which keep incessantly returning to the moment I saw Quince at the Northern Creamery last night. The fight with Damian at the end of the night was annoying, but not unexpected–we had a few like it when we were officially boyfriend/girlfriend. But seeing the hurt and disappointment in Quince's eyes cuts me like ice shards, and watching through the window as he snuggled up to Laura is painful to re-envision. So of course, that's all I can think about.

If I hadn't agreed to Damian's last-minute plans yesterday morning, I wouldn't have seen Quince last night and today I'd be at least a little more capable of concentrating on my homework for small animal care. Maybe.

Screw it. I pull out my phone and send a short text to Quince.

E: *can we talk?*

Staring at the message does absolutely nothing except make my head ache with tension, so I put my phone away and pick up the kitten cup again.

"How many cups have you had already?"

"Only two," I say, smiling up at Cam.

Both of their eyebrows raise.

"Okay, three. But you're late."

They slide into the wooden chair opposite me and pull their sketch pad out of their backpack. "That's because I was finishing this."

Cam pushes their sketch pad toward me, then jams their hands in their jeans pockets, studying a groove on the table with intensity.

I look down at the sketch pad and my throat closes up.

Cam hadn't drawn my birth parents.

On the page in front of me are pencil drawings of my mom and dad. Their hands are intertwined, and mom is looking up at dad with a smile on her face. They look happy and comfortable together; Cam's captured their dynamic perfectly. I saw them like that, holding hands, mom's eyes crinkling as she looked up at dad, just last night, when everyone else was asleep and I had snuck downstairs to grab a snack.

"Cam, what-"

"I tried, Eevee. So many times. To draw your birth parents based on that info in your adoption packet," Cam says, still staring at the groove in the table. "I don't know how many pictures I started, how many I threw away. Nothing seemed right, and I wanted to do something helpful, you know?"

"So you drew my parents?" I have to admit, I'm not following Cam's thinking here. I look down at the drawing again. They really did a great job; it almost looks like a black and white picture it's so realistic.

"Yeah." Their voice is so quiet I'd have a hard time hearing them with all the background noise if it weren't for my super-hearing fae ears. When I glance up at them, I see their ears are flushed red.

"Why?"

They take a shaky breath. "Because they love you. Because you already have a family, one that doesn't leave cryptic clues written in blood. Because maybe your birth parents had a reason for having you adopted. Maybe, I don't know, maybe you're already where you're meant to be."

"It's not about that, though," I say slowly. "It's-"

"Plus," Cam continues, "the fae realm is dangerous."

"You don't get it," I say, surprising myself with how venomous my voice sounds. "You've lived your whole life with parents who have birthed *and* raised you." I push the sketch pad toward them. "Yes, my mom and dad are my mom and dad. Nothing's going to change that."

"But-"

"Nothing," I repeat. "But if you were me, wouldn't you want to know too? I mean, come on, Cam," I add, trying to soften my tone, "you're the one who's into all that fantasy stuff, not me. What would you do if you had found out you were-" I lower my voice- "not human? And there was a whole world you hadn't known about, just waiting to be explored?"

Even with my softer tone, Cam looks like they're about to cry. "I don't know what I'd do," they say in a low voice. They rip the page with the drawing of my parents on it out of their sketch pad and slide it toward me, not meeting my eyes. "Keep it. I made it for you."

I hesitate, then take it and put it in my backpack. "Thanks," I say.

We stare at each other in silence for a few seconds. In the background I hear, "Thanks for stopping at Java Jive, come again soon!"

Cam grimaces at the too-bubbly-for-her-own-good drive thru girl's voice and I laugh. "It's like nails on a chalkboard, isn't it?"

"Worse," Cam replies. The tension between us shatters and we're both still chuckling when Maggie pulls up a chair, a pot of coffee in her hand.

"Thought you could use a refill." She fills my mug, plus two others she had brought over. "What's so funny?"

"Hi there! Welcome to Java Jive! What can I get for you today?" the perky Java Jive employee says into her headset.

We all wince, and Cam wipes at their eyes, still chuckling to themselves.

Maggie shakes her head at us. "You two are awful. Cammie can't help that she sounds like a coffee-addicted chipmunk."

"You winced too, I saw it!" I point a finger at her accusingly.

Instead of responding, she takes a sip of her coffee, then sets her mug down, her face getting that "not-taking-any-shit" look on it I sometimes see when she's interviewing people for her article.

"Tell her."

She's looking at Cam, who's become interested in the groove on the table again.

"Tell me what?"

"I've been holding my tongue for weeks, Cam. We agreed you'd tell her today." When Cam doesn't say anything, she adds, "If you don't, I will."

"Tell me what?" I repeat, because neither of them seem to have heard me the first time.

"It's about Lame-ian." Maggie crosses her arms and stares at Cam.

"Damian? What about him?"

Crap. Did someone see us when we were out last night?

"I was going to tell you guys about our date last night eventually, I swear. It's just, you're not exactly pro-Damian after he broke up with me, and...and you're not even listening to me!"

Cam is on their phone, scrolling through who-knows-what.

"Just wait," Maggie says quietly.

"Wait for what?"

Cam hands me their phone and I look down at one of Damian's social media profiles. The most recent picture he's posted is from a little after three this morning. The location tag says it's in Winona, which means he apparently went straight back down there after our date. And the girl he's with in the picture looks happy to have his arm around her shoulder, his fingers hovering over her breasts as if he's about to grab them.

My first reaction is to toss the phone on the ground and stomp on it, but since it's Cam's phone, I curb that impulse and instead go with my second reaction, which is to scroll through the last couple weeks of Damian's posts.

"I know you haven't unblocked him on social media," Cam's saying, "But I had never blocked him in the first place. I'm not on social media a lot, you know that, so I had forgotten we were friends on there." I tear my gaze away from the third picture I've seen so far of him lip-locked with another girl. Cam looks absolutely miserable. Their face is blotchy, which doesn't pair well with their fading purple hair, and their hands are clenched together in front of their stomach. They're talking to their hands, not to me. "I didn't say anything at first because it seemed as if you were moving on from Damian–you were so focused on that stuff with your birth parents-"

"And Quince," Maggie interrupts.

"I knew something was up with you!" I say, because focusing on Damian and Quince is too gut-wrenching, and focusing on Cam's quieter-than-usual behavior over the last few weeks is easier. "Maggie said she'd talked to you about it." I'm too embarrassed to admit I thought Maggie might have been replacing me as Cam's best friend.

Cam nods. "You know I don't like to butt in to people's relationships. I decided to leave it. Until Damian came back and took you out for ice cream on your birthday last week."

"I wanted to tell you, E," Maggie says apologetically. "But Cam swore me to secrecy. You have no idea how hard it was for me to stay quiet."

"So you guys would've let me make the same damn mistake with Damian, just because you have some moral obligation to stay out of people's relationships?" I don't think I shouted, but they both flinch and an old lady waiting in line for coffee turns around and glares at me.

"No, we wouldn't, that's why we're saying something now!" Maggie protests.

"We would've told you sooner if we had known about your date last night," Cam says, their voice breaking. They're almost in tears again, and I mentally kick myself. "I'm sorry, Eevee. I really thought I was doing the right thing, staying out of your love life."

All my anger seeps out of me and I slump forward, resting my elbows on the table. "Cam, if I'm being stupid, I give you my full permission to butt in and say something."

"Told you she would've rather known right away," Maggie says to Cam.

"You're not going to keep seeing him, are you?" Cam asks me.

"Between last night and what you just showed me? What am I, stupid?"

"Not the brightest bulb on the Christmas tree when it comes to love, maybe, but we'll keep you around, E."

I tell them both all the awkward and disastrous details of what I'm now referring to in my head as the Official Last Date With Damian.

"Are you going to block the new number he's been using, too?" Cam asks.

Annoyingly-perky-voiced-Cammie waves frantically at Maggie, who sighs. "Back to the grind," she says, refilling my mug with what's left in the coffee pot and heading back to the espresso machine. "You better block the blockhead, E!"

"I will!" I shout after her, then turn to face Cam. "But not without saying something first. He may be a liar and a bit of a player-"

"A bit?" Cam splutters.

"-but I'd feel bad completely ghosting him with no explanation."

Cam snorts. "You're nicer than me, then. I'd just block him and be done with it."

"You're the sweetest person I know, Cam," I say as I pull my phone out of my pocket. Cam's lips lift in the tiniest of smiles.

"What are you saying to him? Another Shakespeare quote?"

I had told Cam and Maggie about my previous final text to Damian. "You are not worth another word, else I'd call you knave" is such a great final text. Why didn't I just leave it at that?

"It should have ended with that text," I say out loud.

Cam doesn't dispute this.

"No," I answer. "He doesn't deserve Shakespeare this time."

"Does anybody truly deserve a Bardic insult?"

"Well, yeah. But not the second time."

I show my message to Cam.

E: *we're done, Damian. i don't want 2 hear from u again. hope u have fun with kate or melissa or any of the other girls u been hanging with in Winona. Sry u think im not worth waiting 4. newsflash. i am.*

"Love it," Cam says. They hand me my phone back, and I check that the message has sent before I block the number and delete the conversation. "I'm blocking him now you've seen his pics, by the way," they add, tapping at their phone.

Three more cups of coffee and two chocolate chip muffins later and we're not only finished with our homework, but have made up several nicknames for my ex-formerly-known-as-boyfriend.

Maggie flops down in the chair next to me. "Finally free!"

"Me too," I say, closing my math book.

"Perfect. Now we've got that Lame-ian crap out of the way, we can talk more about…" she looks around and lowers her voice, "that last clue and when you're tracking it down." Her face shines with excitement.

Cam gives her a sharp look. "Eevee-"

"Wants to find out the truth, right?"

I don't want to get in an argument with either of them, so I shrug noncommittally.

"Let me see the notebook again. Please?" Maggie does her best puppy dog eyes.

"Why?" I ask, already digging in my backpack. No one can resist Maggie's puppy dog eyes.

"To see if there's anything we've missed."

All my books, folders, papers, and other random items (like pencils and the bag of fruit snacks I'd forgotten were in my backpack) are out on the table. I rip open the bag of fruit snacks and pop a few of them in my mouth, chewing as I survey the pile. They're kind of stale.

"It's not in there, is it?" Cam asks.

"Did you leave it at home, E?"

I hate misplacing things, but unfortunately it's one of those annoying character traits of mine I just can't shake. It's a rare day when I head out the door with everything I need for the day. "I don't know, maybe?"

I don't think so, though. Today's the first day I've opened my backpack since the bell rang on Friday afternoon.

"When did you last see it?" Cam asks. How many times has Cam had to ask me that exact question since we've been friends? At least a million?

I close my eyes and think. When *was* the last time I had seen my notebook? I try to picture its bright yellow cover with the fairy I'd drawn on it with ink, then picture the page with all I know about my birth parents and being fae.

Opening my eyes, I look at Maggie. "Last time I remember seeing it was Friday morning, when I was showing it to you in the hall."

Maggie takes out a note pad from her apron pocket and writes that down. "Okay, and you don't remember looking at it in any of your classes that day?"

"Nope."

When the mystery of the missing notebook has been thoroughly discussed and documented, we exit the Java Jive. I'm jittery, but not just from the copious amounts of coffee I've imbibed.

If my notebook isn't at home, we think I probably left it somewhere at school, which is an uncomfortable thought at best. The only people I've shared that information with are walking next to me. Well, and Quince. But since thinking about him is confusing and emotionally draining, I refocus my brain on the *other* huge, pressing issue I hadn't resolved yet: when should I go back to Elfaeme to follow the last clue? I don't need my notebook to go back there. I have the map at home in my room, and could technically leave right now.

I could. But should I?

"Think about what I said earlier, about your parents?" Cam asks as we get to our cars. "You've got a great life here, Eevee. They love you."

"I'll think about it," I say, not willing to promise any more than that, my mind already circling back to that last clue and who it might lead to, and what I'll say to them if it does.

Chapter 28

A Mystery Delivery

As someone who recently spent time avoiding a certain person by hiding amongst the bookshelves in study hall, I think I speak from experience when I say: Quince is avoiding me.

There's been a few not-so-subtle clues which have led me to this conclusion. The biggest is his non-presence during study hall this entire week. Oh, and not responding to any of my messages.

Cam says to give him space, but I hate this rift between us–especially because the issue (Damian) is out of the picture. Also, Quince is my only solid link to the fae realm, and if I'm being honest, I feel lost without him. And yeah, I guess I miss him, too.

As Mr. Jenkins drones on about our homework due tomorrow, I entertain the idea of actually leaving a note in Quince's locker on the off-chance he'd read it. That, or hiring one of those planes that write messages in the sky.

Between the two, only one is in my budget, so I tear a sheet of paper out of my notebook.

Dear Quince-

No, that doesn't feel right. Too formal. I tear the paper in half. On the clean half I write: *Hey Quince!*, then wince and tear that half in half. Too informal.

Why is this so hard?

As usual, I find myself relying on Shakespeare when I can't think of the right words to say myself. A quote from *The Merry Wives of Windsor* could work. On the quarter sheet of notebook paper I scribble down a quick message.

Quince–I will one way or another make you amends. (That's the Shakespeare line.) After it I add: *Please. I need to talk to you. I'm sorry, you know. About everything. ~Eevee*

I fold up the note until it's a tiny square and scrawl Quince's name on the front. When the bell finally rings, cutting off Mr. Jenkins mid-sentence, I exit with Cam.

"Put it in his locker yourself," Cam says with a shake of their head when I try to rope them into being my note delivery person.

"Please? If Quince sees me near his locker he'll know it's from me and will throw it out before ever reading it."

They sigh, but still shake their head.

"This isn't because you don't want to butt into my relationships, is it? Because I think we've established I'm okay with you butting in."

"No, it isn't because of that," they say, giving me an exasperated look. "Just don't let him see you, Eevee. I gotta go. Mom and dad expect me at the brewery tonight. Pick you up tomorrow at the usual time?"

"Works for me," I grumble.

They pat my shoulder encouragingly before slouching off down the hall. For someone as tall as they are (I think they're close to Quince's height when they stand up straight), they sure know how to make themselves take up as little space as possible. I watch them melt into the crowd of students, then run my thumb along the edge of the folded up note.

"Here goes nothing," I whisper.

Do I move after this encouraging statement? No, I do not.

The halls are starting to empty and I am in danger of missing the bus when I work up the courage to move from the spot where Cam left me and head toward Quince's locker.

My process is stopped when a teary-eyed Laura shoulders her way past me.

"Laura, what's going on?" I ask, rubbing at my arm.

She's already halfway down the hall, but she half-shouts, half-sobs, "As if you don't know!" and rushes out of sight around the corner.

Her cryptic answer means nothing to me, though apparently she thinks it should. It's distracting enough that I momentarily forget what I'm doing in the middle of the hall until I feel the square of paper cutting into my palm when I clench my fist. Right. The note. A few students still mill about the halls, packing up bags and slamming their lockers shut, but Quince is nowhere in sight. I glance around to be sure, but no one seems suspicious of a girl hanging around Quince's locker for reasons totally unrelated to his dating history, I'm sure. Quickly as possible, I slip the note through one of the metal openings, hoping it doesn't get lost in whatever else he may have in his locker.

"Don't you need to catch the bus?"

"Amelia!"

Her hand is laced tightly around the hand of a kid who I can only assume is shoulders guys from her math class. She's not wrong–her assessment of his shoulders, which I had to hear about for another fifteen minutes just last night, is spot on.

In my unbiased opinion, though, Quince's are better. Not as wide, perhaps, but who's into the whole my-shirt-might-rip-if-I-flex-too-hard thing anyway?

"Eevee? Bus?"

I snap out of my shoulders-related reverie. "Right. The bus."

She stares at me. So does shoulders guy, who seems wholly unconcerned about the bus situation.

"We need to catch it?" she says slowly, as if talking to a kindergartener.

"I should probably get to cross country practice," shoulders guy says, extricating his hand from Amelia's.

I have to say, I did not peg him as a cross country running person on top of being a wrestler.

"Talk to you later?" Amelia asks as he lopes away.

He waves in response, and Amelia grabs my arm. "Hurry!"

We barely make it to the bus, showing up as the bus driver, Bob, is just about to close the doors. He grumbles at us and opens it to let us on, but I know he's not really mad, because when he's mad he yells so loudly and with such intensity that his spit goes flying.

You don't want to be in the first couple rows when Bob's mad.

"Hey, Bob, did you-"

"Still haven't seen your notebook, Eevee. I'd let ya know if it turned up," he answers shortly.

No one's seen my notebook. None of the janitors, none of my teachers, none of my family. And of course I can't remember where I put it, so I've not only been angry at myself about the whole thing with Quince this week, but also at my forgetfulness.

"Thanks for checking, Bob."

I sit down and Amelia plunks down in the seat next to me, already on her phone.

"So what were you doing in the east hallway by Quince's locker?" she asks, not looking up from her phone. "You're usually on the bus before me."

Amelia already thinks I have a crush on Quince. There's no way I'm going to tell her I was leaving a note in his locker.

"And now I know why," I say significantly, elbowing her ribs. "So that's shoulders guy, huh?"

"His name's Trent," she says, her cheeks reddening.

"Yeah, I'll never remember that. He's shoulders guy to me," I tease.

She tosses her long, curly hair behind her and pins me with a scolding expression.

"Kidding, I'm kidding," I say with a laugh. "Geez, you must really like this guy. You never cared when I called whats-his-name Milk Dud Guy last year."

"Benny really liked his Milk Duds," she says, her lips pursing with distaste. "I'll never understand it."

"I'll never understand your dislike of chocolate," I counter.

"It's not that I don't like chocolate, I'd just rather have cheese, that's all."

She turns her attention back to her phone and I breathe a sigh of relief. Awkward Quince-related conversation averted. For now. Knowing Amelia, she'll probably sneak into my room after she should be sleeping and interrogate me then, when she remembers she never got an answer out of me.

I pull my phone out as well. I know it's stupid, that Quince won't get my note until tomorrow morning at the earliest, but the first thing I do is pull up our conversation. He's read the seven messages I've sent him since Sunday, but hasn't responded to any of them.

How can I explain myself and apologize if he keeps avoiding me?

*****

Thursday night dinners at the Acker house are like every other night, except with the inclusion of a no-phones-at-the-table rule recently put into effect because of a certain someone's consistent phone-checking-while-eating habit. Hint: her name rhymes with familia.

Our phones–mine, Amelia's, Jess', and mom and dad's (I don't think mom will allow Greg and Charlie phones of their own until they're both pushing forty)–are in a little wicker basket which usually only makes an appearance once a year on Easter.

Not that I'm expecting a text from anyone. Cam's busy helping their parents at the brewery and Maggie is either picking up a shift at the Java Jive or doing something for the school podcast, or both. Knowing Maggie, it's probably both. And Quince–well. We'll see about Quince after tomorrow morning.

Amelia's obviously expecting a message soon, though. She's shoveling food in her mouth in such large quantities her cheeks are puffed out like a greedy squirrel, and she keeps glancing over at the phone basket where her phone sits, powered down like the rest of ours.

"You aren't being excused until the rest of us are done, Amelia Jane, so why don't you slow down and enjoy your food a little?" dad asks in a half-exasperated, half-amused voice.

In response, Amelia takes a heaping spoonful of mashed potatoes and sticks the whole thing in her mouth, staring at dad the whole time.

"Really mature," Jess mutters.

She's one to talk. Not even two minutes ago I saw her hiding broccoli in her napkin. I pick at the food on my plate. For the last week and a half, I've been getting nauseous at even the thought of eating meat. Under my mom's watchful gaze, though, I choke down a couple more bites.

"By the way, Eevee, a package came for you today," dad says.

"From gram?" I ask. I'm surprised. My dad's mom, who we all call gram, lives in Florida and usually sends our birthday gifts weeks, even months, late. For my tenth birthday, which I had considered to be a pretty big deal, being double digits and all, she had sent my birthday gift so late it had arrived just after Thanksgiving. "But it's still September."

"I don't think it's from gram," dad says. "No return address or anything. You know how your gram is about proper labeling on packages and letters."

I do. I once forgot my zip code on the return address, and I had to listen to her lecture me over the phone about it for ten minutes. I never understood what the big deal was–the letter had gotten to her, hadn't it?

"When we're done eating, you can open it," mom says.

"Can I help?" Greg asks.

"Me too?" Charlie pipes up, always wanting to do what big brother is doing.

I want to say no, but at the imploring looks from them and mom, I relent.

Which is how I end up on the couch with a box on my lap, Greg and Charlie flanking me, and the rest of the family watching in anticipation.

"This feels like Christmas," I say with a grin as I see Jess lean forward.

"Just open it," Amelia says impatiently, her foot tapping.

I move in slow motion, ripping back the tape at the speed of a turtle. It's worth it for the glare I get from Amelia, who, like the rest of us, hasn't had her phone returned to her yet.

Greg and Charlie take over and tape goes flying. In no time the box is open and I peer around my brothers' heads at what's inside.

On top of something wrapped in tissue paper is an envelope with my name on it.

"Is there a card?" mom asks. "Because if there's a card-"

"There's a card," I say, holding up the envelope. "And yes, I'll read it before opening the present.

I turn it over and hesitate. What if it's something awful from Damian? My stomach tightens at the thought. He's been known to hold a grudge. And if it is from Damian, how awkward and embarrassing would it be to open it with my whole family as witness?

Amelia's exasperated sigh cuts through my worried thoughts. Like pulling a bandage off a wound, I rip open the envelope and pull out the card.

On the front is a cutout of a smiling bumblebee with the words "Just Bee-cause" underneath.

Dutifully, I hold it up and show my onlookers.

"Oh for cute!" mom exclaims.

"Who's it from?" Jess asks, now bouncing in her seat.

I open it up and feel my smile freeze.

"Well?" Amelia asks, her foot still tapping out a frantic rhythm on the carpet.

"Yes, Eevee, share!" dad says, adjusting his glasses and smiling.

I don't want to share. But Acker family rules regarding gift-opening are iron-clad. I have to share.

So I clear my throat. "Dear Eevee, Quince told us he is planning to ask you to some fancy event called a Homecoming Dance. Remember, it's always better to be overdressed than underdressed. You may return this after the soirée. S and S."

My cheeks are burning and I have that weird floaty sensation where I feel like I'm hovering above my body looking down on everything.

"Who are S and S?" dad asks with a confused frown.

"Quince is going to ask you to Homecoming?" Amelia squeals, her phone momentarily forgotten.

"It's just clothes?" Greg says, tearing the tissue paper out of the box, his face twisting with disgusted disappointment. "Lame."

"What kind of clothes?" Jess asks, still bouncing.

Charlie reaches his hands into the box and pulls out a dress.

Not just any dress. THE dress. The one Quince had found when we were picking out outfits to wear to the equinox celebration last week. The gorgeous one that starts as a light periwinkle on the bodice and slowly deepens to a midnight blue at the bottom. It's just as beautiful as I remember it, the jewels twinkling prettily as Charlie lifts it up for all to see.

Everyone but my brothers lets out a gasp.

"That dress must cost a fortune!" mom exclaims, rushing over and taking it from Charlie, who is known to have sticky hands even after washing with soap and water. The silky material glows in the lamplight.

"It's gorgeous," Jess says, her eyes glowing as brightly as the dress. "You have to wear it, Eevee!"

"Quince FLORENTZ is going to ask you to Homecoming?" Amelia asks again.

"He did ask me," I burst out. Mom is holding the dress up to her body, but she lowers it at my outburst. My whole family is staring at me.

"He asked me last week Thursday, and I said no, because it was complicated, because I was still kind of figuring things out with Damian-"

They all groan in unison.

"-but I found out three days too late that Damian's even more of a jerk than I had thought-"

A collective chorus of "You think?" interrupts me.

"-and so I ruined my chance at going to Homecoming with Quince, and more importantly, I probably ruined our friendship!"

There are too many eyes, all staring at me. I rush out of the room.

"So, *who* are S and S?" I hear my dad ask as I flee up the stairs to the haven of my bed.

Chapter 29

Plans After Midnight

Sleep evades me. My brain can't concentrate on homework no matter how much I try, and neither Cam nor Maggie has responded to my "HELP I just humiliated myself in front of my family" texts.

Mom dropped off the dress a little while ago, before she went to bed. I keep looking at it where it's hanging against my closet door. In the milky light of the moon it looks delicate, fit for a fairy queen.

My phone buzzes where it rests on my nightstand and I fall partway off the bed in surprise, catching myself with one arm and a leg.

I almost fall over again when I read the notification on my home screen: *New message from Quince.*

Suddenly my hands aren't responding to the signals of my brain because it takes three tries to unlock my phone.

It's been a week since I ran away from Quince after he'd asked me to Homecoming, but it feels like at least a year.

I'm about to open his message, but then I make myself wait an agonizing five minutes because I don't want him to think I have nothing better to do than read his texts.

When the clock shifts from 11:43 to 11:44 I take a breath and open the message.

Q: *you have persistent sisters. and friends. you know that?*

271

My hands tremble, but I manage to type out *im aware. what did they do this time?*

He reads the message immediately. Snakes slither in my intestines as I wait for him to respond.

Q: *Cam and Maggie cornered me after rehearsal, and if that wasn't enough, your sisters have been spamming my social media accounts every five minutes this evening about a dress and how you're sorry?*

E: *i am. sorry. 4 everything i did. and 4 my friends/sisters. I had given Cam & Maggie permission 2 butt in2 my relationships but im regretting giving them so much power*

Q: *i read your note too. have to say, haven't gotten a note in my locker since middle school.*

E: *shut up, im already embarrassed about that*

Q: *ok, ok. 😁 thank you for saying you're sorry. i appreciate it.*

E: *i mean it. its been weird not talking 2 u this last week. forgive me?*

Q: *i almost feel i have to or i'll have Cam, Maggie, and your sisters after me.*

E: *...*

Q: *yes, i forgive you, Eevee. i've missed you this week, too.*

E: *i didn't say i missed u!* 😳

Q: *it was implied.* 😊

Q: *so about this dress?*

I look over at the dress. It really was thoughtful of Sean and Shannon to send it. I'm still not sure how comfortable I'd be wearing it, but it's definitely better suited for a dance than the equinox celebration.

E: *u've seen it b4. @Sean & Shannon's*

I'm tempted to ask him right now if he still wants to go to Homecoming with me, but it's too soon, and do I really want to be the kind of person who asks big questions like that over text?

Q: *ah, THAT dress. they must like you. they don't loan out their clothes willingly, and this is the 2nd dress of theirs they're letting you wear.*

It's not me they like so much as the mystery and secrets surrounding me, I think. But I don't say that to Quince. Instead, I start to type *have u asked anyone 2 homecoming, because*–but my texting is interrupted by another message from Quince.

Q: *so, i've been dying to know. you figure out the 3rd clue? have you met your birth parents already??*

Quince is more like his cousins than he thinks, attracted to mystery like moths to a flame. We're mere minutes past my apology and he's already turned the conversation back to my inscrutable past.

Rocks collect in my stomach and weigh me down as I delete my text about Homecoming. What was I thinking? He had probably asked me in the heat of the moment last week. Now we're back to our status quo: fae friends with a mystery to solve. Besides, he's probably asked someone else by this point.

E: *figured it out. haven't pursued it yet.*
Q: *what?? why not?*
E: *timing? idk??*

Truthfully, as much as I've wanted to go back to Elfaeme since I found the map, I have an equal desire to not get killed or stuck in the fae realm where my phone doesn't work and my friends and family aren't able to come get me (if I could somehow get a message to them).

I'm a bit of a chicken, I'll admit it. I'd prefer the phrase "has a healthy sense of self-preservation."

Legitimate excuses have come up, besides. Work at Gramp's. My Official Last Date with Damian. Working on homework with Cam and Maggie. School.

There have been lots of times where I could have gone, too. A couple times I had even gathered all three of my clues and held the map in one hand and the doll in the other, and almost did it–almost stepped off my bed and into that secluded part of the In Between where I had first visited the fae realm.

But then I'd pause, and my brain with its overactive imagination would kick in. I'd see Folsom's wide eyes and froggy face staring at me, and hear his croaky voice as he asks me to tell him my name and promise to stay by the Reflecting Pool. In my imagination, my legs are rooted to the ground and he laughs, his sticky frog tongue lashing out and wrapping around my head.

I'd see those fae at the Mage Stone who had been staring at me, and they surround me, their eyes all growing to the size of oranges.

The ethereal tree fae inevitably makes an appearance, too, branches whipping at my face and arms as I'm enclosed in a tightening frenzy of twigs and leaves.

If I hadn't abandoned the idea of going to Elfaeme by this point, ice trolls and wyverns and goblins-or-gnomes with gravelly voices all swirl around in my head with the rest of the fae chorus.

My sleep hasn't been too great this week for some reason.

Q: *want to go right now?*

All the images which have plagued my thoughts and haunted my dreams zip through my head, followed by dad's advice he always doles out when curfew comes up.

"Very few good decisions are made after midnight, Eevee."

I glance at the time on my phone: 12:03.

E: *idk, it's late…*

Q: *don't you want to know???*

I pull the cardboard box where I'd been keeping all the clues and adoption info out from under my bed and set it on the bed in front of me. Almost automatically, my hands reach for the baby doll with her orange dress, and I cradle it in my arms. I do want to know.

I scan the framed pictures standing on top of my dresser; in the center is an 8x10 picture with the entire "To be or not to be" speech from *Hamlet* written on its frame in tiny writing. Of all those pictured in the collage–family, friends, even a picture of me and Damian I keep forgetting to switch out–only Cam and Maggie know about my fae side. But I've found it's hard to talk about Elfaeme and my birth parents with them. Cam just sees what haunts me and thinks I should focus more on the family I've got. The picture they drew of my parents is still in my backpack; every time I see it I'm reminded of our conversation this last Sunday. And Maggie's so busy. Even though her excitement is nice, I can't exactly bring her with me, or I risk her life.

Cradling the doll in one arm, I pick up the letter that started it all with my other hand and turn it over to read my birth mom's rushed note for the 742nd time.

P.S. I don't have much time to write this. Your father and I are fae. I know we said not to find us, but I can't stand the thought of not seeing you ever again. I want to see you someday. If you decide you want to find us, just know there will most likely be danger. When you are ready, go into nature. You've lived so long in the human realm, coming to the fae realm won't come naturally to you right away. Find a mushroom circle, or a still pond, or a tree with a hole in it. You'll know what to do from there. When you are ready, follow the clues.

Resolve hardens in me like steel.

E: *yeah, i want 2 know*

12:13. I think I've taken too long to respond, because he doesn't answer. Maybe he's fallen asleep. Some people can fall asleep in minutes, and there's almost ten minutes between his last message and my response.

Another minute passes with no message. He probably fell asleep. I can't say I'm entirely disappointed. What were we going to do, sneak out to the fae realm in the middle of a Thursday night and knock on my birth parents' door (if the moonstone works how the lines suggest it will)?

I'm in my pajamas–a cotton pair of shorts with rainbows and a matching shirt–and pacing my room with a toothbrush in my mouth when a rock hits my window.

Swallowing some of my toothpaste in surprise, I sneak toward the window, peering down into the yard, then crack open the window.

"Quince, what the hell?" I try to say around my toothpaste. It comes out more like, "Winz, wadahow?"

"What'd you say?" he calls up in a loud whisper.

Not wanting to pull a Maggie and try to carry on an entire conversation with a mouthful of toothpaste, I rush to the bathroom and spit. When I get back, Quince is sitting on the end of my bed in a pair of red flannel pajamas, looking around my room in interest.

Closing my door quietly, I turn to him and cross my arms.

"What the hell?"

"You wanted to go check out the last clue, right?"

"Yes, but…" I frown. "You got here really fast. Also, how did you climb up to my room in the time it took me to finish brushing my teeth?"

He waves a hand dismissively. "I have my ways."

My jaw drops. "You-you realm-hopped! You went from your house, to the fae realm, to my house, to the fae realm, to my room! You told me fae can only do that a limited amount each day!"

"I'm fine." His smile is bright and cheery. "I feel great! Are you ready to go?"

"I'm in my pajamas," I protest.

"So am I," he says with a shrug. Swiveling around, he starts sifting through the papers on my bed. "Which one of these is the last clue?"

"This one," I say, picking up the small, folded piece of paper. "It's a map of a spot near where I saw Folsom, on my first trip to Elfaeme."

"I know the spot," he says, pocketing the clue. "Let's go!"

He stands up lightning fast and touches my arm. "Quince, wait!"

The world spins. Or are we spinning? I see trees. My room. More trees. My bed. An owl, eyes wide. My floor. With a wrench, I fling my whole body toward the floor, dragging Quince with me. We land on the rug with a thud that I really hope doesn't wake anyone.

Quince groans and I lift up my head to see him next to me, his face in the rug.

"Are you okay? What happened?" I ask, helping him sit up. We both try to stand, but the room is still spinning (metaphorically this time), so we sit on my rug, our backs propped up on the edge of my bed.

"I'm fine. I think. Just really dizzy."

"Me too. How...what...?"

He starts to shake his head, then stops and holds it between his hands. "I'm not sure. I have a theory, though. You didn't want to go, did you?"

"Not yet," I admit.

His smile is watery and his face has a greenish tinge to it. "I think we just figured out what happens when one fae wants to travel to Elfaeme and the other doesn't."

"Let's not do that again," I say. "Experiment closed."

While we wait for the dizziness to dissipate, I try to collect my thoughts. I turn my head to look at Quince when it no longer feels like a spinning top.

"Quince?"

"Yeah?"

He's still having a little trouble focusing on my face; his slightly cross-eyed expression is both cute and goofy.

This is it. Before I can go anywhere or do anything with him, I have to get the issue of Homecoming off my chest. Even if we're no more than friends, even if he is only interested in me because my past is shrouded in mystery, the fact of the matter is he asked me to Homecoming and I ran, and now it's going to be this big, awkward thing between us unless I say something.

"See any ice trolls lately?" I ask, then cringe internally. I had meant to ask directly about Homecoming, but then my thoughts strayed to how Quince had asked me, and then to fighting the ice troll with him, and somehow that slipped out instead.

"No?" He gives me a puzzled look, then grins. "But you know Glen, on the football team? He looks kind of troll-like, don't you think? I've always wondered…"

"I wonder if Glen is going to Homecoming?" I ask in an overly casual voice.

"Only one way to find out."

Quince must no longer feel dizzy. His eyes have lost the cross-eyed look and his usual playful glint is back. "I'll have to ask him. Hope he's not already going with somebody else. That'd be disappointing."

He takes out his phone and starts scrolling. "Glen, Glen, Glen, where are you, you troll-like hunk?"

I wrestle his phone from him. "You can't take Glen to Homecoming!" I say.

"Why not? You don't think we'd make a cute couple?"

"It's not that, it's-"

"Besides, I'm not going with anyone." His tone is teasing, but he doesn't quite meet my eyes.

"Not even Laura?"

He grabs his phone back from me. "She asked. I declined."

That explains her weird comment to me in the hall today. She must think Quince said no to her because of me.

I take a deep breath. "Before you ask Glen, I thought maybe-"

He's turned toward me again, and his face is so close to mine I can see the light dusting of freckles across his nose and a piece of carpet fuzz in his hair.

"Maybe what?" he whispers.

The carpet fuzz distracts me. I pull it out, my heart thudding in my ears as my fingers run through his soft hair.

"Maybe you could go with me?" I whisper back.

He's going to kiss me. He leans forward until our lips almost touch. I can feel the heat of them on mine they're so close.

"On one condition," he says, his voice barely audible.

"What's that?"

He shifts and his breath tickles my ear. "You let me have one dance with Glen."

I clap my hands over my mouth, but a snort escapes. "Deal."

Sitting back with a grin on his face, he says, "Now that that's settled, are you ready to go find your birth mom?"

Nerves pile on top of nerves. I think my blood consists of 86% nervous energy at this point.

"Yes. But wait." I stop him from touching my arm. "At least give me a minute to put all this stuff away and get a sweatshirt and shoes. It's not exactly shorts and t-shirt weather in the In Between."

I collect everything from the bed and put it into the cardboard box, then tiptoe to my closet and grab a hoodie and a pair of slip-on black shoes. As I close the door, I see Quince's eyes following the dress from Sean and Shannon.

"Not saying you have to wear it," he says, "but it would look amazing on you, you know."

"Flattery will get you nowhere," I retort.

I take a look around my room. This could be the last time I'm in my room with questions about my past clamoring around in my head. Soon, tonight even, those questions may be replaced by answers.

Chapter 30

Glades at Night

The In Between is a completely different place at night compared to the afternoon. Buds dot the limbs of the trees, miniature promises of new life. The leaves which had coated the ground so thickly are decayed and brown, as if they had just spent a season under snow. Here and there, delicate flowers have pushed their way through the layer of decaying matter. I'm not great at identifying flowers, but even still, I don't think any of these can be found in Minnesota.

I'd appreciate their beauty more, I'm sure, if we weren't lost.

"I just need to find the tree," I tell Quince. "If I can find the tree I'd been staring at when I first traveled here, I can find that circle of moonstones."

"Describe the map to me again," Quince suggests, and it takes all my effort not to roll my eyes at him. "Maybe there's another distinguishing landmark we can look for other than a large tree with a hole in it."

"I told you already, I don't see anything around us that's labeled on the map. I don't know, everything looks different in the dark."

"In the circle of moonstones in the wood, one will bring you to me with your blood," Quince murmurs under his breath.

A bat flies by and attaches itself to a tree limb, hanging upside down and staring at us as we walk below it. I yawn so widely my jaw cracks. "Maybe we should just come back in the daytime."

"But we're so close!" Quince protests. His statement loses some of its potency when he follows it with a yawn of his own. "Or we could-" another yawn, "-ask someone for directions or something."

"Who?" I gesture to the bat in the branch behind us. "Aside from that bat, we're completely alone out here. I told you, it was the same when I was here last time. There was no one here except me and Folsom."

"Well, maybe we'll run into him," Quince says. At my look, he asks, "What? Folsom may have his faults, and an unhealthy obsession with regaining his place in the Unseelie Court if my dad's stories are to be believed, but you can't deny he knows this area better than anyone."

"I'm not denying that. I just don't trust him."

Quince scratches at one of his horns. "Then I'm out of ideas. Maybe you're right. We should call it a night."

"More like an early morning," I say after a quick glance at my phone.

Frustration clusters in my chest. It's been an hour since we've arrived in Elfaeme. Why is it we can find a clue in winding wyvern passages within an hour but not if I've been to the place before and have a map?

"What's that, ahead of us?" Quince asks, pointing at a shimmering light through the trees.

"Light. Could it be-"

"Moonstones. That's what I thought, too. Come on!"

Quince grabs my hand and we both run along the path toward the source of light, bursting into the clearing with a chorus of cracking twigs.

"Oh," I say, dropping Quince's hand.

The Reflecting Pool, so calm and peaceful in the daylight, is transformed at night into something magical.

Its surface doesn't reflect the feeble moonlight above us, but instead, emanates a light of its own. The trees, so barren around us still, look lush and green in the pool's reflection. As we watch, the leaves begin to change colors, and soon the reflection matches the way the forest had looked when Folsom had left me here. The image doesn't stay long, however. Leaves fall until all that's left are gaunt branches and limbs.

"I could watch this forever," I whisper, watching as little leaves start to appear on the trees in the pool.

"I could, too," Quince says, his voice quiet. When had he taken my hand again?

I don't want this moment to end. I know from here I can find my way back to the tree and, consequently, to the circle of moonstones. But as soon as that mystery is solved and I meet my birth parents, these moments with Quince will end. What reason would we have to sneak off to the fae realm in the middle of the night together then?

I can think of a lot of reasons for myself, of course. But when the mystery fades, Quince's interest in me will also fade, and just like that, Quince Florentz will be out of my life as quickly as he came into it.

"What are you thinking about?" he asks, squeezing my hand.

"About what will happen after I find my birth parents," I say, trying to be as vague as possible while still telling the truth.

"We'll find them. Tonight. I just know it," he assures me.

"We have a better chance now that I know where I'm going," I say, keeping my voice light.

"You do? Great! Lead the way, Eevee."

We walk around the Reflecting Pool to the path Folsom and I had walked on only a few weeks ago, back before I knew Quince was also fae, before I had told Maggie and Cam, before I knew my fists could erupt into flames or that I could sense the emotions of animals.

It's been a long September.

A question I keep forgetting to ask Quince sneaks into my thoughts. I look over at him. His face in profile is all sharp edges, his mischievous nature obscured by the darkness around us. He'd look almost regal, if it weren't for the red flannel pajamas.

"What are the other rules?" I ask as we walk.

I must have interrupted his thoughts this time, because his forehead crinkles as he looks at me.

"The fae rules? You said the number one rule is that fae can't lie, implying there are other rules. What are the others?"

We reach a fork in the path and I point to show him which way to follow.

"There are lots of rules. But three major ones."

"The number three again," I comment.

He nods. "I told you, fae like things in threes."

"So what are they?"

"The first one you know already."

"Right," I say. "Fae can't tell lies. And the others?"

"The second is your true name, given at birth, is sacred. Share it only with those you trust, because other fae can have sway over you if they know it. And the third major fae rule is, when in Elfaeme, if it looks human, it isn't fae."

Two thoughts war for my attention at this. First, that I have no idea what my true name is. The only name I know is the one given to me by my parents. I can't imagine being named anything other than Evelyn Gray Acker. The thought of being called something else is strange to me, so I push it aside. The second thought: now I know how that tree spirit fae knew Maggie and Cam were human, not fae. Without any markings, or wings, or leaves growing in place of hair, or any other fae-like feature, they stuck out. They looked human, because they are.

"Is this the tree?" Quince asks for the eleventh time since we arrived. This time, though, he's right. He laughs. "Okay, by your excited nodding, I'll take that as a yes. So, where do we go from here?"

I place my hands on his shoulders, turning him. The feathers of his wings brush against my hands as his shoulders shift.

"The moonstones! We've made it, Eevee!"

We both rush through the glade of trees toward the moonstones. In the dark, they are like boulder-sized nightlights, their glow as soft and flickering as a candle's.

"Which one?" he asks when we reach the grassy clearing in the middle of them all. Spinning to look at them, he says, "That tiny one? Or maybe this one that's kind of shaped like a camel's hump? What does the map say?"

"It didn't say anyth-" I start to say, but a glance at the map stops me. One of the moonstones on the map now has a dark red X over it.

I'm about to share this with Quince when a white-as-bones hand snatches the map from me.

"Hey!" I shout in surprise, turning to grab it back.

I freeze mid-turn and feel the blood draining from my face.

The white-as-bones hand is attached to a fae woman with a humanoid upper body and the lower half of a spider. Her mouth opens in what I think is meant to be a grin, revealing two rows of sharpened teeth below a flat nose and eight black eyes.

"Yes?" she says lazily, raising the map just out of my reach, which isn't hard. She's tall, her spider body easily the size of a Volkswagen Beetle.

My pithy retort dies on my lips.

"Eevee, we gotta get out of here!"

Quince's voice in my ear is urgent, scared.

"What's the rush?" the spider lady asks, scuttling a few steps closer. My stomach writhes–a smell of rotting flesh rolls off her, like she sprayed herself with the scent of death.

"Yes, the fun is just beginning," another voice adds. A man with a poison green mushroom on his head in place of hair strides out of the trees, his mouth open in an unnaturally wide smile. He plucks one of the mushrooms growing on his forearm and twirls it in his fingers before popping it in his mouth and chewing.

"Eevee, think of home. Now! I'll meet you there!"

Spider lady and mushroom guy lunge toward us and I close my eyes, not caring if Quince will make fun of me for it later.

I've never been happier to see Slinky stalking across the grass than I am right now.

"That was close," I breathe. "Wasn't it? Quince?"

I whirl around. Aside from Slinky, I'm alone in the yard. "Shit," I whisper. He's traveled between realms too much today–he's stuck in the fae realm. Why didn't I grab him when I had the chance? "Shit, shit, shit."

Slinky meows and cocks his head at me in confusion. "Not you," I mutter. My hands are shaking and sweaty. I don't want to go back, but I have to.

"Tell mom and dad I love them," I say to Slinky before disappearing.

"Get off me!" I hear Quince grunt from off to my left. As I turn to face him, something tears at my sweatshirt, ripping a hole in the sleeve and slicing the top of my arm from elbow to wrist.

I cry out in pain and grab at my arm, feeling woozy and trying not to look at it. I hate the sight and sweet, metallic smell of blood. My attacker, a fae with orb-like, glowing eyes and dragonfly wings, raises his talon-tipped fingers for another strike.

"Eevee, I said to get out of here!" Quince says. His voice is strained and breathy, like he's being choked. I don't dare look away from talon-fingers though.

"I came back, I couldn't leave you here! I thought you were going to follow me!"

"He was occupied." The lazy voice of the spider lady comes from right behind me. All the hairs on my neck stand on end. I look down at my hands, one clutching my bleeding arm and the other clenched in a tight fist. Neither of them have any flame on them to speak of, not even a little flicker. "Why don't you work when I want you to?" I hiss to them. The hand of the arm that's been wounded is going numb and tingly. I can feel my blood dripping, hot, through my fingers to the ground, and I look away again, feeling dizzy.

Talon fingers steps toward me and instinctively I step back. The white hands of the spider lady descend, wrap around my throat, and two sets of hands at the end of black, hairy spider legs, pin my arms and legs. I try to cry out, to struggle, but the hands on my throat tighten and colored spots dance across my vision.

Off to my left I can hear muffled shouts from Quince and the sounds of a scuffle, followed by a horrific crunch of bones snapping, then silence.

My thoughts are sluggish. Is Quince dead? Will I be dead soon, too? My heart races erratically, trying in vain to pump oxygen to my body.

I've never blacked out before, but I think I'm about to, when a voice entirely devoid of emotion says, "Enough."

The hands around my throat and body release and I crumple to the ground, watching dimly as the three fae who had attacked us run to different moonstones and disappear.

Our savior bends and picks up the map where the spider lady had dropped it. He stands over me, and I try and tilt my head to look up at him.

A groan distracts me. "Quince!" I croak.

"Your friend will live," the man standing over me says.

"He needs to go to a hospital," I say. "I heard bones break." My voice is still coming out all croaky, like a frog's.

"That can wait."

The relief I'd felt at being rescued is quickly being replaced with irritation. I manage to push myself up to a sitting position with my good arm and glare up at him. "No, it can't. He needs medical attention. Now."

The man's face gazing down at me is stern, commanding. On his forehead, above eyes the color of storm clouds, is a simple, gold circlet.

"And who are you to give orders to the king?" he asks mildly. His voice still lacks any emotion, but his eyes–they don't leave my face.

"Nightglade," I hear Quince say.

So this is Nightglade, king of the Unseelie Court. The king who allows those in his realm to harm humans without any retribution. I raise my chin and meet his gaze.

"Someone who's concerned for her friend's well-being," I say as steadily as I can.

For the first time, I hear the faintest trace of emotion in his voice. "They were right. They were all right. You look just like your mother."

If I had been standing, I think my legs would've given out beneath me. Pieces to the puzzle start clicking together rapidfire in my brain.

The looks I'd gotten from Folsom and the fae at the Mage Stone.

The extra secrecy surrounding my birth parents' identities.

Sean and Shannon's insistence that I wear a mask at the equinox celebration. They knew.

Quince's words from our talk by the Mage Stone. "There was the whole scandal of the Unseelie Queen Maeve up and leaving King Nightglade, but that was before you were born…"

The former Unseelie Queen is my birth mother.

King Nightglade is still staring at my face as if he were looking at a ghost, and though I sense no anger or hatred from his gaze, I fear for my life, knowing now what he, and a good chunk of the fae realm, apparently, had already known about my identity.

I'm Maeve's daughter.

"What?" I ask, uncomfortable under his scrutiny.

He shakes his head. "I'm trying to understand why Maeve would leave me before telling me we were pregnant. Why she would consent to have you raised by humans." One side of his upper lip curls up in a snarl of disgust.

I blink up at him in surprise. He thinks I'm his daughter–his and Maeve's. But the medical records said my birth father has blond hair and green eyes, and Nightglade's hair is gray, his eyes like steel...and the letter from my birth mother, Maeve, and my birth father...my mind swirls.

I'm in even more danger than I had realized.

"You'll have to come with me, of course," he says. "To be trained properly. Living amongst humans," again, the lip snarl, "has certainly done nothing to prepare you for ruling the Unseelie Court."

This is all too much. I focus on the one thing I do know. "My friend needs help. He needs me to bring him to a hospital."

"A human hospital?" Nightglade's eyes narrow. "I won't allow it. Not even for Gerald's son."

Crap on a stick, of course he knows who Quince is, Quince looks just like his dad.

"I insist you come with me. We have much to discuss."

The part of me which hates being told what to do rises up, giving me a small, molecule-sized bubble of courage. I seize it.

"No." I scooch sideways, away from Nightglade, my hands scrabbling around, searching for Quince.

Nightglade's exterior is calm, but his jaw tightens. "I just saved your life, and the life of your friend. You are in my debt."

"I'll send you flowers."

I keep my eyes open this time, watching as Nightglade's face contorts with anger, then disappears.

Slinky hisses when we appear next to him. I don't know what bones Quince has broken, but he's deathly pale and he doesn't get up when I do. His eyes flutter, and he collapses next to me.

I start running toward the house. "Mom! Dad! Help!"

Chapter 31

Fae Can't Lie

Fae rule number one: fae can't tell lies. So when my parents ask me, point blank, why Quince Florentz has fainted in our backyard due to injuries, I tell them the truth.

There's silence from both of them. Images of me in a straitjacket dance through my head as I wait for them to say something, anything.

After what seems like twenty agonizing minutes (but was probably closer to twenty seconds), dad says, "I'll see if I can get that young man up and moving. We should get him to the hospital."

"His parents should know," mom says. "Eevee?"

"I'll get his mom's number from his phone," I say, rushing after dad.

Relief floods me at their practical response. It's just like my parents to take a bombshell like, "I'm fae, my birth mom used to be Queen of one of the fae Courts, oh, and while searching for her my friend and I were attacked (not for the first time) and he's lying hurt in our yard" and focus on what needs to get done.

Dad's helping Quince up when I get to them. Quince hands me his phone and I punch the numbers into mine.

When I get back inside, mom is shooing a curious Jess back upstairs.

"Eevee, good. You have the number?"

I give Myska's number to her and shift from the balls of my feet to my heels as she dials.

"Go with your dad," she mouths to me.

"Are you sure?" I ask, already backing away toward the garage.

"Yes, I'm su–oh, hello, is this Quince's mom?"

I dash out to the garage and flag down my dad. He stops backing the car out and I clamber into the back seat with Quince.

"Mom said I can come."

He nods. "Probably for the best. We should get that arm of yours looked at, too, in case of infection."

Neither he nor I mention the creature which gave me the possibly infected scratch.

At my side, Quince is silent.

While dad drives, I watch out the window. Now I've had a chance to sit, the adrenaline is seeping out of me, replaced with exhaustion and throbbing pain in my right arm.

"I didn't say anything about you to them," I whisper as we pull into the emergency room parking lot. "Just so you know."

I don't know if he's heard me. If he does, he isn't responding.

His parents meet us at the check-in desk. With no mask to shield my identity as Maeve's daughter, I'm not surprised at the terrified stares they give me when we walk over to them.

"Come with me, Quince," Myska says. She hovers over him as a nurse checks them in. Dad extends a hand to Jerry, who ignores it, still staring at me with a look that's hardening from fear to anger.

"Stay away from my son," he says, his voice cold. The good-natured man I'd met at the equinox celebration is gone. He turns on his heels and marches down the hall after Quince and Myska.

Dad's hand falls to his side and he frowns. "Well, that was rude."

"He's just scared," I mumble. "They know who I am, who my birth mother is."

"Politics," my dad scoffs. "I don't like it in either realm."

Warm appreciation for my dad fills me. I give him a one-armed hug.

"Thank you for not freaking out about everything," I whisper.

"Oh, I'm freaking out," he admits. "My insides have been doing flips ever since you burst into our room with a bloody arm. But I'll be okay. Now," he waves to a nurse and indicates my red-soaked sleeve, "let's get this arm taken care of. One problem at a time."

*****

If I thought I had been miserable after Damian had broken up with me back in August, it's nothing compared to how I've felt since last Thursday night.

I don't know why Nightglade hasn't pursued me, but he's been in my nightmares every night. Not even coffee can help make up for all the interrupted sleep I've had.

What's worse is I haven't been able to talk to Quince about any of it. Mom had me stay home from school last Friday. She told the school office I was sick. I certainly felt sick; I slept all day while my siblings were at school, waking up briefly to take pain meds for my arm, which ached horribly.

By the time Monday rolled around, it was clear from the fifty unread messages I'd left in Quince's inbox that he wasn't checking his messages.

Which is why, early on a Monday morning, I'm standing by his locker, my third cup of coffee for the morning (I had my first two at home before catching the bus) clutched in my hands, fielding dirty looks from Laura while I wait for Quince to arrive.

The warning bell rings. Still no Quince. I finish the last of my coffee, wishing he'd get here so I could make sure he's okay, that we're okay.

As the final bell rings, I slip into my desk for first period, more worried than ever. What if he was more hurt than I had thought? What if he's in the hospital still, on life support or something?

At lunch my mood is so black I expect rain clouds to form over me any minute.

"He's probably just taking the day off to heal," Maggie says as she munches on a limp fry. "I was gone from school for like a week after I got my tonsils out. Hey, Jim!" She waves him over and he sits across from her, next to Cam. "We need to coordinate Homecoming plans still, all of us. We can catch Quince up later. Cam, you talked to your parents about holding a table for us at their brewery, right?"

Cam's parents' brewery, Beer on the Hill, doesn't serve food other than pretzels, but every Friday and Saturday they rotate through different food trucks. This Saturday it will be Tank'o'Tacos, famous for their deep fried tacos. Eating greasy food while wearing fancy clothes may seem like a recipe for disaster, but we like to live on the edge. Besides, those tacos are worth it.

They chat away about Homecoming and I try to catch Jim's eye. He has to know something about what's going on with Quince, they had a musical rehearsal on Saturday that I'm sure Quince wouldn't have missed.

"Eevee, can you ask Quince what time works for him to meet for dinner when you see him?" Maggie asks.

Right. I told her and Cam about Thursday night, of course, but I had left out the silent treatment I received from Quince during the car ride to the hospital and the total lack of communication I've had with him since the incident.

Maybe I can corner Jim during study hall.

Maggie's still looking at me, expecting a response, so I nod, and she, Cam, and Jim resume their Homecoming talk.

Unfortunately, Jim knows even less about Quince's whereabouts than I do.

"He wasn't at rehearsal," he whispers to me. We both peer over to the checkout desk to make sure Mr. Abscons is occupied. He's been on a "silent study time" kick lately. Some of the students have started a petition to have him replaced. I signed it five times already with five different names.

"Where was he?" I whisper back.

"Dunno. He was a no-call, no-show. Which is weird for him. Quince rarely misses rehearsal, and when he has to be gone, he lets Ms. Wilson know weeks in advance. It's strange."

"And you haven't heard from him at all?"

Mr. Abscons glares at us. There's no way he can actually hear us whispering from all the way across the room. We must look like we're doing something suspicious. Or he just hates me. I smacked his face when I opened the door to the library today. How was I supposed to know he was standing on the other side taping up a "Silence is Golden" sign?

When a student raises his hand for help and Mr. Abscons gets up with an audible sigh, I lean over to Jim. "Not even a text from him or anything?"

"No," Jim says, keeping his eyes on the textbook in front of him. "Sorry, Eevee."

On the bus ride home I check my messages again. Quince still hasn't read them, much less responded.

My blood runs cold. What if he can't read them? What if he's somewhere with no cell service, like the fae realm?

Amelia sits next to me, an "I've-got-gossip-but-I-don't-know-if-you'll-like-it" look on her face.

"What?" I ask, sounding grumpier than I had intended.

"You haven't heard then?"

"Obviously not, since I asked what."

She gnaws on her cinnamon gum.

"Spill it, Ames."

"It's about-" she lowers her voice. "Quince."

"I figured."

"You really don't know?"

I shake my head and watch her wind her finger around a wavy tendril of hair.

"Ms. Wilson gave his part in the musical to another kid. She came in to my last hour and pulled the guy out, he's a freshman like me, and when he came back in that's all he could talk about."

"Good for him," I say. My whole body is numb.

"Some people are saying it's because Quince switched schools. Did you know about that?"

"No," I say, watching cars drive by us on the road, "I didn't."

Chapter 32

The Day of the Homecoming Dance

There's something soothing about the monotonous work of washing dishes while Mike's 80's playlist blares in the background. I don't think he's changed the playlist since the 80's, honestly. Listening to the same songs I hear every weekend, I can focus on the scalding water, and the effort of scraping pans, instead of on the fact that today is October 6th, the day of the Homecoming Dance, and I haven't heard from or seen Quince since the night I asked him to the dance and we were attacked.

I'm not harboring any delusions. I've resigned myself to the fact I have no date for tonight. I'd skip it altogether if it weren't for Maggie and Cam.

Maggie had a long rant about this being our last Homecoming together, and Cam, ever practical, pointed out that they weren't going with anybody either, so we could both go solo together. They even sweetly offered to take me, as a friend, if that would get me to go.

At that point, I would've felt like a colossal jerk if I had said no.

"It'll still be fun," Maggie had said, squeezing me with the force of a trash compactor. "You'll see."

When the brunch rush at Gramp's slows to a trickle, Harriet swoops into the kitchen to send people home.

"There's lots of dishes to do," I say when Harriet gets to me.

"Homecoming Dance is tonight, isn't it?" she asks. "Big night, especially for a senior like yourself."

"I'm just going with friends. It won't take me long to get ready." I scrub at the plate in my hands though there's no reason to; it's been clean for a minute now.

"Go," Harriet says in her "no nonsense" voice. "I've got Robby coming in soon anyway, and I don't need two dishwashers on the clock."

"Fine," I grumble, peeling off my plastic apron and grabbing the food scraps I'd saved for Scamp. He hadn't been around last weekend at all, but I'm hoping to see his grumpy face today.

I hold out the napkin of food like an offering. "Scamp! Breakfast!"

No haughty tail flick appears in my vision. Just like last weekend, I deposit the scraps by the dumpster I usually see Scamp run to and head toward my car.

I hope he's okay. He seems scrappy, but he lives outdoors. For all I know, he's been run over or eaten. I drown out my worry for Scamp with music so loud my ears ring as I drive home.

*****

Not even my peppiest playlist lifts my mood. I sit in my car in Maggie's driveway, music blaring, three dresses in my backseat. Two are the ones from Sean and Shannon. The third is a red clearance rack dress I had bought with Maggie and Cam this week when they had insisted on taking me shopping at the Hermantown Mall.

I don't want to wear the dress Sean and Shannon sent me. It makes me think of Quince and how I'll never see him again, because he's somewhere in the fae realm and I'm here in Duluth making plans for my future as a vet tech. Mom and dad helped me get my applications sent out yesterday. I think they're relieved that even though I'm fae I'm still planning on getting a "proper education" and a "sensible job" (their words, as we were filling out the applications together). But Maggie had demanded I bring the dresses as options, and because she wants to see them. I glance at the dresses through my rearview mirror, my stomach tightening into knots.

I can't do this.

I take the dresses from Sean and Shannon and dash to the back of Maggie's house, out of the view of the street, before Maggie or anyone else sees me. Positioning myself behind the bushes on the side of her house, I close my eyes.

Shifting between realms may come as second nature to me now, but it's still awe-inspiring to open my eyes on a brand-new landscape compared to what I'd seen the moment before. The dizziness and vertigo fades quickly as I gaze up at the imposing, ice-covered walls of Sean and Shannon's mansion. Gathering the dresses up in my arms before they get any snow on them, I march up to the door and knock.

"Eevee," Sean says, the door cracked open just enough to reveal one of his icy blue eyes and the streak of black hair falling across the right side of his face. "What a surprise. We weren't expecting company."

"Can I come in?" I ask, holding up the dresses.

"Who's at the door?" I hear Shannon call.

"It's Eevee!" Sean calls back. He opens the door just enough to let me in and gestures for me to come inside. As I step through the doorway, I catch him peeking around me at the snow-covered path.

He strides over to the window once I'm inside and pulls the heavy velvet curtains shut, enveloping us in darkness.

Shannon walks into the expansive entryway, a candle in hand. It illuminates his face, giving his skin a ghostly glow. "What brings you here, Eevee? Is there something wrong with the dress we lent you?"

"No, nothing's wrong with the dress. With either of them."

"I don't understand, then," Shannon says, a puzzled look on his face. "Why are you here if the dresses are satisfactory?"

"I don't want them anymore," I say, holding them out. Neither of the twins move to take them.

"But what about your soirée?" Shannon asks. "Isn't that tonight? Or did it already happen? We've been working on something and tend to lose track of time. In fact, it's just like this one time when Sean-"

"It's tonight," I interrupt hastily at the murderous look on Sean's face. "I just don't need it. I have another dress."

"Oh." Shannon's face falls. I thrust the dresses into his arms.

"Thank you, though. It was nice of you to let me borrow these."

I get ready to leave, close my eyes, start to think of Maggie's house, then stop.

"Why didn't you tell me?" I open my eyes, searching their faces for guilt or unease, but their faces are as blank as if they were wearing masks.

"Tell you what?" Sean asks, all innocence with sharp edges that could cut steel.

"About who my birth mother is. You knew. You both knew, the moment you saw me." I jab my finger at them accusingly, my voice rising. "It would have been helpful to have known about her so I wouldn't have put myself and Quince in danger. Now he's gone, I haven't heard from him in over a week since we were attacked."

This gets an eyebrow raise from both of them.

"Oh, yes, we were attacked by fae when we traveled to the In Between last week. And then we were saved by none other than Nightglade-"

Their eyebrows practically disappear into their hairlines at this point.

"-and now I can't sleep without having nightmares about that night!"

Sean and Shannon exchange a look.

"We like our secrets, Eevee," Sean answers. I huff and don't try to hide my eye roll.

"Wear it," Shannon says, handing me back the dress they had sent. "It really will look beautiful on you."

"I don't care about looking beautiful," I say, angry tears forming in the corners of my eyes. "I just want to know that Quince is okay." I cross my arms, refusing to take it. To my extreme annoyance, Shannon drapes it over my shoulder.

"Take it," he says.

Sean steps forward, his expression inscrutable. "Trust us," he whispers, his breath icy cold on my cheek.

I snort. "Trust you? Never in a million years."

Sean and Shannon grin at each other. "She's smart," Shannon says. "I wouldn't trust us either if I were her."

"Don't trust us then," Sean says. "But wear the dress. Consider it our way of apologizing for not being candid with you from the start."

"Old habits and all," Shannon says with a shrug of his shoulders.

"And keeping secrets is one of our oldest habits." Sean glances at the door, his eyes narrowed. "Now go. Enjoy your dance, Eevee."

"Don't worry about returning the dress," Shannon says. "We know where you live."

I think he meant to be reassuring, but I'm not so sure I like the idea of more packages, or worse, visits, from Sean and Shannon.

"Go," Sean says again, his voice like ice, so I close my eyes and leave before they drape any more articles of clothing on me.

Chapter 33

A Night of Surprises

One dress lighter, I return to the bushes outside Maggie's house.

"Hey, E."

I look up to see Maggie's brother, Zach, grinning down at me through the open window. "Whatcha doing in mom's azaleas? Not spying on me again, are you? I thought that eighth grade crush you had on me was behind you?"

My cheeks have got to be at least as pink as the azaleas I'm crouching next to.

"It is–I'm not–it's just–"

He laughs. "Get on inside. Maggie's wondering what happened to you. She saw your car in the driveway, but when you didn't come in or answer your phone she started pacing around and pulling her hair out."

As if in response, my phone starts dinging with all the messages I'd missed in the few minutes I'd spent in the fae realm.

Cheeks still burning, I make my way to the front door, Zach's chuckles following me as I walk.

"Are you okay? Where did you go? Oh my god that dress is absolutely perfect why the hell did you ever bother letting us force you into buying that red one?"

"Maggie, breathe," I say, feeling a little tension leave my shoulders at the sight of my friends.

I step inside and Maggie beckons excitedly to me, so I follow her up to her room. As we pass Zach's room, I can still hear him chuckling.

Cam is already dressed, wearing black slacks and a green polo.

"You've dyed your hair to match your shirt!" I squeal, dropping my dress on Maggie's bed.

Cam smiles, running their fingers through their hair. "It's not too tacky?"

"It's perfect," I assure them. "You look great."

Maggie hands me a can of Winter's Dream. "You found more?" I ask Cam, hugging them and opening it. My worry for Quince is still there, but I feel it settling, moving lower, replaced by a hesitantly happy sensation.

The afternoon passes quickly. Maggie does something to my hair so it looks sleek and styled. I'm careful as I change into my dress; the scratch on my arm isn't fully healed, and sometimes with movement it'll start bleeding. The last thing I want to do is get blood (real blood) over a dress I've borrowed from Sean and Shannon.

"I think I have...yes!" Maggie closes the jewelry box she'd been rummaging through with a snap. "Here!" She clips a delicate silver butterfly to the side of my head. "This goes perfectly with your dress, don't you think?"

"I look like I'm ready for Cinderella's ball, not Homecoming," I laugh.

"You'll definitely be the best dressed," Cam remarks.

"Oh, who cares about that?" I say, throwing my arms around them both. "I'd go in a trash bag if I could go with you guys."

The doorbell rings. "And Jim," Maggie says, adjusting her pink sequined dress and running to the door.

"I don't know if I'd go in a trash bag for him," I call after her. Cam and I gather up our stuff and head downstairs.

"What, I'm not worthy of trash bag fashion?" Jim asks me. He can't take his eyes off Maggie, who is slipping her shoes on, a big grin on her face.

"Jury's out. It takes a certain kind of person to pull it off."

"Well, I'm willing to try it," he says, tugging at his collar. "It's got to be more comfortable than wearing a tie."

We all pile into Jim's car and head to Beer on the Hill. Maggie and I chant "tacos, tacos!" in the backseat while Cam turns up the music to drown us out.

The moment is almost perfect.

I try to ignore the empty seat between me and Maggie where Quince should be.

*****

"Did they change the taco recipe?" I ask, nearly gagging on my deep fried taco.

"I don't think so," Cam says. They take a bite of their taco, followed by another. "No, good as ever!" they say around a mouthful of tortilla and taco meat.

My stomach growls. I nibble on the chips, which seem fine, and give my tacos to Maggie, thinking back on the one time I'd had dinner with Quince. He had ordered a veggie burger. Maybe fae can't eat meat? It would explain why mom's cooking has tasted weird to me the last few weeks.

"Are you sure that's all you want?" Maggie asks, pointing at the chips and salsa. I nod glumly, and she shrugs. "Suit yourself."

Cam goes up to the truck and brings back more chips and salsa. "Perks of being the brewery owners' kid," they say.

We all wave to their parents, who are behind the counter filling flights of beers for a long line of customers.

At school, the line to be let in to the dance is out the door, which is decorated with so many blue and yellow balloons I'm surprised the school isn't floating away.

"Everyone have their tickets?" Maggie asks as she herds us all toward the back of the line.

"We were supposed to get tickets?" I ask.

She elbows me.

"Yes, I have my ticket," I say, rubbing my side.

The line moves so slowly I start to wonder if we'll even make it inside before the dance ends.

"Hey, no cutting the line!" someone shouts from behind us.

I turn to see who the line cutter is and come face-to-face with Quince "where-the-hell-has-he-been-all-week" Florentz, dressed to impress in gray pants and a dark blue button-up.

"He's with us!" Maggie shouts, glaring at the grumbling kids behind us. She pulls Cam and Jim forward, linking arms with them, and leaving a space in line next to me. Quince takes it and we shuffle forward.

I can't take my eyes off him. How did he get here? When did he get here? Do his parents know where he is?

He catches me staring at him and strikes a goofy pose. "Take a picture, it'll last longer."

I want to punch him, but considering his arm is in a cast, I don't.

"What are you doing here?" I ask out of the corner of my mouth.

He nods toward the school. "It's the night of the Homecoming Dance."

"Yes, but-"

"You asked me to go with you."

"Yes, but-"

"So here I am."

"Yes, but how?" I ask before he can interrupt me again. "I haven't heard from you, you've been replaced in the musical, and people are saying your parents have taken you out of Duluth High."

"All true," he admits.

"I've spent this whole week and a half worried sick about you, about that night, thinking you were angry with me or something after that car ride to the hospital-"

"I'm sorry," he says. I blink up at the sky, willing my stupid tears to go away before they mess up the makeup that took Cam almost an hour to perfect. "I would've messaged you if I could."

"You were there, weren't you?" I ask quietly, still staring at the sky. It's got streaks of pink in it, with the sunset.

"Yes," he says. "And I've been going crazy all week, wanting to talk to you but not being able to."

We reach the ticket table. I hand them my ticket and Quince purchases one for himself. We join up with Maggie, Cam, and Jim, who are in a group near the back of the cafeteria, which has, if possible, even more balloons decorating it than were out front. I thought the theme was a night in Paris?

"The helium company must be making bank on this dance," I mutter. Behind all the balloons, I spot a cardboard cutout of the Eiffel Tower pasted up on the wall.

Jim stares at us as we approach. "Quince. Dude, where-"

"Hey, Jim," Quince says, an overly jovial expression plastered on his face. He claps Jim on the shoulders. "How you been?"

Jim stares pointedly at Quince's arm. "Better than you, apparently. What happened?"

"This and that." Quince shrugs the shoulder of his good arm.

"Jim, I love this song," Maggie says at a look from me. Jim looks like he'd like to stay and talk, but lets Maggie tug him to the center of the dance floor.

"Oh, look, there's Levi from Anime Club. I wonder how he's doing?" Cam says before bolting.

Quince is shaking with laughter. "Your friends aren't exactly subtle."

"No, but that's okay, neither am I."

His smile widens when he looks down at me. "You're wearing the dress."

"Sean and Shannon left me no choice," I say, uncomfortable under Quince's intense gaze. "And when Maggie saw it, she practically threw me into it."

"They told me you'd be wearing it," Quince says, leading me to the dance floor.

"You've seen them?"

"They are currently employing their best deceptive techniques to keep my parents occupied tonight so I could come."

He twirls me, then pulls me in toward him. I spin, coming to a stop when my body hits his. My ear rests on his chest, and I can hear the rapid beating of his heart.

"I thought you were mad at me," I whisper.

He wraps his arm around me. "Why would you think that?"

"The car ride."

Another spin. The dance floor is crowded. Blurred images of dancers wearing all colors pass by my vision.

"What would you say if I told you I didn't remember the car ride?" Quince asks me a few dances later when I'm back in his arms.

I look up into his dark eyes, so serious without their playful sparkle. "I'd say you're lying."

"Fae can't tell lies."

"You're not eighteen yet, you're not bound by the rules. So, technically, you can lie."

"But I'm not."

"How do I know you're telling the truth?"

He goes still, a line deepening between his eyes. "Because I wouldn't lie to you, Eevee."

I want to believe him. I wish I did. "Let's say you're telling the truth-"

"I am."

"What is the last thing you remember?"

He's about to answer when someone taps him on the shoulder.

"What the hell, Quince?"

We pull apart and I see Laura, arms crossed, a murderous expression on her plucked-eyebrows, perfectly-lipsticked face. She's flanked by two other girls who I recognize from the night at Northern Creamery.

Laura launches into a tirade about the show and him leaving them in the lurch and leading her on.

"And then I hear you're at the dance tonight with her!"

She points a sparkly, manicured finger at me, and her friends transfer their angry looks from Quince to me. I try to slip away, to go find Maggie or Cam, but Quince grips my hand so tightly I worry about losing circulation to my fingers.

We are saved from the rest of the rant when Laura's date shows up.

Quince and I exchange a "you-can't-make-this-shit-up" look.

Her date is none other than Glen, the troll-like football player.

"There you are," Glen says, handing a fuming Laura a plastic cup filled to the brim with punch. "I was wondering where you'd gone." He nods to Quince. "Heard you switched schools."

"I'm back for the night," Quince replies while I try and choke down my giggles.

Glen frowns at me. "What's so funny?"

"Nothing."

Quince takes a deep breath. "Listen, Glen, there's something I wanted to ask you-"

I'm laughing so hard I can't breathe as I pull Quince away.

"What?" Glen calls after us, his face contorted in pure confusion.

"Quince, no!" I protest when he tries to go back to Glen.

"Wanna dance?" Quince shouts, ignoring me.

"What'd you say?" Glen calls, cupping his hands around his mouth.

I keep tugging Quince along with me until Glen and Laura are out of sight.

"Hey, you promised me a dance with him," Quince protests.

"You kidding?" I tease. "I can't let you dance with him. He probably has killer dance moves and you'd be gone all night."

"Ah, didn't take you for the jealous type," he says.

We exit the cafeteria and meander down one of the adjacent halls filled with–what else?–more balloons.

"I'm not," I say. "But, who knows when I'll see you again?" I raise my arm to adjust the butterfly in my hair before it falls out, keeping my face turned toward the balloons on my left.

Quince runs a finger along the scab on my right arm.

"You're bleeding a little," he says, the laughter gone from his voice.

"Crap." I rummage through my purse and pull out a tissue, dabbing at my arm. "I really don't want to return a bloody dress."

"Something tells me Sean and Shannon know how to get blood out of clothing," Quince says.

We turn the corner. Bass music thrums through the halls. "I never did thank you for coming back for me," he adds in a quiet voice.

"It was nothing," I mumble, throwing away the tissue in a nearby trash can.

"It was not nothing," he insists, his fingers circling my wrist. I look down at his hand, which is surprisingly cool considering how humid it is in the building with all the bodies and the dancing. "Thank you."

I don't look up at his face because I'm worried if I do I'll see in his eyes what I hear in his voice.

That this is goodbye.

"You're welcome," I say to my feet.

We're both silent.

"You really don't remember the car ride to the hospital?" I ask my shoes.

"Not a second of it," he says. "The last thing I remember is Nightglade appearing, then all of a sudden I'm in a hospital in Duluth and mom and dad are talking about relocating to Elfaeme to get me away from 'that girl' because she means trouble."

"I'm that girl," I say, my mouth twisting. It isn't fair. I can't control who my birth mother is, or the fact that Nightglade thinks I'm his daughter.

"Want to fill me in on what happened when Nightglade showed up?" Quince asks. "That part's a little fuzzy for me."

Mr. Abscons, who apparently got roped into helping chaperone the dance, is glowering at us, all beady-eyed and pinch-faced.

I place my hand on Quince's elbow and lead him out the doors, waving to Cam, who gives us a crinkle-eyed grin before continuing their conversation with a guy who must be Levi from Anime Club.

We make our way through the balloon-infested entrance and out onto the sidewalk. The air has cooled a lot since we arrived.

We sit down at a bench and I rub my arms to stay warm as I tell Quince why his parents think I'm trouble.

He knows the contents of my birth parents' letter almost as well as I do, so when I get to the point in the story where I had realized Nightglade thinks I'm his daughter, Quince gets a pensive look on his face.

"This is bad, Eevee," he says.

"I know," I say miserably.

"I get why my parents are so freaked now," he says. "Nightglade resented when my dad left the Unseelie Court to be with my mom. He's left us alone all these years, but if he thinks my family has anything to do with you or Maeve…"

"I'm so sorry for getting you into this mess."

At this, he shakes his head. "You didn't do anything. I'm the one who reached out to you, remember? Back in the principal's office with old Jeeves?"

"Jives," I say, smiling despite myself. "Yeah, I remember. I still feel awful, though, I-"

He's looking at his phone, but puts it away when I stop speaking.

"Sorry, go on. You were telling me how awful you've been for me?"

This bothers me, because it's true. "Yes, I am!" I point at his broken arm.

"It'll heal."

"And you're not in the musical anymore. You love theater."

He's gazing steadily at me now. "There will be other plays."

"And your parents took you out of school."

I watch his gaze drop to his lap. "That part does suck."

"Jim and Laura have missed you this week." I want to say "and so have I," but I'm not ready to take that plunge, not when a relationship across realms is all we'd have to look forward to for now. That's if he has any interest in seeing me after tonight's obligations are over.

"They have, huh?" He checks his phone again.

"You have to go." It's a statement, not a question, but he nods.

"I don't know how long Sean and Shannon can distract my parents, but I don't want to risk it. If they find out I'm gone they might just lock me in a tower like Rapunzel."

"I don't know, you could totally rock the long-haired look," I tease him.

He must really be worried because his lips barely twitch into the smallest of smiles.

"There you are!" Maggie dashes over to us, dragging Jim behind her. They're followed by Cam, who is sipping a cup of punch. "It's been an hour. We're heading back to my place to hang. You ready?"

Cam, who's known me since second grade and can read my face like a book, lowers their cup and says, "We've interrupted something."

Maggie's hand flies to her mouth and her eyes take on a devilish twinkle as she looks from me to Quince. "Quince, you one-armed player! Alright, meet us at my house when you can."

Jim waves and rushes to catch up to Maggie, who is already standing by his car.

"You can go with them," Quince says, his eyes not meeting mine. "I should go anyway."

"It's fine. I'll get there when I get there."

Sweaty teens with fancy clothes walk by, chatting. I wonder where Amelia is tonight. I know she's here somewhere with her group of friends and shoulders guy.

"I can't head back from here," Quince says. "Too many people."

"Right." I stand. "Where'd you appear earlier?"

"The same spot in the park where we'd been when I took you to Sean and Shannon's."

"I'll walk you there."

"And then?"

He's looking up at me from where he sits on the bench.

"And then we say goodbye, I guess."

I can tell he's not satisfied with my answer, but he stands and falls into step beside me.

"You're not letting this stop you, are you?" he asks when the noise from the crowd is a low hum behind us.

"What do you mean?"

He gestures to his broken arm. "This. My parents' reaction. You're not letting it stop you, right? You're still going to follow that last clue and find your birth parents, I hope."

"I don't know."

I feel his hand slip into mine and let him pull me to a halt. "Don't let this stop you. Please. I'd feel like the worst person in the world if you didn't go any further because of me."

"Let's keep walking." I extricate my hand from his.

"Eevee." He hurries to catch up. "You had so many questions for your birth parents."

"That was before I knew how much danger I'd be in–how much danger I'd put my friends and family and the people I care about in–by trying to find out those answers."

The silence is deafening to me, so I babble on about how Cam thinks I should just forget it all, my birth parents, the fae realm, everything, and focus on the family I've got. I tell him how Maggie disagrees, how she thinks I deserve to know the answers from my birth parents themselves. How Cam gave me that drawing of my parents to remind me of what I've got, and how Maggie has been treating the whole situation like an episode on a crime show or like an article she's trying to write.

We pass the soccer fields, and he listens as I share how my parents don't really know how to react about me being fae and prefer to pretend they don't know, and how I get the feeling they'd rather I stay away from Elfaeme for my own safety. As I'm finishing, we turn onto the path into the grove of trees until we're hidden from view.

Quince slows to a stop. "What do you want?"

"What?" I ask, frowning up at him.

"You. Eevee. Evelyn Acker. I've heard what Cam thinks, and Maggie, and your parents. What do you want?"

What *do* I want? Ever since I was a kid and could understand that my parents were not the same people who were responsible for my conception, I've wanted to know more about those people, at least enough to get some questions answered.

When I found out my birth parents were fae this year, that list of questions only grew.

But so did the danger.

Quince's cast, the scab on my arm, they're physical reminders of the kind of danger that will follow me if I continue to try and find Maeve, the former Unseelie Queen, my birth mother.

"Here's a question," Quince says when I don't answer. "Fast forward ten, twenty years in the future. Can you see yourself being at peace with the unanswered questions? Or do you think you'd regret not at least trying to get the answers while you could?"

I've always hated these kinds of questions. How am I supposed to know what I'll be like ten or twenty years in the future? I have a hard enough time figuring out what the next year in my life is going to look like. And the question seems to be popping up a lot lately, in college applications and senior interview questions for the yearbook.

"I could live without knowing," I say. I think of my family, my friends, especially Cam and Maggie. I could be happy with that life. They may not be related to me by blood, but my parents, my siblings, they're my family. We're the Ackers, and I know we'll stick together through it all, no matter what.

"So there's your answer," Quince says.

And yet…

I shake my head. "I *could* live without knowing. But I don't want to. I want to know. I want to find Maeve, and whoever my birth father is, and learn more about where I came from."

A corner of his mouth tilts upward and he holds out a hand. "I need to go. Come with me?"

"Your parents will freak if they see me. I've already gotten you into enough trouble," I say, tapping on his cast.

He steps closer, and I look up at him. He's framed by the tree branches above us; stars sparkle in the sky.

"I'll take my chances."

His lips meet mine, and it's dizzying and electrifying, and perfect.

When he pulls away, my head is spinning.

"Quince," I whisper. "I don't-" I frown. "Where are we?"

His grin is sheepish.

"No." I look around. Ancient trees, in late stages of autumn. A circle of moonstones around us. "What have you done?" I whisper.

Chapter 34

In the Clearing

"We need to leave. Now." I grab for Quince's arm, but he sidesteps out of my way.

"I don't want to leave."

I grab for him again, and he runs to the other side of the moonstone shaped like a camel's hump. "Remember what happened last time one of us wanted to travel between realms and the other didn't?"

How can I forget? That night has made frequent appearances in my nightmares lately.

I lower my arms. "Why'd you bring me here, Quince?"

He looks genuinely confused. "You said you want to know."

What I want is to smack my forehead. "I do, but not now. Not tonight."

"Why not?"

I splutter. "You're kidding. Tell me you're joking." Realizing my voice is getting louder, I panic and look around wildly.

"No one else is here," Quince says.

He's right. "Why? Where are they?"

The forest around us feels old and hushed, like an ancient library. None of the fae who had ambushed us can be seen.

"No idea. Not here. Do you remember which moonstone the map had indicated was the right one?"

As if I'm going to tell him. "Quince," I whisper, because even though I can't see anyone, the hairs on my arms are all raised and I have goosebumps dotting my whole body, "just stop for a sec."

He pauses to look at me.

"We should go."

For some reason, he looks hurt, even though it's not his estranged birth parents we've been tracking down.

"If not now, then when, Eevee?"

I don't answer; I don't know.

"They're expecting me at Maggie's," I say. "And you said yourself you don't know how long Sean and Shannon can keep your parents distracted."

"When?" he persists.

"Why is this such a big deal to you?" I burst out in a whisper shout.

"Don't you know?" His voice is low, bruised.

A breeze drifts through the clearing, rustling the grasses and my hair. It's icy cold, one of those late autumn breaths of air which let you know ice and snow is on the way.

"Tonight could be it, Eevee." He leans against the trunk of an enormous oak, looks down at the ground.

I walk to him, maneuvering around the moonstones, careful not to touch any of them with my bare skin.

"What do you mean, tonight could be it?"

His face is stony. "Forget it. If you want to go, we can go."

Now I'm the one evading his hand. "Not until you explain what you mean."

He won't make eye contact with me. A flame of anger flares in my chest.

"I know what this is about."

His eyebrows raise. "You do?"

"Yeah. I do." My jaw is tight, it isn't working properly, so my mouth barely moves when I say, "It's all about the mystery for you."

"It–what?"

"Ever since you saw me in Principal Lowell's office and figured out I was fae. First, there was the mystery of the fae girl you hadn't known about. Then, when you learned about my birth mom's note, the mystery only got more exciting, didn't it? You've been almost more obsessed with figuring out the clues than I've been."

He's shaking his head, laughing, which is like throwing gas on a fire.

"What is so funny?" I explode.

"You really think the reason I've been hanging out with you is because you've got a mysterious past?"

"Isn't it?"

"No!"

My laugh is dry. "Sure."

"Eevee, come on."

"Well, what am I supposed to think, Quince?"

"Oh, I don't know, maybe that I like you, you crazy, Shakespeare-loving weirdo."

"So...but...why bring me here?"

"Because you said you wanted to know."

I take a deep breath. This conversation is getting us nowhere. "I do want to know," I explain as patiently as I'm able. "But not now. I don't want to get you into any more trouble."

His face breaks into a smile tinged with sadness. "Don't worry about me. The longer we stand here arguing, though, the more likely it is my parents will see through whatever it is Sean and Shannon are doing to distract them and figure out I'm gone. So…"

Wordlessly, I point to a moonstone to my left.

"That one? Really?"

His mood has lost all melancholy, his face shining with excitement as he bounds to the stone. "This is it, Eevee! This is the night you meet your birth parents! I can feel it!"

I step up to the stone, lifting one of my eyebrows. "You said something very similar last time. And look how that turned out for us."

"Yes, but this time is different," he insists.

"You're back," croaks a voice I've dreaded hearing every time I've visited Elfaeme.

"Folsom," I mouth to Quince.

His eyes widen.

The frog creature himself sneaks out of the darkness, gnarled staff in hand, and comes to a stop before us. How long had he been watching us, listening to us argue? I don't like the way his round eyes reflect the light of the moon.

He surveys the two of us. "Gerald's son and Maeve's daughter. I'm surprised to see the two of you back here so soon."

Every fiber of my being is screaming at me to run, to get out of here.

"What do you want?" Quince asks shortly.

Folsom tsks with his sticky tongue, though it sounds more like a wet suction cup. "Nothing from you, you bastard son of an Unseelie traitor."

Quince looks ready to pounce. I put a hand on his shoulder to stop him from doing anything rash. The feathers on his wings shake with suppressed rage.

Folsom turns his reflective gaze to me. "I never told him. Remember that."

Before I can ask what he'd never told to whom, Folsom hops onto a moonstone and disappears.

"That amphibious pea-brain!" Quince seethes, kicking at the stone where Folsom had been a moment ago. "You should've let me punch him. It's fae like him, with their elitist, outdated attitudes about the Courts, who make it so hard for the fae to unite as one Court again."

I watch him pace. He's limping a bit after kicking the moonstone so hard.

"Maeve could change that, you know," he says to me when he's calmed down.

"Change what?"

"The system, the Courts. She held a lot of sway when she was the Unseelie Queen. I don't know why she went into hiding after having you, but it can't be because she was a fan of how things were run, right?"

"She was probably scared for her life."

Hope shines on his face, and I realize I have to do it. I have to use my blood (easy enough, as my arm's bleeding again) and touch the moonstone which will take me to my birth parents. Not just for me, but for all fae like Quince and his parents and his friend Mindy who are looked down on and ostracized for who they are and what they represent: a blending of the Seelie and Unseelie Courts.

And hey, maybe I'll get my questions answered, too.

"Okay," I say.

Quince stops pacing. "Okay?"

"Yes. Let's go."

He runs to me and wraps his good arm around my waist, spinning and lifting us both in the air until we're revolving in a slow circle above the canopy.

"You've made my night, Evelyn Acker," he says.

This time, I kiss him. My stomach jumps as we descend, our lips still pressed together; he's much more graceful about flying back down to the ground than I am, at least.

When my feet touch the earth, I still feel like I'm floating.

Without a word, I lead Quince to the moonstone the map had shown me. I touch a finger to a drop of blood on my arm, trying not to look too closely at it or I'll get lightheaded, then, one hand holding tightly to Quince, press the finger to the stone.

At first I don't think it's worked. Maybe I remembered wrong and we have the incorrect stone; it wouldn't be the first time I've forgotten something important.

But then the light rippling beneath the stone's surface dims to a red so dark it's almost black, and our surroundings disappear.

The shock of traveling by moonstone hits me and I stagger, gasping, clutching my stomach. Between moonstone travel and nerves, my insides are a mess.

"We've made it," Quince says with relief, then he whoops. "We've made it, Eevee!"

Even though it's night time, I try to take in everything I can of my surroundings, of the place where my birth parents have lived in hiding for nearly two decades.

My first thought is it's peaceful. I can hear a small creek burbling nearby. I think we're somewhere in Seelie territory; the thick trees here are lush with vegetation and the air is humid, like a summer night in Minnesota.

The trees and flowers look more like what I've seen in pictures and documentaries about rainforests, though. And near the moonstone is a cobblestone path overrun with moss.

Quince is already on the path. I jog to catch up to him.

He's looking ahead, his expression eager. "You know, if Maeve is willing to help, my parents might not care as much that I snuck out tonight," he says.

"I hope so. I don't really want to have to climb any towers to hang out with you."

His hopeful enthusiasm is infectious. I feel a smile spreading on my face as we walk.

Because I know. I know that whatever happens when I meet my birth parents, I'll have done it. I won't look back ten years from now and wonder what would've happened.

We come upon a small cottage, its windows dark.

"They're probably asleep," Quince says. "You ready, Eevee?"

My heart is in my throat and my lungs have stopped working, but I nod.

He waits on the path and I walk the last couple of steps to the door.

Images flood through my head: mom standing up to Principal Lowell for me after I yelled at Mr. Jenkins, dad hugging me in the emergency room, Amelia talking on my bed late at night, Jess snuggled next to me during a murder mystery documentary, Greg and Charlie running by my room making raptor noises. We're the Ackers. And whatever the next few minutes might reveal, I know they'll be here for me through it all.

Cam and Maggie were both right. I've got a great family already. And I deserve to get to the bottom of my mysterious past and have some questions answered if I can.

Quince was right, too. I glance back at him and he smiles encouragingly at me. He may have brought me to the clearing tonight, but I know that if I had said no, we wouldn't be here, in front of my birth parents' cottage.

This was a decision I needed to make for myself.

I raise my hand to the door and knock.

A Note from the Author

Every child of adoption has their own unique story. In fact, my personal adoption story only partially inspired Eevee's.

If you are interested in learning more about adoption, here are some resources you can check out:

- Colombian Influence (podcast)
- *The Primal Wound* by Nancy Verrier
- Children's Home Society of Minnesota/Lutheran Social Services http://www.chlss.org
- National Council For Adoption https://adoptioncouncil.org/

Acknowledgments

First and foremost, this book would not be what it is today without my wonderful friend and editor, Laura Cossette. Laura, your input always pushes me to make my stories and characters better. I don't know what I'd do without you.

I have many other people I'd like to acknowledge, without whom this book would have perhaps never been written.

So, in no particular order...

To my uncle, Wes, who put the idea in my head to write a book about a character who is adopted (like me), but whose birth family isn't human. That idea stuck with me for years until, finally, I wrote it. But the idea came from you, and I am eternally grateful.

To my husband, Ty, and my kids, Gavyn and Chase. You boosted me up when I was stuck, you worked through problems with me, and you were my biggest supporters. Ty, our walks in the woods talking about the book, and your interest in the politics of the fae world, helped me build a more interesting world. And Gavyn and Chase, your imaginations are boundless–thank you for letting me pick your brains when I needed the help.

To the very first folks I entrusted my draft to (aside from Laura)–Jenny, Chris, and Elise. Your input was incredibly valuable, and Eevee would not be who she is without it.

To my friends Megan and Sarah, for managing to show enthusiasm while I chatted your ears off about all things fae, and to Sarah for your quick feedback after I asked for your input on part of the book: thank you. Your excitement for the world of Elfaeme and for Eevee kept me interested in the story, especially during the middle part (always difficult for me to write).

To the real Sean and Shannon, thank you for letting me steal your names (and little bits and pieces of your personalities) so I could make intriguing characters for Quince's cousins. I hope you love how they turned out as much as I do.

To my students (especially those in Poetry Club) who knew about my writing journey and cheered me on, even when I revealed so little to you about what the book was about. I know I'm the teacher and the club advisor, but I found myself learning from all of you just as much as (or more than) you learned from me. Thank you.

To my mom and dad, for being amazing parents. I consider myself lucky to have you both as my parents. Let's never stop celebrating my "gotcha" day, okay?

To my grandparents and aunts and uncles and siblings, all of you, for your love and support. It means the world.

To my birth mom, Sue, for supporting my writing passion through the years since we made contact. I'm so glad to have you in my life now.

To my grandpa Tom, for your love of reading and your immediate support of my writing as soon as we met. Your pride in me does not go unnoticed; I hope I live up to the hype.

To Shanna and Rachael, for being available and willing to read through part of the book when I needed an outside perspective.

Last, but certainly not least, to all the authors of all the books I've read up to now (too many to list), for inspiring me, and inviting me into your worlds. I've been so many things, from princesses to wizards to dragon trainers and more. My imagination was ignited when I opened your books. Thank you for sparking the imagination of a little girl who so badly wanted to believe in magic and found it in the pages of a book.

About the Author

El Holly enjoys writing about a lot of things, but her heart is taken by the fantasy genre. Her fantasy adventure series, *Phantasmic Wars*, has been described by readers as "completely unique" and "very imaginative." When she isn't writing, she reads, teaches, drinks coffee, and goes on adventures with her family. She lives in Minnesota with her husband, their two kids, and her favorite fluffball, Mack. Like Eevee, she is adopted. Unlike Eevee, her birth parents are not fae (that she knows of).

El Holly

Books by the Author

Finding Fae (*Finding Fae* #1)

Phantasmic Wars Series
The Book of Imagination (*Phantasmic Wars* #1)
The Quest for the Artifacts (*Phantasmic Wars* #2)
The Waking of the Nightmares (*Phantasmic Wars* #3)
The Hunt for the Five (*Phantasmic Wars* #4)
The Return to Phantasmagoria (*Phantasmic Wars* #5)

Follow me for updates on new releases:

Facebook:
http://www.facebook.com/elhollywrites

Website:
http://elhollywrites.com

Amazon Author Page:
http://www.amazon.com/author/elholly

Instagram:
http://www.instagram.com/elhollywrites

Twitter:
http://www.twitter.com/elholly2

I'd love to hear from you!
eholly42@gmail.com

Made in the USA
Middletown, DE
19 September 2022